THOROUGHLY WHIPPED

TILLIE COLE

Copyright© Tillie Cole 2020 All rights reserved

Copyediting by Stephanie Ward

Cover Design by Murphy Rae Designs

Custom Illustration by Ashley Ranae Art

Formatting by Stephen Jones

French Translation by Célia Gaunt

Paperbook Edition

No Part of this publication may be reproduced or transmitted in any form or by any means, electronic or mechanical, including photography, recording, or any information storage and retrieval system without the prior written consent from the publisher and author, except in the instance of quotes for reviews. No part of this book may be uploaded without the permission of the publisher and author, nor be otherwise circulated in any form of binding or cover other than that in which it is originally published.

This is a work of fiction and any resemblance to persons, living or dead, or places, actual events or locales is purely coincidental. The characters and names are products of the author's imagination and used fictitiously.

The publisher and author acknowledge the trademark status and trademark ownership of all trademarks, service marks and word marks mentioned in this book.

"Always laugh when you can. It is cheap medicine." — Lord Byron

CHAPTER ONE

NEW YORK CITY

"HOLY SHIT," Novah whispered, leaning into me. "Little boy blue blood is all grown up!"

I rolled my eyes. "You do realize he's only a year older than you, right?"

"I've only seen him in pictures, Faith. Unlike some, I haven't been graced with the younger duke's company before this moment. Let me bask in his mighty presence."

"He's not a duke yet. That happens when his old man kicks it and passes down the title. And nobody is *graced* with that dick's presence. He's arrogant and so rich it's made him beyond stupid, and he walks with a permanent pole shoved up his ass. *Il duko* has no redeeming qualities whatsoever," I snapped and folded my arms across my chest to exaggerate my point.

The object of our musings hovered in the doorway to the conference room. He was conversing with Sally, our editor, and Henry Sinclair II, his father. Or, as his father was better known, King.

Apparently, it was quite the amusing nickname among the British elite. Oh, how they must have chortled at the "cheeky" reference to their most famous royals. But to us, his American working-class worker bees, calling himself King Sinclair just made him sound like an entitled douchebag, too full of his own importance.

"Well I, for one, wouldn't mind delving into those khakis the *duke* trainee wears so well and deep fishing for said pole in his pert, tight posterior, if you know what I mean."

I took hold of Novah's arm and met her eyes with my most serious expression. "It's irremovable, Novah. That pole is wedged in deep, like oil-rig deep. You'll need a fucking crane to hoist it out. A *crane*, Novah."

Novah waved her hand in front of her face. "Jeez, Faith. Even that image has my thighs clenching." She whistled low. "I could never be that close to his peach of a tush. I'd end up biting his firm, toned, polo-playing cheek. I know I would. Or at least give it a swift lick. I'm better off keeping my distance so as to not be arrested."

"You're sick." I smirked as she crossed her legs tightly.

"I never claimed otherwise."

"Right, minions!" Sally shouted, standing at the front of the room. The staff grew silent. Our editor clapped her hands with impressive speed. She forced a smile. It wasn't a good look on her. She appeared constipated whenever she attempted "friendly." Or as though she were battling a mild-to-medium case of hemorrhoids.

"Today's a big day here at Visage."

I held my breath, waiting for more, dread seeping into the very marrow of my bones. My skin itched in irritation seeing Henry "Harry" Sinclair III stepping out from behind his father. *No*, I prayed, hands lowering into a death grip on the arms of my chair. I looked up toward the heavens. *God, I know we're not always on the best of terms. I drink, cuss, and enjoy fornicating far too much for your liking, but please, please, please, do not say he is here for—*

"As you may have heard, Mr. King Sinclair is slowly taking a step back from the running of HCS Media Group and focusing solely on his British investments. He is still very much 'in charge' on the global stage, but he has decided to start delegating the US enterprises to his son, Henry Sinclair Junior."

I closed my eyes and felt Novah's hand grip my thigh at this revelation. "So today I have the great pleasure to welcome Henry as the new CEO of Visage Magazine and the New York Journal and everything that falls under that impressive umbrella." The people in the conference room broke out into somewhat enthusiastic applause, and I reluctantly opened my eyes. I'd hoped if I kept them closed, this would somehow turn out to be a bad dream. But as soon as I opened them, my gaze railroaded right into Henry's or, as I liked to call him, the eternally entitled ball-sack.

Fuck my life. What had we mere mortals done in the world to deserve three of these Henry Sinclair jerks on the planet? His father was an asswipe of the highest order, and I'd heard the grandfather, who'd created the empire, had been the worst kind of human being. His grandson had apparently followed suit. Henry didn't smile at me. His nostrils flared and his lip curled up. I wasn't sure if he was silently passing gas or exposing the fact that he disliked me as much as I disliked him.

King Sinclair nudged his son from his malevolent reverie. Henry pulled his hands from his pockets, nodded curtly, and instantly became the leader I was sure he had been molded to be since birth. "Good morning, I'm Henry Sinclair, but please call me Harry. Only my teachers ever called me Henry." He smirked a little at that. I blinked slowly in confusion. I had never seen him smile. This was a barely-there smile and, no matter how brief it was, it indicated *Harry* wasn't always the dour bastard he appeared to be.

"I know most of you have never met me, but I've been living between New York and England for the past few years and am extremely happy to be taking over here at the New York Journal and therefore, of course, Visage." Visage was the in-house style magazine, which went out every Sunday along with the Journal's other Sunday offerings. The in-house magazines of such prestigious newspapers had always been considered the ugly stepsisters in the world of newspaper publishing, but I loved it here. Always had...until, I feared, now.

"For the past few years I have been overseeing HCS Publishing, here in Manhattan, part-time. I've assigned someone else that role, and I will be based in these offices from here on out. I have moved to Manhattan from England for the foreseeable future, as my father takes his steady step back from HCS Media, and look forward to making an already stellar publication even greater."

I didn't know it was possible for an accent to grate on someone to such a degree. As Henry Sinclair III spoke, his too-British, too-posh timbre was akin to nails being scraped down a chalkboard at a slow and torturous velocity. In vain, I tried to control my eye twitching to avoid looking demented.

"I'm gonna come," Novah whispered, pulling my attention from said ball-sack. She dramatically bit her lip. "You think he keeps that accent in the bedroom too?" She cleared her throat and donned a terrible English accent. "Do kindly bend over, dearie, I am about to embark my large royal naval vessel into your splendidly tight vaginal shaft."

A loud snort left my mouth as I tried to bite back my laughter. The sound was like a thunderclap in the small room. Sally swiftly raised her thinly microbladed black eyebrows in my direction, seeking me out like a nuclear missile. Target locked and loaded. I winced under her stern scrutiny; then I felt another set of eyes burning into me. Harry Sinclair stared my way, his cheeks slightly reddened by, I presumed, anger. I immediately straightened my shoulders. I had no idea what it was about this man, but it was like my body positively gleamed at his disapproval, craved his disgust, and preened at successfully pissing him off. I wasn't sure if this was evidence of a new fetish I was developing but, regardless, I couldn't fight the rebellion those narrowed blue eyes inspired.

I waited for public censure from the to-be duke, but Harry just nodded at the room, forcing a tight smile, and said, "Anyway, I am sure we will talk more soon. I'm happy to be here." He looked at his father and indicated, with a wave of his hand, that they were leaving the room. "We have meetings with the other subdivisions about my takeover, so I'll let you get on with your day."

Harry and King Sinclair left the room as elegantly as royalty would retire from their subjects. I exhaled a loud sigh and whipped my head to Novah. "Royal naval vessel, Nove? Really? Vaginal shaft?"

She was still laughing, wiping tears from her eyes, unable to speak. I pushed to my feet and walked to the exit. Sally stepped into my path. "Are you a child, Faith?"

I sighed in defeat. "No, Sally. I'm twenty-five."

Sally turned on her stiletto heel, giving me her back. "Well, you sound like a child to me. Funny, I do not, and will not ever, assign children feature stories in my magazine." With those acidic parting words, she left for the elevators. And that was my boss. A frightening hybrid of Miranda Priestly and—one wouldn't say Hitler exactly, but maybe a lesser dictator. Mussolini perhaps?

"Sorry, Faith." Novah grimaced in contrition.

"It's okay." I felt a pit cave into my stomach. It wasn't from Sally's usual reprimand and threats but from the knowledge that, from now on, Henry Sinclair III would be present in these offices, lingering around me like a bad smell. Harry Sinclair, the famed future duke and heir to the HCS Media dynasty. Billionaire, British, twenty-eight, and arguably one of the, if not *the*, hottest bachelors on the planet. Six-foot-three, wavy dark-brown hair, tousled just enough to make it bedroom sexy, bright blue eyes, and two-hundred pounds of nothing but lean, cut muscle—we'd all seen the paparazzi pictures of him topless at his villa in Monaco. Harry was a walking GQ model, eye candy for the masses...until he opened his mouth and ruined the God-given masterpiece that was his fine exterior.

In truth, Henry Sinclair III was the most arrogant, aloof and coldest man I had ever met. He had such an aura of superiority that even standing beside him made you feel like a medieval maid scrubbing the stone floors of his majesty's castle. And for some reason, I knew that castle would boast at least six turrets and, no doubt, a moat with an impressive girth.

"You think he'll bring up 'the incident'?" Novah asked quietly as we walked past the journalist's cubicles, in the Journal office, to the small Visage quarters at the back of the building. Once in the safety of our two-man cubicle, Novah sat beside me, waiting for my reply. Novah Jones was a red-headed bombshell. Curves out of every 1950s pin-up fantasy and a face that would make a priest throw away his dog collar and bow at her feet begging for a spanking. She was not only a colleague but also one of my best friends. She was Visage's beauty editor. The title suited her well. There wasn't anything that this woman didn't know about makeup and skincare.

"I don't know if he'll bring it up. It was three years ago." I leaned back in my chair and stared at the generic white-tiled ceiling. "He never has before. Then again, I have only seen him once since, and it was in passing. A very *awkward* passing."

"But he was never directly your boss before. He had no official power over you then." Novah leaned over me. She took an unopened PR tube of lipstick off her desk, ripped off the packaging, and began to paint my lips. "He was the son of your boss, who you crossed paths with a few times. Now it's entirely different. You're his bitch now." She smiled widely at my painted lips. "Oh, I knew this would be your perfect shade of red. More orange and less blue in its undertone." Novah stepped back and held up a mirror in front of my face. "With your olive skin, dark hair, and espresso eyes, I knew this color would make those full lips pop, you gorgeous tanned bitch!" I rubbed my lips together. It felt nice on my mouth. Not too drying and I loved a good red lipstick.

"Love it," I said absently; then I proceeded to dramatically drop my head to my desk with an audible thud. I groaned at the memory invading my mind. "I called him an overprivileged cockface, Novah. An overprivileged cockface who needed nothing but a good spanking and a thorough fucking. And he heard my every word. And now he's my boss." I peered to the side. "Help me!" I cried pathetically as Novah sat on the end of her desk.

"I can't, gorgeous," she said and took her place at her desk chair. "This is one hole you're going to have to crawl out of on your own. Or should that be a cave? And you know I'm claustrophobic."

Novah patted my head like one would a puppy, moved to her computer, and began writing her column for this week's press. I stared at the grains of wood in my desk and thought back to last year and the moment I'd shoved one of my size-eight red Jimmy Choo rip-offs into my big, stupid mouth. I had interned at The New York Journal one summer, when I was twenty-two. Everything had been going great until I'd met a man with bright blue eyes and silky brown hair. Then everything went wrong. So completely wrong.

CHAPTER TWO

THREE YEARS AGO...

"YOU GOT THIS, FAITH," I said to myself as I stepped through the door to the conference room where the interns were meeting. About ten interns were already present. Smiling at the mix of boys and girls as I passed, I moved to the back table, which offered coffee and muffins. I poured myself some coffee and took a seat in the back row.

"Hi, I'm Faith," I said to the girl beside me. Luckily, I wasn't shy. It always helped in situations like this.

"Jayne," she said and shook my hand. I introduced myself to the people around me. In minutes, my nerves settled. Too busy talking to Jayne and a beefy jock type named Blake, I didn't see who sat beside me until I turned my head, and I had to clench my jaw to hide my reaction. Fuck me...the guy was beautiful. Tall and dark and those blue eyes... He was wearing a ridiculously nice suit and was rubbing his eyes like he hadn't gotten a lot of sleep last night. Or maybe he was nervous.

Feeling like this day had improved immensely, I extended my hand. "Hi, I'm Faith."

I held my hand out for so long that my muscles started to ache. The man eventually stopped rubbing his eyes and glared at my outstretched hand. His lip curled as if my fingers were covered in shit. I pulled my hand back with rising anger. Blue Eyes reached into his jacket pocket and pulled out some Advil. He dry swallowed a couple of pills and folded his arms across his chest. Ah, he had a headache. That explained things.

"Rough night last night?" I asked. I pointed to the beverage table behind us. "There's coffee and muffins there. Caffeine and sugar might help you feel better." Blue Eyes kept facing forward, not even acknowledging me. "Hello! Did you hear me?" I said, my hairs standing up on the back of my neck in irritation. Was he sick, or was he really this rude?

"I heard you loud and clear."

"Oh. I was worried there was something wrong with you." I tried again. "I'm Faith." When I was met with silence, I added, "And you are?"

"Will. You. Stop. Talking." As the words left his mouth, I tensed in complete shock. His jaw clenched and he flicked his lofty gaze at me before looking back at the front of the room. Second by second, my shock turned into red-hot blazing anger.

"Excuse me?" I hissed. "Stop talking?" But Blue Eyes didn't even flinch. "You can't speak to me like that."

"I can and I did," he said, and I realized he had an accent. British. English.

"How dare you!" I snapped, just as someone entered the room. "You won't get far here if you treat people like this—" I was cut off as Colin Frank, the internship program director, entered the room and clapped his hands to get our attention.

Seething, I tried to listen to Colin talk about what the internship entailed. I bit my tongue in fear that I would give the English dick beside me a piece of my mind. I had earned this internship fair and

9

square. I wanted to work for HCS Media in some way in the future. I wouldn't let some stuck-up twat ruin my chances.

"You'll report to me," Colin said, "but we have Henry Sinclair of HCS Media here for the summer, and he will also be present sometimes. He is here to see how things are done at the New York Journal." Before I'd even had time to wonder where Henry Sinclair was, Blue Eyes got to his feet. He fastened his jacket button as he stood; then he walked to the front of the room. With every step he took, I felt my excitement about this internship lessen.

Colin shook hands with Blue Eyes. "Let me introduce you to Henry Sinclair, heir to the HCS Media Group."

Henry's cold eyes settled on mine, as I shrank back into my seat, and his cheek twitched in annoyance.

Oh shit.

After introductions had been made, Colin invited us all up to meet one another. I watched Henry shake the hand of each of the interns. Then it was my turn. But just as I went to introduce myself, Henry gave me a blank stare and turned and walked out of the room.

I was a damn statue.

"What have you done to piss him off?" my new friend Jayne asked.

"I talked to him," I said, forcing a nonchalant smile. As Henry's broad back disappeared from sight, my resolve set in. I'd clear the air with him the next time I talked to him. I would smooth things over.

I DIDN'T smooth things over.

The next day I caught Henry behind the desk in Colin's office. "Oh," I said, putting down the envelope I'd been tasked with dropping off. Henry didn't even acknowledge me. I should have walked out of the office, but I was a stubborn bitch. And, apparently, I didn't know when to leave well enough alone. "Look, I know we started off on the wrong foot." I edged toward the desk. He didn't even look away from the screen. "We're going to be here all summer, right?" I tried to smile, but it was so forced I felt like my face had just been injected with an ungodly amount of Botox and I had yet to learn how to move my facial muscles. "Can't we just be friends?" I shrugged. "I promise I don't bite."

Henry sighed heavily and, looking directly at me, said, "I do not care to make friends, Miss Parisi. This isn't a summer camp, this is a New York City publishing company. Now kindly do the job you have been hired to do." I radiated anger, I knew I did. But Henry Sinclair was the heir to HCS Media. He was King Sinclair's son. I was never winning this battle.

Closing the office door behind me, I vowed to not let a stuck-up little rich boy ruin this for me. I would kill the prick with kindness. And I did. All summer long, whenever he gave me a task, I responded with a spritely "Yes sir" and gave him a wide saccharine-sweet smile. Each time I addressed him this way, his eyes flared with annoyance. His silent censure helped me get through each day. I chose to live my life loudly and with joy. He was brooding and miserable. I knew who had the better deal.

Then came the party at the end of the internship program. A summer of hard work ended on that night. We interns were dog-tired and run ragged after a summer of fetching coffee, printing and copying documents, and basically being everyone's bitches. But I knew I'd proven my worth, and the editor of Visage, the Journal's magazine, seemed to have taken a shine to me, and she wanted me to intern for her next year. Life was good. My exhaustion couldn't dampen my mood, and I entered the ballroom, nodding my head to the music, already three large glasses of wine deep. I had a good buzz zipping through my veins, and I was ready to let loose. Jayne and Blake waved me over to the rest of the interns, and the shots and liquor flowed.

"Don't look now, but your best friend has just entered the party." Blake nudged my arm.

I turned and saw Henry Sinclair walk into the ballroom, his usual expensive suit and patronizing scowl firmly in place. "Ugh," I grunted, but I forced a smile and an enthusiastic wave when his eyes met mine. I laughed when his glacial stare turned from mine and he beelined for Colin and the other execs, who had gathered around another table.

"You're playing with fire," Jayne said and handed me a large Moscow Mule.

"He's a spoilt little rich boy who hasn't had a damn bit of hardship in his entire life." I clanked my copper mug against Blake's. "And he can suck my massive dick!" I took his hand. "Now, my boy, we dance!"

Hours later, feet throbbing and highly intoxicated off one too many Moscow Mules, I had to make my third trip to the bathroom. Stumbling off the dance floor and slurring along to the lyrics of "It's Raining Men," I collided into a hard wall. No...my hands patted down the wall. It was covered in silky material and seemed to sport some seriously rock-hard abs.

Like I was living life in slow motion, I lifted my head, only to see Henry Sinclair glaring down at me in thinly veiled distain. I tried to gather my composure and step away, but the room kept tilting to the side, taking me with it. Henry sighed loudly and guided me to a seat. His large hands wrapped around my biceps and placed me in the chair. Even in my vodka-riddled state, I could appreciate that the man would be able to seriously throw around a partner in the bedroom.

I started to laugh at that titillating visual, only for Henry to curl his luscious lip in censure and say, "Really, Miss Parisi, at your age one should know how to conduct oneself in public. This is HCS Media, not a trashy gossip rag. Pull yourself together before you re-enter the ballroom and take our good name down with you." With that, the pompous douchebag walked off, leaving me raging like a thunderstorm. Why did he always have to be such a twat? I'd hoped he'd get better as the summer went on. He hadn't.

Blake and Jayne found me on the chair I'd been dumped in.

"What happened?" Jayne asked, giggling drunkenly. I regaled them with what the asshole had said. Then, smirking and letting my dangerous mouth fly, I said, "Henry Sinclair the Third is nothing but an overprivileged cockface. An overprivileged cockface who needs nothing but a good spanking and a thorough fucking!" I held up my hand for a couple of well-earned high fives. It took me a minute to realize my friends had become frozen statues around me, no fives of any kind being given.

As I lifted my eyes, I saw Henry standing before me. His blue eyes were positively livid as he looked down his regal nose at me in disgust. Crouching, he picked up his handkerchief, which had been perfectly placed in his suit pocket, off the floor and walked away.

"Shit!" I shouted, but the sound was lost to the music from the ballroom. So I said it just for me.

THAT WAS THEN. And now he was back. And this time he was in charge.

I lifted my head from my desk, stood up, and poured myself the strongest coffee I could from the break room. When back at my desk, I opened my computer and began answering the write-ins. Hopefully, I wouldn't have too much direct contact with Harry. In all the time King Sinclair had been in charge here, I'd never once spoken to him. Sally was my editor. I was sure that things would remain the same.

Two hours later, I realized I didn't know shit.

CHAPTER THREE

"MISS PARISI?" A man was suddenly at my desk. "I'm Theo, Mr. Sinclair's assistant. I've been sent down to get you for your meeting."

"Meeting?"

Theo nodded. "You received an email earlier. Did you not get it? You were expected on the tenth floor fifteen minutes ago for your one-on-one."

Of course I was. I turned to Novah. She pressed on computer keys and brought up her intranet emails. She grimaced. "He's right. I have one later. I've just seen it too."

"Awesome." I groaned and got to my feet. I straightened out my black dress and ran my hands through my hair. "Okay, ready," I said to Theo and followed him out of the office and to the elevators. Theo was about forty years old, if I had to guess. Cute. Like Penfold from Danger Mouse.

"I like your lipstick," he said, smiling at me over his shoulder.

"Thank you, sweets." I'd forgotten I was even wearing it. "Novah tells me it's my perfect shade, apparently."

"Spanish?" Theo asked, eyes narrowing on my features.

"Italian. At least my papa is. My mom is American, but from

Scottish parents. She's a pale, blond beauty. I get my coloring and attitude from my papa. He's from Parma in Italy. I get my potty mouth from my mom. Scots sure know how to throw the f-bombs."

Theo laughed. "The perfect combination," he said, just as the elevator doors opened to the tenth and top floor. The floor of the bosses or, as I liked to refer to it, Dante's fourth level of Hell. Theo led me to the office that King had previously occupied. I'd never been there before, but we'd all heard about the famed Sinclair office with the black door. That asshole ruled with an iron fist and had reduced many a journalist to a weeping baby simply with one look.

Theo opened the infamous black door. "There you go, Faith." I smiled at Theo as I passed him. "Good luck," he whispered ominously as he shut the door, trapping me inside.

"In here, Miss Parisi. Sometime today would be good." The sound of Harry's deep voice cut through the room. I winced at his shitty attitude. Forcing my feet to move, I rounded the corner and found the bastard sitting behind his large mahogany desk. His hands were steepled as he sat back on his plush leather desk chair, which may as well have been a damn throne. His dark eyebrows were pulled down as he watched me approach. I held my chin high, refusing to be intimidated by him. Harry didn't break his stare; he just gestured to the seat opposite him. "If you don't mind, Miss Parisi. I have a day full of appointments that will now all run late because of you." I exhaled a long, controlled breath, trying to calm my hot Italian blood.

"I didn't see the memo. Sorry. I was working on my column." Harry's face didn't change. He reached for a piece of paper on his desk.

"Yes. 'Ask Miss Bliss.' Your very...interesting page, correct?"

"Yes," I said through gritted teeth.

Harry read something on the page. I lowered my gaze to his clothes. I wanted to roll my eyes but managed to refrain. He wore his usual ridiculously expensive suit, jacket off, tie tightly in place. His shirt sleeves were rolled up to his elbows, showing his muscled forearms, sprinkled with a dusting of dark hair. And then there was his handkerchief. The fucking stupid handkerchief that sat in his shirt pocket in a perfect little triangle. I wanted to pull it out and toss it out the window, preferably with Mr. Sinclair III following closely behind. I couldn't help the tiny smirk that pulled on my mouth at that happy visual. Harry looked over the page he was reading. His eyes momentarily narrowed on me; then he resumed his reading.

"And this is what seventy percent of our Visage readership want the magazine for?" he said in disbelief and flicked the paper with his hand. "Your column?"

Pride swelled in my veins. "Yes. Or so the surveys tell us."

Harry's eyebrows rose. "Well, you certainly have a way with words, Miss Parisi." He leaned forward, reading, "I want my wife to do anal, but she's reluctant. Any advice on how I can convince her? Sincerely, Mr. Smith." I fought back the laughter bubbling up my throat at the question coming so politely and eloquently from Harry's mouth. "Are the questions usually of this...nature?"

"You mean sexual, Mr. Sinclair?" I said innocently, dying inside at how hard it apparently was for him to say anything referring to sex.

He didn't even flinch at my veiled attitude. "Well?"

"Yes. They are all of that nature. I now offer only sex advice. It was an organic shift. Started off encompassing any advice, but quickly became more carnally themed. It's what the readers seem to want from me. It's the advice I give best."

"And advice you do give." There was no hint of amusement in his expression or tone. "Let us see what you said to this Mr. Smith. Ah," he said dryly. "*Dear Mr. Smith. If you want to introduce your wife to the wonderful world of anal sex, I say lead by example. Buy the biggest strap-on you can find, gift it to your beloved, and encourage her to let loose and rip the shit out of your rim for the better part of the night. If you can show her the delights of such backdoor ventures, I'm sure she'll comply with your wants. Sincerely, Miss Bliss.*"

I fought back my smile. That was one of my personal favorites. Harry placed the piece of paper on his desk and regarded me with shrewd and assessing eyes. "You most certainly have a way with words, don't you, Miss Parisi?" I felt the hairs on the back of my neck stand on end, knowing what he was hinting at. He obviously remembered our summer together as clearly as I did. "And you most certainly enjoy sharing your advice, yes? Freely and without filter." His fingers drummed on the desk. "And it's award-winning too, so you must be truly gifted." *Henry Sinclair the Third is an overprivileged cockface who needs nothing but a good spanking and a thorough fucking.* My advice for him ran through my mind like an annoying song you can't remove from your head.

"Thank you," I said, refusing to let him see me shaken. "It appears people get a kick out of it."

"Some people apparently do."

"But I want to eventually move on to feature stories too," I said, trying to lead us out of dangerous territory. "I love my column, and Visage, and always want to keep it. But I also want to showcase my writing beyond answering the many 'Mr. Smiths' that write in." Harry placed a finger to his mouth, listening. "Sally knows this," I said. "We're just waiting for the right story to come up for me to cover."

"You can write features?" he asked, doubt and a patronizing tone laced in his voice. That just pissed me off.

I painted on my fakest smile. "I graduated top of my class with a degree in creative writing from Harvard and a master's in feature journalism from Columbia. I assure you, Mr. Sinclair, I am more than qualified to write features."

"Then I look forward to reading your first masterpiece, Miss Parisi. Until then, sex advice for the masses it is." He focused on his computer, tapping at the keyboard. When I didn't move, he glanced at me and said coldly, "We're done." Harry gestured toward the door.

Keeping my forced smile firmly fixed on my face, and my hands beside me so I didn't lash out and slap him upside the head, I rose from the chair. I felt his evil eyes on me as I walked out of his office and toward the elevators.

"Hope that went okay, Faith!" Theo said from behind his desk as I tried to keep my shit together.

"Awesomely!" I said chirpily and stepped into the elevator, my hands shaking with anger. Just as the doors were about to close, I shouted, "What a fucking *dick!*" Someone's hands caught the doors and they began to open. I held my breath. It couldn't be. Surely nobody was *that* unlucky. I sighed in relief when a man in a suit, probably in his mid-fifties, stepped in, staring at me like I was insane. "Tourette's," I said, laughing and pointing to my mouth. "Not a direct slight toward you, I promise."

The man gave me an awkward nod and faced the doors, keeping as far away from me as he could. Pulling out my cell, I texted my roommate, Amelia, and our neighbor, Sage.

Code 5! We're going out tonight. I need to drink and dance. No excuses.

Within seconds I had confirmation that both of them were in. Back at my desk, I got a thumbs-up that Novah was in too. Knowing I had a night to unwind, I relaxed in my chair and opened the latest email:

My husband came home late last Friday night and when he undressed and came to bed, I saw lipstick marks around his penis. What advice do you have?

I cracked my hands, flexed my fingers on my keyboard, and swiftly typed my reply for this week's column: *Wine and dine him, take him to bed. Smother his cock with Nutella, then nibble off his pubes like you're tearing corn off the cob. Watch the fucker scream then Lorena Bobbitt his ass! Badda bing, badda boom—no more lipstick on his cheating dick!*

Screw Harry Sinclair and his cold blue eyes. I was damn good at my job.

CHAPTER FOUR

"SHIT, FAITH, THIS IS HIM?" Sage asked as I sat beside Amelia on our green velvet couch. I grabbed the large glass of red wine she had poured for me. Sage sat opposite us on the edge of our thrift store coffee table.

"That's the prick," I said, shaking my head at how perfect someone so freakin' awful could look in photographs.

Novah sat on my other side. "Yep, that's him, Henry "Call me Harry" Sinclair. Bachelor of the century and Faith's archnemesis." Novah nudged me and laughed when I hissed at her like an angry cat.

Sage went back to searching his phone. "Well, well, well," he said and held out his cell again. "Who is this bit of candy on his arm?" I squinted, trying to fight my way through the wine haze that had descended over my eyes. I saw a tall blonde with green eyes, arm firmly linked with Harry's. He was in a black suit, top and tails, and a mustard cravat, while she sported some monstrosity on her head that appeared to be two cocks fighting—of the avian variety, not the phallic. Although seeing two actual dicks thrashing it out on a bowler hat would have been a vast improvement on this feathered shitshow, which had no place as head decoration.

"What the hell is that on her head?" Amelia tipped her head to the side, trying to work it out.

"The trainee duke and his lady friend are at the Cheltenham races, *dahling*," Sage mocked. "It's where the who's who of England go to show how money and fashion proves you don't have to have taste. And where they drop ungodly amounts of money on horse racing to disguise how small their teeny-tiny members are."

I laughed as Sage winked and Amelia ripped Sage's cell from his hand. She read the photo caption aloud. "Rumored couple Lady Louisa Samson and the Viscount of Surrey, Henry Sinclair III, attend Cheltenham races." Amelia looked at me. "Viscount?"

"That must be his title now," I said. *Viscount*. Good Lord. That sounded even more conceited than *duke*.

Amelia passed me the cell. I studied the picture and the statuesque blonde linked to Harry's arm. Her hair was cut into a long bob, and she sported a true English rose complexion and a patronizing smirk on her dusty pink lips that I instinctively wanted to slap right off her face. How did someone simply exude the attitude of "I'm better than you" from a picture?

"She looks just as pompous as he does," I said and beamed a huge smile. "Match made in heaven! They deserve each other. Now..." I gave Sage his cell back and got to my feet. "Are we hitting the club or not? I'm dangerously low on alcohol, and in this bra my breasts are shoved up so high that they touch my chin. If we don't get to the club soon, I'm afraid it'll be dangerously close to cutting off my capacity to breathe. I'm not wasting another second on Duke Dumbfuck, his bobblehead blonde, and their many acquaintances with terrible teeth."

I held up my glass of wine like a warrior leader giving her speech before a major battle. "Tonight, I want to shake my shimmy like my ass working for tips and, preferably, drag a hottie into the bathroom to rehydrate the stark desert my poor little vagina has become. And I want to make so many bad decisions I'll have my priest rolling out of his confessional booth on Sunday from sinful exhaustion." I brought my glass to my lips. "Cheers, hookers! Let's get wasted!"

As we stepped out of the apartment building, I breathed in deeply. New York was firmly in spring; the blistering cold of winter a distant memory. I smiled as the warm breeze kissed my face. Sage threw his muscular arm over my shoulders and pulled me in the direction of the club. As we walked down the streets of Brooklyn, I asked, "So, Sagey-baby, any news on your love life?"

Sage sighed. "I've exhausted the many fuckboys on Grindr and my Prince Charming hasn't found me yet, so that would be a huge fat zero on love-life news." I patted Sage's arm and laid my head on his shoulder. When Amelia and I had moved into our Brooklyn apartment two years earlier, Sage had quickly become our honorary roommate. He lived in the apartment opposite us. He'd come over for drinks one night and had been our third musketeer ever since.

"He's out there. I know he is," I said and kissed his cheek. Sage was eternally hopeful that his soulmate was out in the world just waiting to meet him.

Ten minutes later we were in the club and walking into the main room. I loved this place. We did clubbing two ways: down and Brooklyn dirty, as we called it, or bougie and boogie. Tonight was the latter. The music was epic, as were the drink prices. But we had that solved.

Tapping the bar, the bartender nudged his chin my way. "Hey, gorgeous," he said, licking his lips as he scanned me from head to foot. It was a nice try. He looked about twelve, and babyfaces just didn't float my boat.

"Barkeep!" I called. "We'll have four of your best Diet Cokes."

"Diet Cokes?" The bartender frowned. "That's it?"

I firmly nodded my head. "And make sure it's the good stuff." Babyface walked away and I cast my gaze around the club. Smoke filled the air like the fog over London, green laser beams cut through the dance floor like peridot blades, and the highly expensive DJ spun his tunes, the clubbers surrounding him like rats to the pied piper. I glanced up, seeing the darkened VIP balcony starting to fill with people. We'd never been up there, of course. It was for the rich Manhattan types who slummed it down in Brooklyn a few nights a month.

"Four Diet Cokes," the bartender said behind me. I handed him the cash. "Keep the change." I winked, feeling like a baller, and walked back to my friends, who had bagged us a table at the back. It was strategic. This wasn't our first bougie rodeo.

"Drinks!" I said and placed them on the table.

Amelia checked to see that the coast was clear. "Now," she said hurriedly and I reached into the top of my dress.

My friends watched me as I felt along my breasts, along the side seams of my bra, until... "Gotcha!" With a wide smile, I unscrewed the secret spout in the bra, pulled one breast from my dress, and began pouring.

"It may have been expensive, Faith. But that bra is paying for itself!" Novah took a large sip of her Diet Coke, now mixed with the vodka I'd smuggled into the club.

"You're telling me. But shit, I feel for women like you, Nove. These things weigh a ton. I can feel my spine bending irreparably as we speak."

"I know. You may think I look good now, but come to me when I'm fifty and I'll be answering the door like Quasimodo, nipples dragging along the floor. But instead of repeating the *bells, the bells*, it'll be *my tits, my tits!*"

Laughing, I aimed for my drink, squeezing the hidden pouch lining my bra for the vodka that had gathered at the base. Someone tapped me on my shoulder, scaring the living shit out of me. I spun, still squeezing my tit, and shot a squirt of vodka straight into some poor guy's eye.

"What the fuck!" he said, wiping the liquid from his face. I quickly fumbled with the bra's pouch and tucked myself back in. "What the hell was that?" he asked, face reddening with disgust.

"She's lactating, asshole," Amelia said. "What do you think it was?" As I met her eyes, she grimaced and shrugged, mouthing, *I didn't know what else to say!*

"Then why the fuck does it taste like vodka? Oh god!" he said, face paling. "I got it in my mouth!"

As he spat at the floor, Novah leaned forward over the table, affronted. "Listen, pal, you try raising a baby without alcohol. Don't you dare judge a mother for doing the best she can!"

"Fuck this," the guy said, walking away. "Bunch of freaks."

"Oh my god!" Sage said and burst out laughing.

"Lactating?!" I said to Amelia.

"I panicked!" she said. "I'm not loud and feisty like you. I had to think on my feet! I didn't want us to get thrown out!"

I was laughing so hard tears filled my eyes. "And Novah. Don't judge a mother for doing the best she can! What the—?"

"He fucked off, didn't he? Nothing like a whiff of *eau de commitment* to scare off the boys!"

I fixed the genius that was my vodka-smuggling bra, and we clanked our drinks and downed half our glasses.

"Shall we have this dance?" I asked my best friends. We moved to the dance floor, and I got lost in the pounding music. The beat pulsed in time with my heartbeat, my skin heated from the bodies swirling around us, brushing against my limbs, and I felt the day's awful events slipping away.

A tall blond guy came toward me. He was good looking, and I smiled in encouragement. He would do nicely. It'd been a while since I'd lost myself dancing with a man, and even longer since I'd had a night between the sheets. I wrapped my arms around his neck, and our hips ground to the beat. Turning my back to his chest, I felt his hardness press against my ass.

Song after song rolled on, and the night was looking ever more promising. I lifted my hands in the air and placed them behind my partner's neck; then I felt the hairs on the back of my neck rise. It was as though someone was watching me. I looked up, my eyes immediately seeking the VIP balcony...and my gaze crashed into a familiar blue stare.

The heat infusing my muscles instantly cooled. My body froze. The guy I'd been dancing with tried to keep me moving with his hands on my hips, but when I didn't move, he walked away.

"Faith?" Amelia asked, pulling on my arm. "You okay?"

"Shit!" I said, my gaze still fixed on the balcony. "It's Harry Sinclair."

"What?" Amelia asked, confused.

"He's here."

Immediately all of my friends looked up at what held my attention. Harry rose from leaning on the balcony. He never moved his eyes off me, but without any form of greeting, he turned away and disappeared into the depths of the VIP area.

"Damn!" Sage said. "That guy is..." I glared at my friend, warning him with my laser eyes not to be complimentary. Sage shrugged. "Sorry, baby girl, but that guy is hot as fuck!"

"Ugh!" I said. "*One* night. I needed this one night to dance my problems away." Feeling irritated beyond measure, I combed my fingers through my hair. "I'm going to the bathroom."

"I'll come," Novah offered.

"No, it's fine. I won't be long. You guys keep dancing." I weaved my way through the packed dance floor, heading for the bathrooms. I cut down the back hallway, turned right, and then smashed right into someone's chest. "For fuck's sake!" I screamed, stumbling backward and, in my quintessentially clumsy way, I landed firmly on my ass.

I stared at the ground and prayed a hole would cave under the tiles and swallow me right up. In my drunken state, I smacked the floor with my palm. "Come on, kraken! I'm waiting! You have a willing victim! And I'm juicy. Particularly my ass!"

Suddenly, a hand hovered in front of my face. Realizing nothing was coming to eat me, thus saving me, I grabbed onto it and was hoisted to my feet. Another hand steadied me by holding my arm.

The vodka I'd consumed was well and truly in my bloodstream now. The room swayed from side to side.

"I am pretty sure a kraken is a mythological creature from the sea. If you wanted something from the earth, you could maybe try summoning a balrog, or something of its ilk."

The room quickly righted itself into a steady focus, and I closed my eyes. I didn't want to look up. I knew that voice. I knew that accent.

Eventually, I opened my eyes and met the stupidly stunning face of Harry Sinclair. "Miss Parisi." His lips were tight and his eyes shrewd. He wore no hint of a smile. Did the guy have a perpetual pissed-off stare?

"Viscount Sinclair," I slurred back, victory soaring through my blood when I saw his eyes narrow at my use of the title. I'd hit a nerve. Good to know. My eyes dropped to his attire. He wore dark jeans with a crisply ironed white shirt, open at the collar, and a navy blazer. And, lo and behold, a silver silk handkerchief sitting offensively in his blazer pocket. He looked good. Goddamn it, he looked so fucking *good*. Why did his unstyled dark, wavy hair have to fall so perfectly? Why?

"WHY!" I gasped for breath when I realized I'd screamed the last word aloud, my shrill voice cutting through the echo of the music from the main dance floor. Harry frowned at my outburst, viewing me as if I had just escaped an asylum. I challenged him, with a tilt of my chin, to say something. He kept his mouth shut.

Harry's gaze fell to my clothes. I stood proud, knowing I rocked this dress. I might be the clumsiest, most accident-prone woman in all of New York, but I knew how to dress to accentuate my curves. I waited for the begrudging compliment Harry would have to give me. I would relish it, knowing it would cause him nothing but discomfort and would wound his pride. But when he finally opened his mouth, he said, "Miss Parisi, it appears your breasts are leaking."

My eyes widened and I glanced down at my dress. The impressive bust that I had been sporting had burst and deflated, leaving me with my usual C-cups and two rings of wetness dripping vodka onto the floor. "Perfect," I said and forced a strained smile. "You got a glass?" I flicked my soggy breasts. "Drinks are on me."

"I think I'll pass," he said, his eyes boring into mine. He tucked his hands into his pockets and his mouth twisted. He looked like he wanted to be anywhere but here right now. "You make this a habit?" he asked, looking down his nose at me like only the upper class seemed to be able to do. I was sure they taught it in those fancy-ass schools they all went to—How to Be a Pretentious Bastard 101. "This is the second time you have collided with me while being intoxicated." He shook his head, as if in censure. "Though thankfully the first time your drink was in your hand and not dripping from your undergarments."

Harry glanced down to his blazer, jaw clenching. He took his handkerchief from his pocket with regal ease. I had to hold back my laugh when he started pressing it to the expensive fabric and I realized the vodka from my bra had also stained his clothes.

The dirty look he threw me only heightened my amusement. "Send me the dry-cleaning bill," I said and held my hand against my mouth. I had no idea why seeing the usually pristine Harry Sinclair trying in vain to wipe vodka from his blazer caused me such amusement.

"No need. I have plenty more," he said, beginning to fold his handkerchief back into its perfect little square. He tucked it precisely back into his pocket.

"Ball park figure, how many of those do you own?" I pointed to his handkerchief. "You seem to have quite the collection."

"I couldn't possibly say." His cheek twitched, I presumed in annoyance at my question. He regarded me suspiciously. "Are you mocking me, Miss Parisi?"

"Me!" I said, placing my hand on my sodden chest. "Never. I think they're just...spiffing!" Balancing—or trying to—on my heels, I said, "Alas, I must bid you a fond farewell, my viscount, the powder room waits for no lady." I brushed past Harry as quickly as I could, stumbling to the bathroom, no doubt looking like Bambi on ice. As soon as the door was shut, I exhaled and shut my eyes. *Why me? Why do these things always happen to me?*

When I opened them again, I walked to the sink and stared at myself in the mirror. Two large round wet stains greeted me. I moved to the hand dryer and began drying my dress. My thoughts immediately went to Harry Sinclair. He didn't seem the type to be in a club. I wondered who he was with. Then I chastised myself for even caring.

The door was smashed open, and two women came barreling in. "He was, by far, the hottest guy I've ever seen in my life."

"And he had an accent." These women were both blond and pretty. "If I'm not under him tonight, then I may as well go back home to Oklahoma and marry Jimmy Burns. That guy out there was the reason I came to New York. I bet he's amazing in bed. The quiet ones always are."

Harry. Of course they were talking about Harry.

I snorted a laugh. The one who had been talking gave me the side eye, seeing me dipped into a limbo position under the hand dryer blowing on my breasts. She curled her lip. I rolled my eyes, dipping back as far as I could, widening my smile. Shaking their heads, they left, and I hoped to god she collared him. Lord knew the viscount needed a good fuck. Maybe then he'd learn how to crack a smile for once in his life and maybe loosen up at work. Hell, in life!

Once my dress was dry enough and appeared to not be a total write-off, I walked back into the hallway, sighing in relief when it was empty. Instead of going back to my friends, I headed straight to the bar. I was buying us a bottle of prosecco, whatever I could afford. I had my credit card with me, and I was seizing the day and using it.

The bartender sighed as he saw me coming. "More sodas?"

"*Au contraire!*" I said smugly. "A bottle of prosecco." I handed him my card. He winked as he took it. I quickly grabbed his arm, stopping him in his tracks. "But make it the cheapest you have." He shook his head in exasperation.

"Make that a bottle of Cristal. On me." An arm reached over me, and the bartender nodded. He handed the stranger my card. When I turned, a blond man with gray eyes smiled down at me. He read the name on my credit card. "Faith Parisi. I believe this is yours."

He was a handsome bastard, and when he smiled, my breath caught in my throat. "And you are?" I asked.

The bartender came back with the Cristal and four glasses. "On my tab," the mystery guy said. I waited for him to give me his name, but instead he pulled a black business card from his pocket and handed it to me. "If you're ever feeling adventurous," he said, pointing to the card, "don't lose this. It's your golden ticket to the chocolate factory, Charlie." Then, kissing the back of my hand, he moved away through the crowd like a ghost. I lost sight of him as he disappeared into the mass of bodies and smoke. I glanced down at the card, all kinds of confused. A phone number was on the back, and a code of some kind. When I flipped the card over, one word was spelled out in richly embossed silver: NOX.

The breath left my lungs, and my mouth dropped open. I turned and grabbed my champagne; then I made my way back to our table as fast as my shaking legs would carry me. My friends were already there when I returned.

"There you are! I was about to gather a search party!" Amelia lifted her brows in surprise when she saw the Cristal. "What's all this? Did you win the lottery and not tell us or something?"

"Long story. But I was bought this." I then held out the card to Novah.

Within seconds she looked at me and whispered, "You lucky bitch."

"What is it?" Sage said and took it from Novah. His eyes widened. "Faith. Forget the lottery. You've just hit the jackpot with this."

"What is it?" Amelia asked. She read the card. "What the hell is NOX?"

"It's a sex club," I said, still stunned with disbelief.

"A what?" Amelia choked.

"A sex club. A *sex* club, she says!" Novah said dramatically. "It's not merely *a* sex club, it's *the* sex club! The sex club of the elite. The rich and famous. All kinds of high-powered people go there. It's a damn fortress. People pay a fortune to get a membership there, that or—"

"You get invited," Sage said, looking at me like I was a damn mythical creature who'd just stepped into this world on the back of a pink unicorn. "To be invited is more than rare. But if you do, you get a free membership."

Novah started jumping up and down. "Fuck, Faith, you just got invited to NOX!" Novah grabbed the champagne. "Wait, who invited you? Did he buy you this too? What the hell happened when you went to the bathroom?"

"Some hot blond guy approached me at the bar."

"Wait, wait, wait!" Amelia said, making a slicing motion at her neck. She stood in front of me. "Faith. Firstly, what the hell? And secondly, you're not thinking of going are you? A sex club, Faith? A sex club?"

"I like sex," I said and shrugged. It was true. I did. I wasn't a shy little wallflower. I had a healthy sexual appetite and made no apologies for it. I was a single woman in New York; I both worked and played hard. But then I snapped my eyes to Novah. "My feature." I felt breathless at the sudden excitement soaring through me. "Sally said to go to her with a feature that my readers would want to read. What better feature for a sex advice columnist to write than about the most infamous and mysterious sex club in all of New York, if not the world?"

"Shit, Faith." Novah nodded so fast she resembled a bobblehead. She quickly poured the champagne into the glasses. "You're right. This is it. This is it!"

"It's a sex club, Faith. You'll have to do things. Really fucked-up things," Amelia said, trying to bring the rest of us back to Earth.

"Sounds like heaven to me," Sage said, throwing me a high five. I met his hand and saw his excitement for me shining in his gorgeous face.

"Are you really going to do this?" Amelia said. I saw the worry in her expression. Amelia and I had gone to college together. She was now an archeologist who worked at The American Museum of Natural History. We'd shared a dorm at Harvard and had been best friends from the day we met. She had always been quiet and reserved. I was loud and, *not*. She was like my sister. My overprotective sister who worried about me.

I took her hands. "Amelia, this is my chance. You know I've been waiting for this, an opportunity for a real feature. And it's sex. I *love* sex. I've never been shy about that. I've experimented, have no plans to settle down anytime soon. Going there doesn't scare me. If anything, I'm ridiculously intrigued." I looked to Novah. "You think Sally will go for this?"

"I think Sally will piss her pants when you tell her you've got an in at the most exclusive club in the Western world. Do you realize how long people have been waiting for a story on that place?"

"Shit," I said, the reality of the situation beginning to sink in. I read the card again. NOX, the notorious sex club. The one no one talked about, but everyone wanted to know about. And I had been invited. *Me*. Even with running into Viscount Douchebag and ruining my favorite vodka-smuggling bra, my night had just turned out to possibly be one of the best.

I'd been invited to NOX.

A sex club.

I'd never been more excited for anything in my life.

CHAPTER FIVE

"YOU INFURIATE ME." Harry's harshly spoken words washed over me, causing my skin to bump in their wake. "You talk too much. Everything about you is too much." Harry's teeth nibbled along my neck as he pinned me against a wall in his office with his broad chest. "I can't stand that I want you. I hate your voice. I hate the smirk you wear when you think you've bested me somehow." Harry's tight hand held my wrists above my head; his other hand palmed my breast, sending bolts of heat between my legs. I throbbed everywhere, my breathing uneven.

"Good," I said, cheeks flushed and skin too hot. "Then the feeling's mutual." I groaned, tipping my chin to the ceiling as Harry kissed along my throat, my jaw, and my cheek. "I hate your condescending voice, your stuffy accent, and the way you think you're better than everyone else." My breath hitched as his hand slipped down from my breast, lifted my dress, and ran along the seam of my panties. "Shit!" I moaned as he yanked my panties down my thighs. They pooled at my feet. I stepped out of them. Harry's eyes clashed with mine. I hated his perfect eyes and his long, dark lashes. I hated his smooth skin and how

his hand felt touching me so intimately. And I hated how much I wanted him, needed him, craved him.

"One time," I said and watched his nostrils flare in response. "One fuck to get it out of our systems." I pulled my hands down from his clasp and started unbuttoning his fly. Heat flooded my veins seeing his eyes roll back as I took his length in my hand. He pushed a finger inside me, and I almost came on the spot.

"I need to be inside you," he said and moved my hand from his dick. Then he lifted the hem of my dress, pulled my legs around his waist, and slammed inside me. Our mutual groans were thunderous as they echoed around the vast office space. Harry tucked his head into the crook of my neck as he pounded into me. I wrapped my arms around his shoulders as I was thrust into a maddening state of ecstasy. "Christ," he moaned as he filled me, his talented thrusts sending shivers down my spine. I was too hot, the pleasure was too much. Then Harry lifted his head and smashed his lips to my own. I didn't want his kiss. I didn't want to feel his lips against mine. I didn't want to taste his tongue. But as he kissed me, as his hot tongue dueled with mine, I wanted it all. I wanted all of him, inside and over me.

"I hate you," I murmured against his lips. "I despise you."

Harry just groaned, snapping his hips faster and faster until I was a burning flame. "You infuriate me," he retorted, his perfectly graveled voice causing my nipples to harden as they pressed against his chest. "You both incense and madden me." I cried out when Harry's teeth scraped along the skin of my collarbone, before his gentle tongue traced a path to my mouth and he kissed me again. He kissed and kissed me until my lips were swollen and his taste was tattooed into my senses.

He thrust faster and faster until I became an inferno, my hands clawing at his shirt. "Now!" I cried out as blistering heat engulfed me and I shattered apart. It was nothing I'd ever felt before. It was too much yet I still craved more.

"Fuck!" Harry cried, then came inside me, his hands on my ass pulling me so tightly against his hips that there was no air between us. I gripped his shoulders, gasping for breath. I hated him. I really, really *did. But as his dick twitched inside me, bringing another flash of pleasure to my core, I wanted more. I craved him like the worst addiction, his curtly spoken words and arrogant and contemptuous attitude my much-coveted drug of choice.*

Harry stilled against me, drawing back slowly. As I met his eyes, I saw the flare of distain; I knew it was reflected in my own. But then his mouth crashed to mine again, and I became utterly consumed. It didn't change anything. I loathed him. He detested me. It didn't change anything at all...

"Faith? Are you there?" The sound of Mom's voice pulled me from reliving the dream that had accosted my drunken psyche last night. Hell, not dream. *Nightmare.* Harry and me...I pushed the images from my head. Of Harry pressed against me, inside me, making my toes curl in pleasure... "Faith? I know you're there, you're breathing funny." I focused on the here and now, and not the fact that my thighs were trying to clench together as I walked, just remembering the steamy vision.

"Mom! I'm here. Sorry about that. The sidewalk's busy this morning. How are you?" I was walking from the subway to my office building, chatting on my cell. I caught my reflection in a glass building as I made my way to HCS Media. I was glad I was wearing my huge sunglasses. The warm day was too bright for my hungover ass, the dream still had me flustered, and I looked like crap.

"We're good, sweetheart," Mom said, but I heard a hint of sadness in her voice. It instantly crushed me.

"And Papa?"

"He's at the shop." Mom paused. My feet suddenly did too. Some Wall Street douche plowed into my arm from behind, sending my Trenta extra-strong coffee sloshing to the sidewalk.

"Prick!" I called out to him. The asshole flicked me the finger without even looking back. I tucked myself against a nearby building, kicking the coffee off my shoes. I had some on my skirt too, but this time I didn't care if it stained. All I cared about was Papa. "Mom, what's wrong?"

Her silence told me it was bad. Really bad. Eventually she said, "The shop's landlord has given your father only a matter of weeks to find the money for the back rent, or..." She trailed off.

"Or what?"

Mom sighed. "Or we lose it."

"Mom," I whispered, a lump clogging my throat. I couldn't imagine Papa not having his tailoring shop. It was his life. His passion. It would break him. I knew it would.

"It's okay, Faith. This isn't your problem. We'll work something out. We always do."

"If it's your problem, it's mine. We will figure it out. Us three. Okay? We can't lose it. I'll think of something. I promise."

"Okay, sweetheart," Mom said, but I heard the flicker of defeat in her trembling voice. My eyes welled with tears. I loved my parents. We were a team, us three. We'd never had much money, but we'd had an abundance of love and I'd never needed any more than that. Mom cleared her throat and asked, "Are you still coming for dinner on Sunday?"

I laughed, chasing away my sorrow. "I come every week, Mom. You never have to ask. Yet you always do."

"I just like to be sure. Now, you better get to work or you'll be late, lady."

I checked my watch. "Shit!" I hissed and started running toward my building. "I'll see you on Sunday, Mom. Kiss Papa for me!" I ran into the building, catching the packed elevator just as the doors closed. I squeezed myself in next to a pack of journalists all suited and booted for the day. I prayed with all that I was that the elevator didn't break down. I'd been trapped in this steel contraption twice already. With this many people, it would turn from *Mad Men* to *Lord of the Flies* in five seconds flat.

As the elevator rose to each floor, jerking as it stopped to let people out, I fought back the wave of nausea threatening to project from my mouth a la *The Exorcist*. I could still feel the vodka, wine, and champagne sloshing around in my empty stomach, reminding me of my stupidity in getting that drunk on a work night. That, paired with a sex dream about Harry Sinclair, was enough to make anyone sick. I practically cried with relief when the elevator landed on my floor. I rushed to my booth. Novah was there already and immediately helped me shed my jacket and purse.

"She has a meeting in twenty minutes. You'd better hurry if you want to catch her."

I kissed Novah on the cheek and sprinted for the elevator. I pressed the button repeatedly until the doors opened, and I rushed inside. I took a deep breath, grateful it was empty, and pressed the button for the tenth floor. Just before the doors began to close, someone slipped inside. The minute I smelled a familiar addictive cologne—fresh water, mint, sandalwood, and musk—I knew exactly who it was. Despite myself, I couldn't help but bask in the scent. Why did the asshole have to smell so damn good? And all I could see in my mind was me pressed up against the wall of his office, him plowing into me like his life depended on it. I cleared my throat when it became too hard to breathe at the memory.

"Miss Parisi," Harry said, and I begrudgingly lifted my head. He glanced back at me over his shoulder. The doors to the elevator closed, and it began climbing to the tenth floor.

"Viscount Sinclair," I said as cheerily as I could muster with a drumline marching in my head. At this moment, I was at a solid minus three out of ten on the happy scale.

"Harry," he corrected curtly. "No need for titles." His shoulders tensed. "But if I were being pedantic, I would inform you that my current *title* is Viscount Sinclair, but I am *addressed* Lord Sinclair."

There was *no* fucking way I was ever calling him *Lord*. "I'll stick to calling you Viscount, if that's okay. It rolls of the tongue better." Harry sighed, I presumed at my stubbornness. I couldn't help but childishly stick out my tongue at his broad and ridiculously muscled back. Then I waved two raised middle fingers in the air in an impromptu and highly juvenile rhythmic dance.

I quickly dropped them when he glanced over his shoulder again and asked stiffly, "I trust you had a good time last night?"

My lips kicked up at the side. "I sure did." What would Mr. Prim and Proper say if I told him I had been invited to a sex club after we'd talked? The girl with vodka-flavored nipples had been asked to the most prestigious underground adult playground, despite her clumsiness. He'd probably choke on his own prudishness. Then again, if he fucked anything like my dream, maybe he'd fit right in.

Harry glanced down at my skirt and shook his head. "Seems you have had another accident, Miss Parisi. Tell me," he said smirking. "Do you actually imbibe the beverages you purchase or simply prefer to wear them as outfit accessories?" My eyes fell to the coffee stain that graced the front of my lilac pencil skirt and the flecks of latte on my nude heels. At least my jacket had protected my white silk shirt, so I would be half presentable to Sally.

"Fluids are the new black, Mr. Sinclair, haven't you heard?"

Harry raised a dark eyebrow at my retort. "Is that so?" I caught the mirth in the slight lilt in his deep tone.

Fluids. I'd just said *fluids.* Jesus H Christ.

"Not *bodily* fluids," I said quickly. Harry's head tilted to the side as I tried to remove the epically sized shoe that was currently jammed in my mouth. "I mean, we all saw how Monica Lewinski went down when she showed the infamous dress to the world." My eyes widened. "Not *literally* saw how she went down." I pointed my finger at my crotch, circling that general area to exaggerate my point. I snatched my hand back and forced it to my side when I realized I was guiding my boss's eyes directly to my vagina. "I mean, she did *literally* go down on old Bill, you know, to get the bodily fluid on her dress in the first place and all, but—" The elevator suddenly dinged and the doors opened, saving me from falling further down the fluid-themed rabbit hole. "Oh, thank God!" I said, breathless from the train wreck my verbal drivel had become.

"Miss Parisi," Harry said, something like amusement glinting in his eyes, as I collapsed against the back of the elevator, exhausted from all the talk of fluids. He stepped out onto the tenth floor and walked off toward his office.

"Yep," I muttered to myself and headed to Sally's office on the opposite side of the floor. "All that from a girl who is about to battle for her first feature." Clara, Sally's assistant, wasn't at her desk when I arrived, so I knocked on the door.

"Go away!" Sally's harsh voice sailed through the door.

I turned the knob and quickly entered Sally's office, firmly shutting the door behind me. Pulling the treasured NOX card from my bra, I put it on the table. "We need to talk about my upcoming feature in Visage." Sally's eyes narrowed on me in confusion; then she looked down at the card. Those narrowed eyes swiftly rounded and widened with shock.

"You've been invited?" she said, peering at me over her severely edged black glasses. "Is this real?" She picked up the card and admired the quality stationary and the expensive embossing of the font. "Holy shit, Faith! This is real, isn't it?"

"I was invited last night." Sally was on her feet in seconds and marched to her door. She bolted the lock and faced me.

"This needs to stay between us. You will tell no one."

"Okay." I sat on the visitor's chair as Sally rushed behind her desk and sat down too. She steepled her hands and glared at me. I wasn't sure if she was excited or pissed off about this development.

"You realize the kinds of people that go to that club, Faith. Money, power, people that could both elevate and destroy us." It was the first time I'd ever seen Sally look nervous. Her left eye was twitching, the thick lenses of her glasses forcing me to watch it in a magnified fashion. When her head began ticcing and her perfectly slicked-back black hair began falling from its gelled prison, I knew I was losing my chance.

Leaning forward, I said, "You wanted something that'll hook in my readers. Sex. BDSM. You can't move these days without reading or watching some alpha dude being all primal and domineering with his love interest and her gushing liters at his every command. We need to capitalize on that. Dip into the whip and anal bead pool and bathe in it a little. Let's give our readers wild sex on a silver paddled platter. Let's dildo up and jump on the gag ball bandwagon." Sally's lips pursed and she sat back in her seat, regarding me as predatorily as a cat studies a mouse. "I can do this, Sally. Let me do this. I'm a damn good writer and you know it. This is going to work. Trust me."

The wait for her to speak seemed to drag, my pulse acting like a countdown clock throbbing in my neck.

"This will be your one chance, Faith," Sally said and I felt my heart kick into a sprint. "But you don't tell anyone about this. Fuck knows who in this building could be a part of the club." She paused. "What if you're recognized? The story will be over before your first flogging."

"I did some research," I said. "I got up early this morning. Seems it's all anonymous. Hoods and masks, all identities hidden. Very *Eyes Wide Shut*, hopefully without the devil worshipping and cult aspect, of course. Though that would be the story right there. I'll do whatever it takes to pull the wool over their eyes."

Sally pointed her taloned finger in my face. "You continue 'Ask Miss Bliss,' you're not leaving that column. Don't even think it. It's too important for our popularity."

"Understood and I would never give up the column. It's my baby, my very naughty baby."

"Eight weeks," Sally said. "Enough time to understand what happens there and not long enough to get in too deep. Understood?"

"Understood."

Sally drummed her lengthy acrylics on the table. "This...a story this big, this interesting...it could be our summer feature, Faith." I momentarily lost my breath. The summer feature. Every year Visage published an extended edition. At its heart was a prime feature. The biggest exposé or human-interest story of the entire year.

"I understand," I said, and Sally shooed me away from her desk with her hand.

As I stood, she said, "Discretion, Faith. No one is to know a whisper about this until it's done. Not your colleagues, friends, and especially the powers that be." She pointed toward Harry's and the other top dog's offices. "We don't want the story drowned before we've even given you a chance to, what did you say, 'dip into the whip and anal bead pool and bathe in it a little'." I laughed at what I'd said. Sally didn't. "Discretion and epic writing. Find a hook and roll with it. We all want to know what's happening in that club. We want to know who is there and what they're up to. And if they NDA you, which I'm sure they will, we need to work around the legal jargon and create a story that lets us vanilla fuckers—literally—feel like we've been in kink heaven with you." Sally tilted her glasses down her nose and peered at me over the rims of her frames. "You must do whatever is required of you to get that story, Faith. You understand that?"

"Yes."

"*Whatever* is required of you." Sally smirked. I'd never seen amusement in her expression before. It scared the hell out of me; she looked like a mountain lion about to attack. "Let's pray you have the stamina and pain threshold for such a task." She trilled out a single mocking laugh. "Oh, to see you trussed up in chains with a gag ball in your mouth. Maybe whoever gets to play with you will eventually get you to shut up."

"Ha! I'll be their biggest challenge yet," I said, feigning hilarity at her snark. I cast her a strained smile and quickly left her office.

Despite Sally's acidic tongue lashing, I felt like I was walking on air as I headed down the elevator and toward Novah. She jumped up from her seat and followed me to the bathroom. Once inside, I locked the door, after making sure no one else was in the cubicles. I switched on all the hand dryers and faucets to drown out any noise. Novah watched me with the eyes of a hawk. Then I stood before her. "She wants it to be the big feature."

Novah's mouth dropped open. "Are you fucking with me?"

"No," I said and Novah grabbed my arms and started screaming. I couldn't help screaming either. "Shush, shush!" I said after ten seconds of good shrilling. I pulled Novah closer. "No one is allowed to know. I carry on as normal. Write 'Ask Miss Bliss,' but at night…"

"Get the shit whipped out of your tush and become the daughter of Chaos."

"Huh?"

"NOX. The Roman goddess of night and the daughter of Chaos."

"Okay. I didn't know who NOX was. So that was helpful. But yes to what you said about the whipping of said tush." As I said those words, the reality of the situation crashed down upon me. "Fuck, Nove." My hands trembled slightly. "What am I going to be stepping into?"

"Copious amounts of come and other bodily fluids, I imagine. Oh, and lube. They'll have that shit on tap." I pulled the card from my bra and stared at the number. "No time like the present, hey babe?"

Nodding, I reached into my pocket and pulled out my cell. I could do this. I loved sex. Was pretty fluid. Experimented in college as most people did. This was just another experiment, with the holy award of gaining the big feature at the end. What were a few bruises and mass orgies to land that baby? Orgasms as payment? I could cash those checks all day.

"Okay," I said on a deep breath and punched the number into my cell. It rang exactly three times before someone picked up.

"Membership number?"

"I was given a card last night," I said, stumbling over my words, and waited for the other person to speak.

"Code on the card."

"Two, one, six, eight, three."

I waited in silence, Novah leaning in close to listen. "It's gone quiet," I mouthed to Novah. She leaned in further, pressing her cheek to mine. The man came back on the line. "I'll text an address to this cell number. You must visit that address within the next two hours. You'll be contacted afterward with further instructions." With that the phone went dead.

"Well, that wasn't creepy in the slightest," Novah said and I shook my head in shock.

"It's like the Mission Impossible of sex clubs," I said. "This message will self-destruct in sixty-nine seconds." I winked at Novah just as an address came through the cell.

Novah was on her cell in no time, googling the address. "It's a clinic," she said, "not too far away."

"Well," I said and turned off the dryers and faucets. "I'd better get my ass to the clinic quick smart. I've got a sex dungeon to join."

"THERE IS no part of me that hasn't been searched, poked, and swabbed," I said as I entered my apartment later that night. Sage and Amelia were sitting on the couch awaiting my return. I'd been texting them the developing story as the day progressed. Sally had sworn me to secrecy, but that didn't include these two or Novah. I told them everything.

I slouched onto the couch and winced. "Front or back passage?" Sage asked, eyebrows dancing.

"Both. The side, vertical, and horizontal ones too." I took the glass of water Amelia offered me before she slumped to my other side. I drank the water in one go and rolled my neck, closing my eyes as I rested the back of my head against the couch.

"They took so many tests from me today my head is spinning. Earning my master's degree was easier than that medical exam. Who knew there were that many STDs you could catch? And the fucking vampire nurse savaged my arm to get blood. I was sure it was a test of endurance. Knowing my luck she'll be the head dominatrix and loves nothing more than blood play. My poor veins had performance anxiety and ran away when the needle came calling. They got prick shy."

"Let's hope the rest of Faith doesn't get prick shy," Sage said and I elbowed him in his ribs, wiping the smug look off his face.

I grabbed my purse and pulled out the NDA I'd been given to sign, scan and send back. "They told me to have my attorney look at this for me. I'm not allowed into this place until it's signed. After being Nurse Nightmare's pincushion for the better half of three hours, I'm getting into that club ASAP." I handed it to Sage. "And since you're my attorney..." I batted my lashes at him, and Sage took the NDA and went to sit at the table.

I felt Amelia's worry hovering over me like an annoying fly that keeps buzzing by your ear. "Amelia, I'm fine."

"You good with anal?" she asked and I choked on my tongue.

"What?"

"Fisting?"

"Amelia!"

"Pegging?"

"Amelia!"

"Squirting, queening, figging?" she continued.

"What the fuck is figging?"

"Having a piece of ginger shoved up your asshole. It burns, Faith. It goddamn burns and some people love it." I blinked at my friend, realizing she was completely serious.

"Shit. I'll never look at the Gingerbread Man the same way again. Was it the Muffin man who did this figging? Did he degrade Gingerbread in such a way? The dirty bastard."

Amelia ignored my joke and asked, "You okay with CBT?"

"The therapy?"

"Cock and ball torture, Faith. Cock and ball torture."

I covered Amelia's hand. "Out of everything you have just said, that seems the most exciting to me. Who wouldn't want to clamp their hands on a pair of balls and make some asshole scream?"

"You're not being serious about any of this, Faith!" she said, exasperated.

"I am, Amelia."

"You didn't even know what queening was, I could tell by your face."

"I still don't."

"It's when you pop a squat and smash your vagina into someone's face. That's it. You just sit on someone's face. Queening! It's a whole thing."

I couldn't help it. I burst out laughing. Amelia's mouth twitched until she finally joined in. "Pop a squat? If that's the truth, then I'm screwed! I can't squat to save my life. I'd kill the poor asshole who wanted to chow down between my legs. With my thigh strength I'd land on the guy's face and wouldn't be able to get back up." I looked across the room. "Sage! Is vaginal asphyxiation a thing?"

"Sure," he said, without taking his eyes off the NDA. "Any kind of asphyxiation is a thing."

"Faith—" Amelia pulled on my arm.

"Amelia. I love you. And bless your innocent heart, but I can only imagine what you had to go through to research those terms today." Amelia was quiet and not at all adventurous. I adored her for doing this for me.

"I sat in the Hall of Human Origins amongst the life-sized Neanderthals. I swear at one point they were peering over my shoulder, looking at my laptop, gasping along with me."

"Gasping, huh? That another sexual activity?"

"It is, actually," Amelia said and my laugh dropped. "It's when you choke someone out as they come. They pass out for a few seconds and it's meant to be akin to what some would deem ecstatic."

"Wow."

"Wow. Exactly, Faith. These are the types of things you will be walking into blind. I know you're not some virginal princess, but to these people, you are. This isn't hooking up with some random guy in a bathroom. This is real scary sex play."

Leaning over, I kissed Amelia on the cheek. "I love you. And I appreciate you. I just want you to know that. But this is happening, sweets." Sage flopped down beside me. "Well?" I asked him.

"It's ironclad, as I thought it would be." It deflated my hope of the big feature like a pin being stabbed into a blow-up doll. "But not impossible. You'd have to leave out any names, any facial descriptions—anything that could expose the people you meet, or fuck. But as for your experience, what you do and have done to you, you're good to go."

"Argh!" I screamed and dived on Sage. I wrapped my arms around his neck and kissed him on the cheek. "Sage, would you like me to queen you in thanks?"

"What?" he asked, nose wrinkling in confusion.

"Smash my hoohaw on your face."

"Erm...I'm good, Faith, thanks."

"You sure? These are the delicious treats one might expect from me from now on. I shall become well versed in all things kink."

"One hundred percent sure, baby girl. Though if you find a handsome man who wants to deliver me treats, I won't say no."

"What if he wanted to shove ginger up your ass?"

"Then I'd say call me Mr. Moscow Mule."

I barked a laugh and slapped Sage's buff chest.

"I can't with you two," Amelia said and curled up on the couch away from us. "Each of you is as bad as the other." I dove forward and cuddled into her arm. Amelia laughed and pushed me away.

"You want me to scan this and shoot this over?" Sage asked. He had an office setup like no other in his apartment.

"Yes please."

Ten minutes later, Sage was back in our front room and the signed contract had been sent to NOX. The nerves I had been fighting all day were starting to kick in. It was done. I was going to be attending NOX.

Just as I got up to grab a drink, my phone rang. I fumbled with the device, luckily avoiding dropping it for once in my life. "Hello," I answered hurriedly. Sage and Amelia muted the TV and watched me.

"Tomorrow night. Seven p.m. Come fully shaved, no hair on the genital area, and be clean. Your hair must be tied up. You will be sent the address an hour before your arrival time. Don't be late. You only get one chance at NOX, don't waste it." The call clicked off, and I looked at my friends with wide eyes.

"Tomorrow night," I said and took a deep breath. "I go tomorrow night."

Tomorrow night I would discover what was hidden behind the high walls of mystery that surrounded the infamous club. I would commit myself to getting the story, no matter what I must endure. I, Faith Maria Parisi, would enter NOX, my eyes—and, no doubt, my legs—wide open.

CHAPTER SIX

"YOU CAN DO THIS, FAITH," I chanted to myself as the cab began to slow. My black three-quarter length trench coat was pulled tightly around my waist. The man on the phone last night hadn't given me a dress code. So I'd dressed in my sexiest get-up and hoped it would suffice. I wore a fitted black dress and my best five-inch heels —it was a tad ambitious for a lady of my balance ineptness to try for such great heel heights, but I felt the night required something bold. I was entering a sex club after all. Maybe I would discover some handsome man who had a fetish for clumsiness.

My hair was swept up in a mass of waves on the top of my head, a gazillion bobby pins holding it in place. My makeup was heavy and glamorous with my new red lipstick matching my nails. Chandelier earrings hung from my ears. I feared I looked like an extra from Jersey Shore. But I was here now, and I had to pull up my big-girl pants and face the floggers.

The cab came to a stop in the center of the Upper East Side and I stared at the towering townhouse, perfectly situated beside its pretty neighbors on the idyllic tree-lined street. It was made of white stone with Romanesque columns standing like guards at the all-glass entrance. The glass was opaque and I couldn't see inside. It was all very Roman Pantheon in its awe-inspiring aesthetic. And its facade suited the name of the club. The goddess and daughter of Chaos would be proud of this Italian architecture. As beautiful as it was, it looked like just another ungodly expensive home in New York. This infamous club was hiding in plain sight. From the street one would never know the carnal delights it offered inside.

"You getting out?" the cab driver snapped, interrupting my inner musings.

"Calm your tits, Mike," I said, seeing his name on his cab license, hanging from his mirror. "I'm out."

I stepped out onto the sidewalk, my gaze traveling up to the very top of the building. It was at least five stories tall. How many rooms could a building like this boast? I could only imagine the amount of rope and latex that it must take to satisfy the clientele behind the thick walls.

"You got this, Faith," I said again and began climbing the steps, carefully trying to stay upright on my skyscraper heels. I rang the bell and waited for the games to begin.

A butler, of all people, answered the door. He must have been at least in his late seventies, his gray hair and the heavy wrinkles on his face giving his maturity away. And he dressed as any butler would, in black pants and a matching jacket, with a white shirt and black bow tie around his neck.

"Do you have your card, Madam?" he asked, as though he'd been expecting me, his softly spoken English accent sailing to my ears like a gentle breeze. His accent soothed, where Harry Sinclair's voice felt as annoying as a cheese grater over my ass.

I reached into my pocket and handed him the card. He moved to an iPad-looking contraption on the wall in the foyer and typed something in. "ID?" he asked next. I handed over my driver's license. He scanned it on the same device.

He smiled at me when the machine beeped and flashed a green light. Handing me back my ID, he bowed and said, "Welcome to

NOX, Miss Parisi." He gestured for me to enter the large white marbled foyer. The front door shut and locked behind us. "All new sirens are required to meet in the basement."

"Sirens?" I questioned.

He gave a silent nod. "This way, Miss Parisi," Alfred said. I didn't know his name, but this was all very Batman, so the name suited him well. Well, if under his bat suit Batman was wrapped head to toe in a gimp suit and liked to lick people's feet after wrestling them in Jell-O.

Alfred led the way, walking a fraction ahead of me. He'd only made it a few feet when I choked on my own saliva. "Is all well, Miss?" Alfred asked, turning to face me.

"Very," I rasped through my raw throat, trying to keep my eyes from bugging out of my head. "Please, continue." I smiled in encouragement. Alfred resumed the lead, and the source of my choking fit swiftly came into view. Alfred's suit looked like the typical attire of a well-trained British butler to the queen herself but, on closer inspection, the entire ass of the pants was missing, showcasing his saggy behind for all the world to see. I couldn't tear my eyes away from his slightly flat cheeks as he led me to a set of stairs and we began our descent.

I averted my eyes from the elderly man's ass and set my sights on the sweeping marble staircase that led to the upper floors. I tried to listen for any sounds of sex or, at the very least, mood music, but all that could be heard was the clacking of my heels on the marble floor. Rich red carpet covered the landings and the center of the stairs, and an extensive number of vases filled with bouquets of flowers sent a sweet fragrance around the space. Artistic masterpieces, so big they belonged in museums, adorned the walls.

I was so busy admiring the view I tripped on a stair, grabbing the handrail for balance, and I viewed the pictures up close. They were Renaissance-style paintings of men with their heads between women's legs, women having sex with men in all kinds of Kama Sutra positions—men with men and women with women. This was no ordinary Upper East Side town house.

Darkly stained wooden doors made a maze of the hallways. The farther we descended, the more I wondered just how big this townhouse truly was and how many people it could hold. My mind boggled at how many bottles of lube one must purchase to keep such a sexual frenzy going strong through even one night.

As we reached what seemed to be the basement, two ornate doors sat on opposite sides of the landing. These were not dark wooden doors like those in the rest of the house, but appeared to be made from pure gold, with Roman figurines carved into the illustrious panels.

Alfred led me to the right and turned the knob. "In you go, Madam." I edged cautiously through the doorway, and a female dressed in a full-body PVC latex catsuit greeted me. I found myself standing in a black box. There was no other name for it. Both the walls and floor were jet black, illuminated only by dim red lights cascading from the ceiling like dusky twilight.

A mask covered the woman's face. It was a full-face mask, only showing her red-painted lips. And at the top of the mask, she sported the huge ears of a rabbit. As hard as I tried, I couldn't make out her face under the lagomorphic coverage. Only her eyes. And the vivid shade of purple shining back at me proved that even eye colors were disguised by the clever use of contacts.

Anonymity, it was NOX's key to success, after all.

"Welcome to our club. You were scouted by our resident reconnoiter to become a beloved NOX siren." The curvaceous woman talked in a seductive, though slightly robotic, tone. "Sirens are those who have a natural sexual magnetic draw. Those who can lure and tempt our members like forbidden fruit and help make their greatest fantasies come to life."

A siren. I had been scouted to be a siren. I didn't know the specifics, but from the little information there was on NOX online, I wondered if a siren was a kind of sexual pet.

"Do you consent?" Bunny asked.

I closed my eyes, giving myself an internal pep talk. *You can do this. You will enjoy this. You can do it.*

"I consent," I said, opening my eyes and gaining the gleaming smile of Bunny.

"Then please follow me." Bunny moved to one of the black walls and pushed it open. A door opened to what appeared to be a changing room. If changing rooms were gothic in decor with booths made to look like medieval stone dungeons.

Bunny led me to a booth. There was no curtain on the door; it was exposed, just like I imagined my body was about to be. "This is your uniform. You will wear this each night you are in NOX. You are a siren to our members. It is the role you will play. Having sirens present is just one part of the theatrics here at NOX. Part of the fantasy we offer." She unhooked a pair of cuffs from the wall. "Members may want to chain you to themselves if you allow it. Or tie you to the many instruments in the main room."

"Right. Gotcha," I said, feeling like Alice stepping into a really perverted Wonderland, and looked at the rest of my "uniform". A black velvet bustier, black French lace barely-there pants, stockings, and stripper heels. There was something else on a hook, but I failed to comprehend what it was.

"You gave us your sizes on the form you filled out." Bunny indicated for me to enter. "Your clothes will be stored until it is time to go home." Purple eyes stared at me as I moved into the booth. Bunny didn't move. I gave her a tight smile when I realized she was going to watch me undress. As I shed my trench coat and dress, Bunny remained unmoving.

"Pussy shaved?" she asked and edged closer to me as I pulled down my panties. Her mouth kicked up at the side. "Good." She winked at me. "Nice lips." I knew she wasn't talking about the ones around my mouth.

"Thank you?" I said, my response lilting up like a question. I was a confident woman. But even I was feeling slight nerves at all of this.

I took a deep breath, shed my bra, and stood there in the nude, trying to pretend that it was no different than being at the gym. I'd never been to the gym, of course, but I'd heard about women swinging low and free, legs perched on benches as they aired out their nether-regions and chatted about the day's events, their cheating husbands, and the pool boys they were screwing in secret in the guest house.

"You get hot in that thing?" I asked Bunny, pointing to her catsuit, trying for small talk as I put on my French lace panties, stockings, and garters.

"My master enjoys PVC."

"That a yes?" I smiled, winking at her this time.

At her mute response, I tried to put on my bustier with zero success. Bunny's hands quickly took over, and she started tying the laces for me. She yanked on the laces, swiftly ripping the air from my lungs. My hands slapped on the wall in front of me to keep my balance.

"Shit. Careful," I said.

Bunny kept pulling and pulling until I was sure she'd cracked a few ribs. "Can you breathe?" she asked sweetly.

"No!" I squeaked.

"Perfect," she said and fastened the laces. She bent down and placed the new heels on my feet. I was glad; I feared if I tried to bend over, I'd crash headfirst into the wall and be unable to get back up.

Bunny reached for the one item of clothing I couldn't make out. I could barely see over my cleavage, it was thrust so high up my chest, but as she stroked the semi opaque fabric, I suddenly realized what it was. "A veil?"

"A veiled mask." She placed it on my head and hooked a clasp at the back of my skull to keep it in place. The lace fabric fell over my face, dropping to the bottom of my neck, inhibiting my sight. A curtain of black beads created a second layer over the lace. I could only see through it a little. I guessed that was the point of the design.

"Our greatest rule here at NOX is to keep our faces covered at all times." Bunny's mouth went close to my ear. "It might seem daunting at first. But believe me, you will love it. It is like nothing else, taking pleasure anonymously. You will feel freer than you ever have before once you just let go."

"I'll take your word for it."

"At no time will you remove this veil," Bunny said, back to business. "If you show your true identity at any point, you will be vacated from the club. Maître will not tolerate any form of disobedience. It does not matter how much or little you have paid for a membership, the rule is absolute. Do you understand?"

"Maître?" I asked, my journalist's ears pricking up almost as tall as Bunny's. *Maître*. French for *master*. The rumors of a French ruling master were almost as famous as the club itself.

Bunny gave the first wide smile I'd seen from her. "Our Maître. The master of the club. The architect of all of this." Her voice changed from the monotone I had become accustomed to into an excited and heated lilt.

Stepping back to admire her work, Bunny nodded and took the black leather cuffs and, as gentle as a mouse, began fastening them to my wrists. I stared down, able to see her delicate hands locking them firmly in place. I stared at the sight, unable to look away. I was here. I was a NOX siren. And I was suddenly terrified.

"There," Bunny said, skirting her finger up my bare arms. "You are perfection now. Civilian clothes are so dull. There's nothing like lace and leather and latex to make you embrace your femininity."

Bunny led me through another door. As I entered, I squinted through my veil. The room held a few women dressed just like me. There were two men there too, dressed in leather pants and nothing else. If my mythological knowledge was correct, sirens were traditionally perceived as female. Then again, we were in the twenty-first century and men could damn well be sirens too if they wanted to be. NOX was clearly progressive. That was a tick in my book.

"Sit down here," Bunny said. I dropped to my knees, sitting back on my haunches like the other sirens were doing. Bunny spoke to a man at the front of the room. "She is the last," Bunny said and walked away.

The man at the front of the room was dressed in PVC pants, his torso bare. A floor-length cloak with a large hood was wrapped around him. The hood covered half of his face, but I could see the mask he wore, of the Venetian variety. Gold, with short red feathers adorning the edges. "In NOX no one will use their names. It helps us protect our identities." I caught sight of his rippling abs. "In your role as a siren, you must always answer with "Yes, sir" or "Yes, ma'am" when speaking to members. That includes me."

"Sir" moved back to the front of the room. "Soon you will enter the main body of NOX. We have an array of members here. It is not only singletons who gain membership. Many of the people who attend NOX are couples too. We scout and invite sirens into the club for those wishing to experiment, to add other members to their sexual endeavors. And for your own pleasure too." I could hear my heart beating in my ears, nerves swooping in my stomach.

"As a siren, your experience in NOX could be vast. You might find yourself playing the part of a submissive, or a sexual pet to a master. Or the person or persons you join may want *you* to be in charge, they might desire to serve *you*. We all have different sexual preferences and needs and that stands for you too. As a siren, you hold a great power. You are desired here, practically revered and worshipped by our members. You can refuse any advances, of course. And you are in the lucky position where most of the members' pleasure will be focused on you." I was getting hot. The air seemed to crackle around me.

"Whoever you partner up with, it is up to *you* to decide what you will do with them, what you like and what you don't. NOX is *everyone's* greatest sexual fantasy come to life. We want it to be yours too. You are not less than because you do not pay a membership, on the contrary. We want all our members to feel safe and to enjoy themselves."

He paused and began walking up and down the room. Like the

changing rooms, this room was dark with low lighting. "If you do not want to participate with someone, politely decline. No one will argue. If they do, they will be removed. Everything we do here is one hundred percent consensual." When he stood at the top of the room again, he said, "Now that has been said, we are ready."

A door opened and immediately the low dulcet tone of trance music came pounding into the room. Screams and moans of ecstasy sailed on those heavy beats and slammed straight into my chest.

I got to my feet and followed the other sirens into the main room. I glanced up through my veil and, even with hazy vision, my eyes widened at the sights before me. I could only describe it as a vast basement of debauchery. Men and women writhed in every part of the space. Dim red lights seductively kissed both naked and clothed bodies. A pit at the bottom of the room swirled with enraptured bodies like a moving oil painting being crafted by an erotic artist—kissing, oral sex, fingers and toys, intercourse, and heads thrown back, mouths screaming out in pleasure. My mind raced at the thought of being in the center of that pit.

What would it be like to be touched by that many people?

I jumped in shock as a hand skimmed up my leg. I looked down, under my veil, to see a man in a cloak and mask lounging on the floor, with another man kissing along every inch of his bare stomach. "Join us?" he asked. He smiled at me under his red demonic-horned mask.

"Sorry," I blurted, my nerves taking over. "I'm just window shopping for now." I winced at how pathetic I sounded.

I stepped away and quickly searched the room. As Bunny and Sir had said, all faces were covered with masks—cats, bunnies, masks in Egyptian and Venetian styles. Demons, angels, and multicolored carnival facades. Vibrant pink, red, and black eyes stared at us as we passed through, contacts disguising the members' only distinguishable features.

A high-pitched scream cut through the hypnotic music, and my head snapped to the left. My mouth fell open as I clapped eyes on a woman, wearing an outfit made only from leather straps, tied to a St

Andrew's Cross. She was getting whipped by a man in a gold mask, carved with an evilly laughing mouth. Pink welts littered her skin. The man saw my interest.

"Come. I'd be honored to flog you too."

"I would, but I...erm...I have too sensitive skin," I said, mumbling my words. "I bruise like a peach." The man bowed at me then went back to whipping his partner. I tried to seek out the other sirens. My stomach rolled when I saw them joining couples, some entering other rooms.

Come on, Faith, I said to myself. *Stop being such a pussy.*

I moved through each room, the sights melting into one libidinous blur. Two women were strung up from the ceiling by ropes like roasting hogs at a barbeque. Human tables and chairs were scattered around the floor, people's feet and drinks resting on their backs. Men and men kissed, women and women groped, and orgies ten people deep rolled on the biggest beds I'd ever seen.

My feet faltered when I saw men dressed as ponies trotting by, a mistress in red PVC holding their reins and whipping them with a large crop when they displeased her. My head throbbed in sync with the trance music at sights I'd only ever seen in films. Hell, some I'd never seen at all. Amelia had been right. This was more than I'd ever bargained for.

A "pony" stopped beside me. The mistress ran her crop down my arm. "Are you interested?" she asked.

Pony play was too friggin' much for me. "Sorry. I'm allergic to horses," I said and scurried away, face blazing at my stupid excuse. I needed a break. I needed to gather my thoughts and kick my own ass for being such a wimp.

I searched for somewhere to go, unable to find my way around. I passed fully stocked bars, where NOX members lounged and drank, laughing with friends like they were at any other bar in Manhattan. Thong-wearing submissives acted as tables. One man lifted his sub's face and pushed her between his legs without interrupting his conversation with his friend. His jaw clenched as she blew him in front of us. Then I turned to my right, just as a woman smashed her crotch over the face of a man wrapped in chains beneath her.

"Queening," I whispered, a traitorous nervous laugh slipping from my mouth as I imagined Amelia's face, seeing this in action.

I saw what I assumed was a bathroom beside the main bar. After darting across the floor, avoiding the many offers flying my way, I pushed through the door...only to stop dead in my tracks. It wasn't a bathroom. It was a dark room with several swings attached to metal frames, some wooden crosses, and I couldn't make out what else. Four women were swinging from the leather swings, which held their wrists and ankles. I began backing away. "Sorry," I said to the man in the center, holding a whip made of horsehair.

"Join us," he said, "we have room to spare." I started shaking my head. I backed away, praying I'd find the door that second. My shoulder bumped a metal pole, knocking me offtrack. I stumbled in my heels, but I managed to find purchase on the frame of an empty swing, which stopped me from hitting the floor.

It all happened so fast. My unsteady grip on the metal swing caused it to topple over...knocking down all the other swings in the room. It was a cacophony of metal crashing against metal and screams from the women tied up in leather swings and unable to get away. I tried to help the man stop the wreckage, but it was in vain.

My cheeks flamed with embarrassment as the bar staff entered the room to help. When the final crash of metal ended, I felt several pairs of eyes fixed on me.

"Whoops," I said, grimacing under my veil.

A hand landed on my back. Through my veil I saw the familiar Venetian mask of the "sir" who had been tasked with watching over us tonight. He led me through the club. I kept my eyes to the floor. I'd fucked up. I was going to get thrown out. I just knew it. Sadness swept through me. I wouldn't get the feature. Sally was going to kill me.

Sir led me to the room we had started in that night. "Are you okay?" he asked. I wanted to cry at how nice he was being to me.

"Yes." I sighed. "Believe me when I say this is nothing new to me. I'm a bit of a calamity."

"No one was hurt," he said, but there was also no reassurance that I wasn't about to be thrown out on my lace-clad ass. Sir started to say something, but the phone on the wall rang. It made me jump. Sir answered it. I tried to hear who was on the other end, but I couldn't. "Okay, Maître."

My eyes widened. Maître. The legendary master of the club.

"Yes, Maître," Sir said and hung up the phone. He turned to me. "Maître has requested your presence."

I was rooted to the spot. Maître wanted to see me. *The* maître. I'd heard of him, of course. Rumors of NOX in New York were nothing to the secret whisperings about the man that ruled the club with an iron fist. The mysterious Frenchman who ruled his sexual kingdom from his throne, his loyal subjects worshipping at his feet.

The door behind us opened, and Bunny came through. "She is to be taken straight to him in his quarters," Sir said to her.

"Yes, sir."

Bunny led me from the room and toward black padded elevator doors. As the doors opened, it was to find the elevator covered wall to wall in red velvet.

Bunny pulled me inside and pressed the button for the top floor. "Be honest," I said, "am I getting kicked out?"

"I have no idea what Maître wants. He's not an easy man to read. He mostly keeps to himself."

Great. That didn't help me at all.

The elevator opened, and Bunny led me to the landing. I looked around the impressive upper floor. There was only one set of double doors to be seen. A massive chandelier hung from the ceiling.

We arrived at the doors, and Bunny rang a bell. A green light flashed and she led me inside. The perfect sound of Andrea Bocelli hit me first, his beautiful voice sailing into my ears. It immediately made me feel calmer, my nerves settling some.

Through the cover of my veil, I peeked at my surroundings. The room was large and gothic in style, in keeping with the rest of the house. Erotic pictures, as in the foyer, hung on every wall. I swallowed hard as all the contraptions I'd seen on the main floor were scattered around the room. And then some. Certain devices in this room looked straight from The Spanish Inquisition's High Inquisitor's torture chamber.

Maître was prepared to play. He was prepared to play hard.

"Kneel down," Bunny ordered, then whispered, "Maître is a master in every sense of the word. He is a dominant in the bedroom. If he wants to play, and you agree, he will require you to be submissive to him. You must decide whether or not that kind of pleasure appeals to you." Bunny's words circled my mind as I dropped to my knees. A submissive. Could I be a submissive?

Then I heard a creak on the wooden floor.

"Maître," Bunny said, awe thick in her voice.

"*Pars,*" a hard voice said. I held my breath as the word rang out, in stark contrast to the beautiful classical music lacing the air around us.

"Yes, Maître," Bunny said and left the room.

In the heavy silence, I could hear myself breathing heavily in anticipation of meeting the infamous man. Then, "Look up." The command was spoken in a thick French accent.

Obeying the Maître, I looked up and saw a man casually sitting on a large wooden throne-like chair, one leg draped over an ornate winged arm. I lost my breath seeing his entire torso exposed, his chest and abdominals tanned and blessed with tight muscles. He wore black silken pants and nothing on his feet.

My eyes roved to his face. As with the other men, a cloak covered his head and a mask covered his face. It was a white mask similar to that worn by The Phantom of the Opera, but this version of the mask hid more of his face. Bright silver eyes pierced through the holes in the mask, staring back at me. Contacts. A curve of the mask near his mouth exposed one side of his full lips.

Maître, I thought, feeling my stomach clench.

I froze as he got to his feet, moving with the confidence only a man so sure of his power and sexuality could display. He bent down until his eyes were level with mine. I was transfixed by this mysterious man.

Maître pushed back loose strands of hair off my veil. This close, he would be able to see a glimmer of my face through it. As I met his stare head-on, Maître's eyes flared and the exposed part of his lips curled up in amusement.

"So, you are the source of all the commotion." It wasn't a question.

I nodded and sighed in defeat.

I waited for him to tell me I was banned from NOX forever more. What I didn't expect was for him to say, "You will do, *ma chérie*. You will do for me very well."

CHAPTER SEVEN

MY CHEST ROSE and fell in quick succession. The deep scent of mahogany and tobacco swept around me as heavily as the cloak Maître wore. His head cocked to the side as he admired me from top to toe.

Maître got to his feet and moved back to his throne. I couldn't take my eyes away from him. I had never seen someone so magnetizing in my entire life. His hand rested on his cheek, gently tapping the white porcelain mask. "You were scouted as a siren?"

"Yes, sir," I said and he stilled.

"I am *Maître*. You will call me as such. I am no 'sir'." He leaned forward. "This is my castle. I am the master, not a subject."

"Yes, Maître," I quickly corrected.

I was rewarded with a large smile. "You learn quickly."

I huffed a laugh. "When I'm not wrecking rooms full of sex swings, I'm generally a smart cookie."

His head tipped to the side again as he studied me. I couldn't read his expression due to the mask and the silver contacts, so by the quirk of his lip I didn't know if I had misspoken or he was impressed.

"You speak without being told to."

"I know," I sighed, then tensed. "Are you going to punish me for that now? For what happened downstairs?"

"Do you want to be punished?" The way he said *punished*, his voice rising at the end of the word, caused a rush of wetness to gather between my legs.

"Do you want to punish me?"

Maître lounged back on his throne as I asked him that question. He lifted his leg and laid it over the winged arm, mirroring the way he had been sitting when I came into the room. The operatic Italian music flowing from the speakers calmed me like a soothing balm. I spoke Italian, of course. It was as much home to me as English. Though I had never been in a home like this—full of crosses, walls of floggers, canes, and whips, what appeared to be stocks, an intricate wooden bench of some kind and, in the corner of the room, what looked like a giant birdcage.

"Do you like the look of the cage, *mon petit chaton?*"

I blinked. "Little kitten?"

"You are curious like one, *non?*"

Maître pushed to his feet and walked straight to me. I wanted to peel the mask off and see the man underneath. He had me more than intrigued. Maître's hand moved to the mass of hair on my head. Deftly, and with a gentleness that made my skin shiver, he began threading the bobby pins from my tresses, dropping them to my feet in a haphazard pile. My hair fell like a heavy curtain to the middle of my back.

"You will never wear your hair up again." He bent his head down until his cheek was hovering beside mine. "I'll need something to grab hold of when I fuck you. If you consent to this, of course."

Every part of my body was taut and turned on, my stuttered breath betraying how impossibly aroused I was right now. I felt like Maître would simply have to stroke his finger on my bare shoulder and I'd splinter apart. Curiously, I felt safer here, alone with Maître in his room, than in the main room with everyone else.

Maître circled where I knelt. He was tall and broad with cut muscles that flexed with every small step. "I haven't fucked a siren in quite some time. Have never trained someone solely for my liking." He walked back to his throne, sat down, and stared at me.

"Never?" I whispered. He shook his head silently.

He leaned forward. "Tell me." I waited for him to continue. "Why did you refuse so many offers in the main room?" He had been watching. "I check the main room throughout the night, ma chérie. I must ensure my members adhere to the rules." His eyes narrowed. "I saw the new sirens all joined in...except for you." I closed my eyes, embarrassment taking me over. "You do not want to be here?"

"Yes, Maître," I said quickly, opening my eyes. "I do. It's just that room..." I shook my head. "It was. A lot to take in at once. I..." I decided to be honest. "I don't know what happened. I just got a case of cold feet."

Maître came forward again. Moving behind me, he placed his mouth at my ear and whispered, "And now? In this room, with me. Do you have the same *cold feet?*"

An involuntary moan slipped from my mouth as my blood heated to boiling temperatures at his close presence. Maître lifted my hair in one hand, like a rope, and I felt his breath on the back of my neck.

"No, Maître." My voice was raspy. "No cold feet at all."

"Do you want to play with me, ma chérie? Do you want to be my siren, my submissive? Do you consent to being mine?"

There was only one answer I could possibly give. "Yes, Maître. I give my consent to being all yours."

"*Bon*," he said and tightened his grip on my hair. Not hard enough to cause pain, but enough to make me still and fall under his command. I froze in shock at how quickly my body had fallen under his direction. He dropped to his knees behind me, and his free hand moved to my panties and slipped underneath the lace. I hitched a breath at his touch, my thighs instinctively sliding apart.

"You're so wet, mon petit chaton," he whispered and moved his fingers to my clit. I moaned out loud, my head falling back against his hard chest. "Do you want to come?"

"Yes," I said, moving my hips to try to get his fingers to move. Maître pulled on my hair and his fingers stilled. "No!" I protested. "Don't stop. Please!"

"One," he said, his mouth at my ear. His lips ran up and down the side of my neck, his warm breath causing my skin to bump in its wake. "Do not give me commands. Ever." The deep timbre of his voice held me captive, the tight fist in my hair keeping me firmly in place against his chest. "I don't respond to orders."

He pressed those soft lips of his to my hot skin, dusting whispers of kisses on my neck, the gentleness in stark contrast to the firm grip he commandeered in my hair. My fast breathing was loud enough to be heard over the operatic music playing all around us, the string section soft in melody and sweet in tone.

"And two," he said, pulling my head so far back the back of my skull rested on his shoulder as his lips kissed my earlobe. "You will address me at all times as Maître. I am your master in this club. I am your sovereign, your leader and king. To not address me as such is disrespectful, and I do not tolerate disrespect in this *chambre*."

"Yes, Maître," I whispered, using all the breath I had left in my lungs. My eyes fluttered closed when his fingers moved from my clit to my entrance.

Maître kissed along my jaw, my legs turning to Jell-O as he pushed a single finger inside me. I cried out, leaning against him to keep from falling. "You smell like strawberries," he said, pushing his finger in and out of me. "Of lychees and blossoms." I moaned when he hooked his finger and hit my G-spot.

"Yes," I whispered, and his finger stopped moving. "Yes, Maître," I corrected. "It's my perfume."

"See?" Maître moved his finger again, adding a second. "For that you shall be rewarded." I moaned. It felt so good. "I can teach you many things, mon petit chaton. Many things."

His hand moved from my hair to my bustier. He freed my breasts, one by one, and my bustier fell an inch, to my waist. With one hand, he began circling my clit with his thumb. With his other hand, he rolled my nipple in his fingers. "I will teach you all of the things I like. You will obey me. In return, you will be pleasured like you have never been pleasured before."

"Yes, Maître," I said, my stomach tightening as my orgasm began to build. It was a rising wave, ready to crash into me. I needed more. He had just touched me and I needed so much more.

"You will submit to me. You will become mine and, in this chambre, I will own you."

"Yes, Maître, yes!" I cried and arched my back when the fingers at my clit moved faster and the fingers inside me pushed at my G-spot over and over again. His minty breath ghosted over my face, and his hand palmed my breasts. Maître was everywhere all at once, no part of me unaffected by his presence.

"Come." One single uttered command from his mouth and I shattered. I orgasmed so strongly it stole my breath and strength and the tiny morsel of inhibition I had left.

His hands didn't stop, just pushed and pushed and drained me of all the pleasure I could muster. I bit my lip at the too-heady sensation until it became too much and my body jerked, unable to take any more. Maître slowed his fingers inside me, moving his other hand from my breasts to push my hair from my face and neck.

"That is just the beginning. You have no idea what is yet to come. What awaits you in my chambre with me." I wanted it. Wanted everything he offered. "I will break you, mon petit chaton. I will break you apart and rebuild you until you live and breathe only for my touch. Oui?"

"Yes, Maître."

"We will have fun, you and I," Maître said, laying a final kiss on my neck before moving away from me. I placed my palm on the ground just to stop me from falling over.

Once he was towering over me, he ordered, "Kneel." I knelt on the floor, straightening my back. I was wet and hot and thoroughly sated, and all he had used on me were his fingers, lips, and voice.

Maître moved back to his throne, and I noticed how hard he was.

I lost my breath at the sight. As he sat back down, he said, "You will return to me tomorrow night at eight p.m. You will enter this room and kneel while you wait for me." Maître reached into his silk pants and pulled out his dick for my viewing. My eyes widened as he began stroking it lazily, as if the action were nothing at all. I felt that ache between my legs begin to build again. "And you will bring with you a list of your hard and soft limits."

"A l-list, Maître?" I stuttered, unable to take my eyes away from his hand. He was huge.

"Hard limits are what you do *not* want me to do to you. Things too far out of your comfort zone." Maître's hips rolled slightly on the throne. I was transfixed at the seductive sight. His jaw clenched and his skin flushed at the pleasure he was bringing to himself. "Soft limits," he said, his French accent thickening as he fell deeper into his pleasure. "Are things you may like to try on occasion, or if the opportunity is right. Anything not on those two lists is bon."

Maître hissed and his hand started to work faster. I moved my hand between my legs, too turned on by his touching himself to think of anything but joining him.

"Stop," Maître ordered. He turned on his throne, and his legs widened so I had a full view of his self-pleasure. My hand froze. "You will not touch yourself for the rest of the night." Maître stroked his hand faster and faster, licking his lips. It didn't matter that I couldn't see his face. I saw the tension building in his bare torso and the defined V that led to his crotch.

"You will kneel on that spot until I tell you to go home." Every part of his being exuded carnal appetite and sin. "If you do not, then you do not return to me tomorrow night. You never come to NOX ever again. You leave now, and will forever have had only a glimpse of what would have awaited you if only you'd learned to submit and do as you are instructed."

His silver eyes were locked on me, daring me to defy him. I moved my hand from my crotch. "Clasp them behind your back," Maître said, nudging his head toward my hands.

One by one, I placed them behind my back, and I entwined my fingers. Maître worked his hand faster and faster over his length, never looking away from me as he brought himself closer to climax.

"You will sit like this for the rest of the night," he repeated, then stilled, clenching his teeth and grunting as he came, semen landing on his tanned washboard stomach. Slightly breathless, but impossibly composed, he added, "And you will watch me come repeatedly until you are released." He smirked. "You may think me a sadist." He stroked himself again. "Maybe I am. That is for you to find out."

As the night moved on, my legs grew numb and my eyes felt raw from having watched Maître masturbate four more times before me. Each time he had ordered that my hands stay behind my back. I didn't know how long I could stand sitting like this. I was wet and so flustered I could barely function. Maître hadn't said one more word to me, just sat on his throne, hard gaze locked on me, daring me to rebel.

Just when I felt I couldn't take any more, the sound of a gong being hit vibrated through the room, making me jump. Maître had been watching me, cheek resting on his hand, for the past hour. He was testing me. Measuring how much I wanted this. Wanted him. Was willing to be under his control.

In this moment, I didn't think I'd ever wanted anyone more.

"Rise," he said when the sound of the gong stopped. I tried to move, but when I did, I found that my legs were completely dead from sitting in one position for too long. Maître came across the room as I attempted to get to my feet. Placing his hands on my arms, he hoisted me up. He was incredibly strong. I grimaced and willed myself not to moan as the blood that had been so harshly denied to my legs rushed into my muscles and veins like a dam breaking and swelling the rivers.

"Tomorrow," Maître said. Just before he turned away, he said, "Maître Auguste." He reached out and ran his finger down my cheek, over my mask, and down to my neck. His touch stole my breath. What was it about this man that made my own body betray me? "You will call me Maître Auguste." The way he said *Auguste* wrapped around me like a Fall breeze threading through my hair.

He waited, with a steely gaze, for me to answer. "Yes, Maître Auguste."

"Tomorrow, mon petit chaton. You and I...we shall play."

Maître Auguste walked past his throne and toward a doorway that took him out of sight. The door behind me opened and Bunny walked in. She stopped dead when she saw me, flushed and exposed.

"This way," she said. I followed her and tried to wrap my head around what had just happened. It felt like a dream. But when I thought back to his fingers inside me and the scream that had ripped from my throat as I collapsed against him, I recalled every single stroke with perfect clarity.

We entered the elevator, and Bunny pressed the lowest button. We descended, and as the doors opened, we were in a vast white space with antique golden mirrors, showers, and marble walls and floor tiles. It looked like an ornate French spa.

Other women occupied the space, changing from their fetish wear of choice and into "civilian clothes," as Bunny had called them. Their masks remained in place. I was led past them, and curious stares followed me.

"You caused quite the commotion tonight. First, in the swing room," Bunny said. I grimaced in embarrassment at that memory. "And now they all want to take a peek at the siren who has lured in Maître."

Bunny stopped at what appeared to be a private changing room. She handed me a card. "This is a personal carrel just for you." She pointed to the door. "This changing room belongs to Maître's submissives. Their *exclusive* room." Bunny pointed at the lock. I scanned the card over it, and the door opened. My eyes rounded when I peered inside. It was almost as big as my apartment. It was decorated in all golds and whites, and a bathtub in the center of the room was perched on gilded feet. A huge shower was in the corner, and a toilet was in a closed-off room. Couches, a fridge filled with water. And...

"A closet," I said and walked to the tall golden doors. I pulled them open to find outfit after outfit hung up on white padded hangers. My eyes widened at the sights. Leather and lace and chains.

"Maître's specific tastes," Bunny said and pointed to my current siren attire. "You will no longer need the standard siren uniform. Each night you arrive, an outfit from this closet will be waiting for you." Bunny led me to white elevator doors at the end of the room. "There are three buttons. The top is for Maître's chambre. You will go directly there every night after you change. You will only see the members of the club if he brings you down to the main floor." She pointed to the middle button. "This is for this floor. For you to change at the beginning and end of the night."

"And the bottom button?"

"Is where a town car will await you. They will pick you up from your apartment and return you home."

"Wow."

Bunny gave me a smile and brushed past me. "Your clothes for home are hung up in the end closet."

"How many people have used this room?" I asked.

Bunny turned to me, her purple eyes softening. "None. This is the first time it has been used." With that, she departed. The door clicked shut, locking everyone else outside.

I scanned the room and, still stunned, made my way to the closet and found the dress and trench coat that I'd arrived in. I dressed and pressed the bottom button of the elevator. As it opened, a large underground parking lot met me. While other people were climbing into parked cars in the lot, mine was waiting for me at the private elevator exit. "Miss," a driver said, getting out of the car, and he opened the rear door for me. I climbed inside, smiling at him. The windows were tinted so black that no one would see inside. The cars filed out into a tunnel that opened onto a deserted back road.

"You've thought of everything, haven't you, Maître Auguste?" I said and sat back on the leather seat, closing my eyes. Maître's masked face sprang to my mind, along with that arrogant flicker of a smirk he had frequently given me.

I inhaled a deep breath when my pulse started to race. His voice, his accent, his cut and ripped body, which had pinned me to him. And those lips, the lips that delivered such soft kisses, and those hands, which had made me come so hard it was akin to reaching nirvana.

Maître Auguste. I ran his name around my head, looking out the window as we crossed the Brooklyn Bridge. My body felt alive just remembering how I'd felt in his presence. And I would be back there tomorrow night to play.

At that thought, I smiled.

CHAPTER EIGHT

"ELECTROSTIMULATION?"

"Hard limit," I said, as Novah added that to what we'd deemed the "Oh, fuck no!" list. Novah had found a list online of typical BDSM sex practices. The farther we went down the list, the more I realized what deep shit I was in.

"Riding crops?" Novah asked next. I sat back in my chair in our cubicle, feet up on my desk, hands steepled as I considered each option.

"Soft limit," I replied. Novah added that to the "Never say never list of things I might try".

"Blindfolds?"

"I'm okay with that."

"Ropes?"

"Passable."

"Vagina worship?"

"Highly encouraged."

"Forced exercise?"

My feet slammed on the floor and I whipped my head to Novah with breakneck speed. "Hard limit. *Really* fucking hard limit. Who the hell would put someone through that kind of torture?" I shook my head in disbelief. "Barbaric! Whip me, cane me, tie me to a St Andrew's Cross, but do *not* force me into a set of jumping jacks. That's a definite addition to the "Oh, fuck no" list!"

Novah laughed and wrote it down. "You know, these things seem pretty excessive, Faith. You sure it's that kind of club? Isn't there a strong difference between a true hardcore BDSM dungeon and a sex club for the rich and famous?"

I nodded. "I don't think it is for sadists, it's more for exhibitionists with so much money they get bored with life and thus suddenly decide dressing up in a pig mask with a sign around their neck saying 'touch me' seems like a good idea." I took a long drink of my coffee. "But I'm not taking any chances with Maître. He wants to own me, Nove. I can feel it. I need to have all parts of my bare ass covered."

"No, what you can feel is the remnants of the hardest orgasm you've ever had, and it's frazzled your brain." Novah held my arm. "Faith, you're acting like a man."

I laughed, but I let my mind drift back to Maître Auguste behind me, his talented fingers causing me to scream. "It's true," I admitted in defeat. "And that was nothing, Nove. *Nothing* to what was happening in the rest of the club. Nothing to what all those devices and contraptions in Maître's room promised."

Novah rolled her desk chair beside me. "Just go with it, Faith. You never know, this might be the best thing that has ever happened to you. I mean, the elusive Maître of NOX picked you to be his personal siren. On your first night. Granted, it was because you almost maimed innocent people, but still. It's an incredible thing. It's like you've won the lottery twice. Think of all the material you'll have for your feature."

I squeezed the arms of my chair just thinking about watching Maître pleasure himself on his throne, with those alien-like silver contacts practically boring laser beams into my eyes as he watched me for any sign of disobedience.

"It was, without doubt, the best orgasm I've ever had in my life."

"And you said he was hung." Novah's eyebrows danced. "Just wait until that piece of hot salami is served on your moist platter."

"Please never utter that sentence again. My lady boner just totally deflated."

"Faith! Are you finished with your column?" Sally barked as she whizzed past us like a hurricane.

"Almost!" I called back, scrambling forward to my desk. In truth, I hadn't even started it. I had wasted too many hours researching hard and soft limits and kink practices. "Shit! What time is it?" I asked Novah.

"Five." Novah grimaced.

"Double shit!" I spat and downed the rest of my coffee like it was a shot of cheap-ass vodka. "Think, think, think," I said, piling up the emails for my "Ask Miss Bliss" page, trying to find ones that were spunky enough for this week's magazine.

"We don't go to press until midnight, Faith. You've got time."

"I don't. I have to be in Maître's room by eight, kneeling down and awaiting my trip to hedonism!" Novah stood and started putting on her coat, as did most of the office. I panicked. "Help me!"

Novah kissed my head. "Can't, sweets. I've got a salon appointment. These red tresses don't grow naturally, you know."

"Traitor!" I said and made my eyes focus on the first email I'd printed off.

I've recently begun having sex with my boyfriend, and on our first night I squirted as I came, drenching both myself and my antique patchwork quilt. I'm afraid it will happen again and, worse, my boyfriend cannot swim. Any advice? From H.R. Brown.

Loading up my computer, I wrote: *Invest in some waterproof sheets for you, and repurpose the quilt as a wall tapestry far out of squirting range. Buy a snorkel and swimming cap for your boyfriend. Ride his dick like it's Aquaman's trident and be safe in the knowledge that the next time you gush, your precious belongings and boyfriend will be safe from imminent drowning. Live wet and wild, Miss Bliss.*

I typed like a mythical Fury high off her tits on a six-pack of

Red Bull and quickly wrapped up my agony column. When I looked up, it was to see Frank, the janitor, slowly making his way into Visage's office. The lights were low and I was the only writer left.

"Hey Frank!" I called as I ran past him, jacket, purse and, more importantly, my list in my hands.

"Hey, Faith! Be careful out there. The rain is really coming down."

"Will do, Frank! Bye!" I ran to the elevators and pressed the button repeatedly until the doors opened. I rushed inside, only to come up short when I saw Harry Sinclair.

His head snapped up in surprise. "Miss Parisi," he said, rising from a slouched position against the back wall. "I didn't think anyone else was left in the building." The doors shut behind us, and I quickly pressed the button for the lobby.

"Yeah, had to work late," I said and watched the floors begin to count down. I wanted to take a shower at home and change before going to NOX, but I couldn't be late. Despite myself, I was practically bouncing with excitement about what tonight would bring.

Just as we reached the second floor, the elevator's lights flickered, and the steel box jerked to a bumpy stop. "No," I said, when the cable above groaned. "No, no, no!" I started slapping my palm on the door. "Not again! You piece-of-shit elevator! Not again!"

"Miss Parisi?" Harry's voice said from behind me. "May I?"

For a second I'd forgotten that Harry was behind me. Oh. My. God. I was stuck in this godforsaken elevator. I was going to be late for Maître and, worse, I was trapped here with Harry Sinclair.

I pressed the button for the lobby repeatedly, so fast my wrist was at risk of developing a nasty case of carpal tunnel. When that failed to work, I tucked my things under my arm and ran my palms up and down all the buttons on the grid. No lights. Nothing. It was completely dead.

"*Cazzo!*" I shouted, the feisty Italian in me taking over.

"Miss Parisi!" Harry said more sternly. "Please move. Although you appear to be an expert in lift maintenance and repair, I'm afraid this time your talents seem to have failed you."

I closed my eyes and stepped aside, mentally talking myself down from bitch slapping the English asshole. *He's your boss, Faith. Let's not get fired when you're finally getting ahead.*

"Sinclair House, elevator three," Harry said into the emergency phone. "Thank you." He hung up and turned to me.

"That was my next option," I said, sinking into the wall. The lights above us flickered again then suddenly plunged us into darkness. A shrill, banshee-like sound traitorously fled my mouth, and I launched forward when the elevator jerked again, convincing me that we were about to plummet to our immediate demise.

In seconds the elevator stilled and the dim emergency lights came on, blanketing the small space in musty yellow light. I counted to ten, trying to slow my panicked heart. It wasn't until my breathing had calmed that I realized I was wrapped around something hard, smelling of mint, sandalwood, and musk.

My eyes widened feeling rippling abdominals flex against my chest and back muscles moving against my palms. As I slowly lifted my head, my gaze passed an open collar, the lightly tanned skin of a corded neck, and an incredibly strong clenched jaw with a hint of dark stubble, and came to a stop at a pair of bright blue eyes that were narrowed and watching my every move.

With awkwardness reigning, I smiled widely and said, "Well, of all the places in all the world, fancy meeting you here." Realizing I was wrapped tightly around Harry like an overly attached spider monkey, I quickly unlatched my arms from his waist and stepped back.

Flustered, I pushed my hair from my face and moved to the far side of the elevator. "I was just checking you were okay. Some people can be scared of the dark, you know? I was just doing my civic duty in protecting a visitor to our fine country."

"Is that so?" Harry asked, his face as stoic and unreadable as ever.

"Yep."

Silence screamed around us, and I realized that I would never complain about the terribly played piano music filtering through elevator speakers again. Silence in general made me twitchy. Marrying that with the high anxiety of being stuck in a premade metal coffin gave me the unstoppable urge to fill it with noise.

"So, you work out?" I asked Harry, who lifted his head. Apparently, the floor had been a more interesting view than the clearly unstable agony aunt across from him, who now knew his clothing measurements intimately.

Harry raised a single eyebrow. I pointed to his body, circling his torso and arm region. "Hard," I said, instant regret settling within me as the word slipped from my mouth. "Muscles." I winced. That wasn't any better. "That I was wrapped around. That I felt. The abs and back and—"

The emergency phone rang and Harry answered it, leaving me free to exhale in embarrassment and lean my head back against the wall. Every time I was around this man my mouth never failed to betray me.

"That is not the best news," Harry said tightly to whoever was on the other end of the phone. "But thank you. We shall but wait."

As he hung up the phone, I felt my hopes for a hot and steamy night with Maître plummeting as deeply as the Titanic. Harry sighed. "They had to call for the elevator repair service."

"Great." I slid down the cold metal wall to the floor. Harry watched me, opening another of his shirt collar buttons, laid his jacket on the floor, and sat down. I couldn't help but laugh.

"Something amusing, Miss Parisi?"

"Afraid you'll get your tush dirty on the elevator floor?"

"This is a three-thousand-dollar suit."

"Of course it is."

Harry tipped his head to the side like I was a puzzle he was trying to work out. "You are here late."

"Had to finish off my column. As you know we go to press tonight, and I was a little behind."

"I shall look forward to this week's Ask Miss Bliss's offerings," he said and ran his hand across his forehead as though he were fighting a migraine. "Anything particularly enlightening this week?"

I shrugged. "Squirting, herpes, and cock rings were the solid standouts."

"Quite," he said, and I thought I caught a slight flicker of a smile. It was gone so quickly that I wasn't sure if I'd imagined it. I once hit my head in the bathtub and swore I saw a mermaid swimming toward me during the subsequent concussion. I believed this could be akin to that. I felt the back of my head. I hadn't hit it during the breakdown, I didn't think.

"Are you hurt?" Harry's voice changed in tone and he sat forward, narrowing his eyes to see me better in the low lighting.

"No, thought I might of hit my head. But I'm good."

A minute fluttering sensation moved under my sternum. I shook my head, not having a clue what it was. I rubbed my hand across my chest. "You have anxiety attacks?" Harry asked, nudging his head toward my hand.

I nodded. "Don't like the dark much. Or should I say, I don't like the dark when I'm trapped inside a steel box that is dangling from a single cable in thin air." But I knew what a panic attack felt like. The sensation I was feeling now had nothing to do with anxiety. Strange.

"We will be out soon."

I checked my watch. I was running so damn late!

"Are you in a rush?" Harry asked.

"Kind of." I gave Harry a tight smile. "I just have somewhere I need to be." I decided to omit the fact that I had a sexual Dom waiting to teach me all the secrets of pleasure in the most interesting of ways, an experience I hoped to write about in a big feature that Harry Sinclair knew nothing of. "You?" I asked, trying to polite.

He shook his head. "Afraid not."

"No hot date?"

Harry huffed a laugh, and I thought I might faint at the sight of him smiling, even if it was only a small hint of a grin. "No hot date."

I studied my boss. He was only a few years older than me. Was ridiculously handsome and a billionaire to boot. He came across like an absolute prick, but he wouldn't be that way to everyone. Surely some people warmed to him. He must have some potential suitors in his life. He was frequently photographed with that Lady Louisa Samson for one.

"So," I asked, filling the dead air. "How are you settling into New York?"

"Well. I have been coming back and forth to Manhattan for years. I know it well. It is fine."

"Not as good as old England, hey?"

"England is home." His expression made me breathless. It was a look of pure love. He said "home" with such warmth I felt it deeply within my heart. And I knew that feeling too.

"You're Italian?" he asked. He pointed to the grid of buttons. "*Cazzo*. If I'm not mistaken, that's a swear word in Italian, is it not?"

I burst out laughing in shock at the word slipping from Harry's prim and proper mouth. "Yes," I said. "It's Italian. And it's a bad word." He waited for me to continue. "My papa is Italian, from Parma in Emilia-Romagna. The north."

"I know Parma well."

"You do?" I asked. "I've never been. Though it's my dream."

"You've never seen your father's home?"

My smiled died and my gut clenched. "No. They could never afford it when I was younger." I didn't want to add that they had saved up for years to go back last year, but it had all been stolen by a man Papa had trusted like a brother.

I'd never cared for money; it had never been a notable factor in my life growing up. Apart from the obvious—needing a house to live in and food on the table. But of late, it had been a huge factor to my parents. Good people who had been deceived by a bad man.

"But you are from New York?" Harry asked, pulling me back from the sadness I feared I'd drown in one day.

"Hell's Kitchen." I smiled, thinking of my youth running through the streets in the summer with my friends, the theaters, and neighbors gathering on stoops to chat and drink and laugh. "I live in Brooklyn now."

"A true New Yorker," he said with no discrimination in his voice. It reflected an easy affection toward those born and raised in the Big Apple.

"And you?" I asked.

"Surrey."

"I'm guessing that, unlike me, you didn't grow up in an apartment though."

"Not quite," he said, lip hooked up at the side. "Do you have siblings?" he asked awkwardly, like he was clutching at anything to make things less strained. If we were being honest, there was no love lost between us, so I was surprised he was trying so hard to engage in conversation. If it made the time pass more quickly and with less pain, I could put my animosity aside and engage in meaningless small talk with the viscount.

"Nope. Just me." I winked. "Couldn't let anyone else share my spotlight, could I?"

"I fear not," he said; then he glanced at the emergency phone as though he were wishing for it to ring and rescue him from this uneasy situation. "I believe God broke the mold when He made you, Miss Parisi."

"A defective model?" I joked.

His blue eyes met mine, reminding me of a cerulean sea. "I wouldn't say that." That strange feeling was back underneath my sternum. What the hell was it?

I cleared my throat. "So, do you have siblings?"

"No," he said. An air of sadness seemed to wrap around him for a moment, before it quickly faded away. "But I have a cousin I am particularly close to. He is my pseudo-brother, I guess. My best friend."

"Is he in England?"

"Yes."

"You miss him?"

"Very much."

An ache burst in my chest when it occurred to me that Harry might be lonely. I had always viewed him as uptight and distant, cold and unapproachable, which I supposed didn't make for easy friendships. And he certainly appeared to be all of those things. But I had met his father, who was a complete and utter prick.

It couldn't have been easy growing up with King Sinclair. From the outside, it seemed like Harry had a very sparse social life outside of HCS Media. He always gave me the impression that he was wound so tightly he was about to snap. That he didn't have a clue how to operate if he wasn't looking at people with utter distain and ensuring he could be viewed as nothing but powerful and prideful. For all I knew, every assumption I had about him was correct.

"Do you have hobbies, Mr. Sinclair?"

"Harry," he said. Then, "Just the usual, fox and badger hunting. Pheasant and grouse shooting. All when in season, of course."

My mouth fell open in disgust. "Are you kidding me?"

"Yes, I am," he said, deadpan. It took me a moment for his response to sink in.

I shook my head, laughing. "Damn! I was just about to rip into you about the barbarism of blood sports."

"God forbid," he said dryly. "But that's what you expected, did you not? The stuck-up English aristocrat taking part in those typically nefarious sports of ours."

"I mean," I said, "if the three-thousand-dollar suit fits."

When he smiled knowingly, dimples caved into his cheeks. As if he needed to be any more handsome. "Fear not, Miss Parisi, I find blood sports as atrocious as you. In fact, I have put a great deal of money into banning them altogether."

He undid his cufflinks and rolled up his sleeves to his elbows. I checked the elevator for fire. I was suddenly getting really hot. He sat back and slouched against the wall.

"But to answer your question, I like rugby, lacrosse. And I ride horses." My head immediately went to the man dressed as a pony last night in NOX. I snorted a laugh at the thought of tearing the equine mask off his head, Scooby-Doo style, and finding Harry neighing underneath.

"You normally find things of the equestrian persuasion so amusing?"

I waved my hand in front of my face in an attempt to calm down. "Sorry. No. It just reminded me of something funny."

"Clearly." Harry checked his watch. His cheek twitched as though in irritation. "And you? What are your hobbies?" he said absently.

Well, Harry. As of last night, I am a member of NOX, you know the infamous sex club? I guess you could say my hobbies are heading in the delightful direction of orgasming, nipple-play, and giving really good head.

In reality, I said, "Are drinking vodka and judging cooking shows from my couch considered hobbies?"

"One could argue the point, I suppose."

Conversation faded, yet I felt Harry's gaze on me. He was probably wondering what demon was punishing him by trapping him in this elevator with me. I checked my watch again and hope drained from me. I had the sneaking suspicion that Maître Auguste would see lateness as a final strike against me and swiftly revoke my membership from his club.

Just as my hope had begun to run out, the elevator rattled, the main lights lit up the place like a Christmas tree, and it began to move down—thankfully not at a breakneck speed.

"Thank God!" I cried and jumped to my feet. Harry slowly got up too, taking his jacket off the floor and tossing it over his shoulder like a Burberry catwalk model. When the doors opened, a man in a boiler suit was waiting for us.

"All fixed," he said.

"I could fucking kiss you!" I said, patting him on the arm; then I raced toward the entrance.

THOROUGHLY WHIPPED

"Then why didn't you?" he shouted after me.

Rain thrashed against the glass windows. Screw the subway tonight; I'd be splurging on a cab. Just as I burst through the doors, a sheet of rain slapped me in my face. "Shit!" I shouted, running toward the road in the freak tsunami that seemed to have hit New York in the last few hours.

Trying to keep my list dry, I tucked it in my jacket pocket, and I threw my other arm into the air to hail a cab. Ten minutes and a thousand full cabs later, I felt like crying. No one would see me in the rain anyway, and if someone did see me and ask me what was wrong (which they wouldn't, of course—we were in New York), I would simply tell them that I was a voluntary sexual submissive in training and was about to miss my chance with a French master because I got stuck in an elevator with my boss, who I was pretty sure hated me.

A car suddenly stopped and I exhaled in relief. When the window wound down, I saw it was Harry Sinclair. "Why are you standing in the rain?"

"Water is out at home." I pointed to the sky. "Thought I'd use nature's own source as my shower tonight."

"Are you joking?" he asked, eyebrows pulled down.

"Of course I'm joking!" I shouted back, water soaking through my pale-pink shirt, likely giving everyone in New York a peep show. "I'm trying to hail a cab, but seemingly every taxi in Manhattan is being used tonight."

"Get in the car, Miss Parisi."

"No. It's okay," I snapped, done with every part of today, especially taking orders from an Englishman with a strong sense of his own superiority.

I moved away from Harry's car to finally flag a damn cab. But life, wanting to keep me firmly locked into the disastrous theme for the day, saw to it that my heel slipped into a crack in the pavement and I swiftly tumbled on my ass. My jacket, purse, and list went sprawling on the sidewalk.

"Why!" I screamed at the sky, only to be rewarded with a

mouthful of rainwater, which I swiftly deep throated, choking and spluttering within an inch of my life. As I coughed like a Dickensian street orphan with tuberculosis, a large hand wrapped around my upper arm and lifted me to my feet.

"I said get in the bloody car, Faith, before we both catch our deaths." Harry's familiar voice cut through the car horn-filled symphony of Eighth Avenue, and his impressive strength deposited me onto a warm leather seat. The passenger-side door to whatever stupidly expensive designer car this was slammed shut.

Harry rushed around the hood and slipped into the driver's side, holding my things. "Are you forever this stubborn?" he bit out, and his usual shitty and cold attitude erased any glimmer of warmth I had felt in the elevator. "Just when I think…" He shook his head, cutting himself off. I was glad. I couldn't be bothered to hear what his highness wanted to say.

Harry placed my sodden jacket and purse in the back seat. Just as he started his ignition to get us the hell out of here, the list fell out of my jacket pocket and landed straight into his lap.

I prayed to whoever might be listening that the rain had ruined it, smudged the ink at least. But when the car plunged into a heavy silence and I looked over to see Harry reading the list on his lap, I knew it was bone dry and I wanted the ground to open up and swallow me whole.

Harry's long, dark eyelashes glistened with raindrops as he scanned the list. His nostrils flared and he raised his head. Handing me the list, he quickly pulled the car out into traffic.

"Brooklyn, you said? That's where you live? Whereabouts?"

I begrudgingly reeled off the address, and Harry punched it into his GPS. The air between us crackled with tension. What had he read? More than that, what the hell must he think? Why hadn't he said something? Did he think me a freak? And why the fuck did I care? I hated him. Okay, not hated, but severely disliked him. I didn't care to be in his good graces.

Thought after thought raced through my head at such an overwhelming speed I became dizzy. When it all became too much to stand, I blurted, "I don't want to be pissed on!"

Harry didn't take his eyes off the road, didn't even show the slightest reaction to my outburst. "Fortunately, I used the bathroom before I left the office."

"No, I didn't mean I thought you would piss on me. In fact, out of everyone I know, you would be the last person I'd expect to do that." We stopped in a line of traffic and I rued the day that I found out what uro-fucking-philia was.

Harry rubbed his forehead, clearly affected by the direction of this evening too. "Miss Parisi, can we please stop talking about urine. I feel it is never an appropriate topic for civilized conversation."

I quickly scanned the list, wondering what else he may have seen. I groaned at the fifth from the top. "Fisting. Did you see the line about fisting, rough or otherwise? It's a list of what I *wouldn't* do. Not a bucket list."

Harry blew out a long breath. "Miss Parisi. Please. Stop."

"I saw you read it. And just wanted you to know that I don't want to be spit-roasted."

"Spit-roasted?" he asked in clear exasperation.

"Double penetrated. One in the front, one in the ass. Double stuffed, you know?"

"Not intimately."

I realized my index fingers were pointed toward each other, acting out exactly what double penetration was.

Lowering my hands to my lap, I closed my eyes and tried to think of a lie that would make sense to explain my having such a list. Sally had told me none of the top bosses could know about NOX. Harry was the CEO. I didn't want him to pull my feature, when I'd barely started, to avoid upsetting his high-flying, powerful friends who lived under the many unusual masks I'd seen.

My eyes opened. "It's for my column," I said. "I've been compiling a list of preferences that are a little *out there*. You know, things I may discuss on the column at some point, that people might find interesting."

Harry sighed. "You certainly live an interesting life, Miss Parisi. I don't think I've ever met anyone quite like you."

I stared straight ahead, unsure if I'd just been slighted in a polite, gentle way. "You called me Faith," I blurted. I had no idea why that was the prominent thought in my head right now. Harry had never called me by my name before. And he had lifted me off the ground. Carried me in his arms and against his chest to his car. A car that had seat warmers.

His jaw clenched. "Slip of the tongue. It was unprofessional of me."

"As unprofessional as seeing 'large anal plugs' on an employee's private list?"

With that the car came to an abrupt stop. "Is this your building?" Harry asked. The rain had lightened from torrential to a hazy mist.

"Yes. This is my place."

Harry reached for my jacket and purse. Just as he did, my cell chimed. I immediately checked my purse and read the text.

A car will pick you up. Don't be late.

It was from a number I knew belonged to NOX. Harry's car's incredibly complex dashboard clock told me I had to move my ass. "Shit," I said and dove from the car. Harry walked around the hood and handed me my now heel-less shoe. "Thank you. And thank you for the ride home."

"Let me see you to your door."

"No! That's okay," I said, waving my hand in an awkward kind of goodbye as I reached the handrail of the stoop.

"Faith?" I turned around and saw Sage coming up the street.

"Sage!" I said in relief.

Sage walked past Harry, eyes widening when he met my gaze. *Harry Sinclair?* he mouthed and I smiled tightly at Harry over Sage's shoulder. Harry's face was as hard as stone as he watched us. "Faith, you have no shoes on."

"Carry me," I whispered. Sage frowned in confusion but did as I asked. He swept me up into his arms, heading for the door.

Harry was a statue on the sidewalk, muscled arms folded over his chest. "Good day, Miss Parisi," he said neutrally and got back into his car.

"He thinks I'm a fucking moron," I said to Sage when we were safely inside our foyer and Harry was gone.

"What do you care? You hate the guy, right?"

"Right," I said. "Of course." I pointed to the elevator. "Quick smart, my good man. Maître is waiting, and his private car is picking me up any minute."

The elevator closed and took us to our floor. "Why was your boss here anyway?" Sage asked. "That was him, right? I recognized him from all the pictures online."

"Yes, but it's a long story, and right now I have to prepare to potentially get my ass spanked by a sexy Frenchman."

"Just another ordinary day then," Sage said, shaking his head in amusement.

"Just another ordinary day."

Faith, I heard Harry's voice circle in my head as I undressed. Not Miss Parisi, but *Faith*. As I plunged myself under the hot shower stream, the sound of his voice only got louder.

Then I remembered when, in the elevator, he'd smiled. That goddamned dimpled smile. That weird fluttering underneath my sternum came back again. I closed my eyes. Those canes Maître had on his wall seemed more appealing to me by the minute.

As I heard Harry shout a worried *Faith* one more time in my stupid head, I prayed that Maître flogged the living hell out of me tonight.

I didn't like *Viscount Harry*. He was a pompous and prideful ass...I just needed to keep reminding myself of that fact.

CHAPTER NINE

"WELL, it's a good thing I'm body confident," I said as I stared at my reflection in my private changing room in NOX. Bunny had told me last night that the outfits in my closet had been chosen for Maître's specific preferences. It seemed Maître Auguste liked leather, but also very little of it.

I wore a bra and panties set, but the cups of the bra were conveniently absent, exposing my bare breasts to the world. To compliment this look, the crotch of the panties was missing. Everywhere else, I was completely naked. I slipped my veil over my hair, which I had worn down as instructed, and over my face, anonymity firmly in place.

With a fortifying breath I made my way to the private elevator, holding my list of limits in my hand. As the elevator doors shut, I laughed in mortification thinking back to Harry reading it in his car. If I'd told him I was coming here, then at least I would have had a reason for clutching a list of sexually deviant activities like I was safeguarding the Holy Grail. I wasn't sure if he'd bought the excuse I had given him and, honestly, I shouldn't really care if he thought I was a more than adventurous nympho. He was my boss. And that was that.

The elevator opened and butterflies began to flutter in my stomach. I turned the doorknob and it opened, revealing to me the chambre. Lowering to my knees, hands on my thighs and head down, I waited.

Several minutes passed before I heard a door opening and, through my peripheral vision, saw Maître's bare feet and black-silk-clad legs as he made his way to his throne. Looking up from the safety of my veil, I saw his cloak around him and the Phantom mask on his face.

"*Bonne nuit,* mon petit chaton." His deep and gravelly voice exuded pure sex. My nipples hardened just at the sound of his voice.

Maître was quiet as he regarded me. When I flicked a glance up at him, I saw him watching me with his finger resting on his mask's cheek. "Do you have the list I asked for?"

"Yes, Maître Auguste."

"I do like hearing my name from your mouth." I didn't know why, but I beamed at that.

"Now, crawl to me, mon petit chaton. Crawl to me and leave your list at my feet." I knew I should have been offended by the degrading command. But instead my breathing quickened, and my skin grew hotter at the level of dominance in his voice.

Slowly, I moved to a crawling stance. Maître waited silently for me to do his bidding. On all fours, I moved, trying to keep in time to the music. It sounded like Wagner. When I arrived at his feet, I laid the list down.

"Give it to me." I handed it to Maître. "Now kneel and wait." I did as he said.

An attack of nerves assaulted me as he read the list. Would he think me unsuitable for the club? Last night had already given him doubts. My list of hard limits was extensive.

"Bon," Maître said neutrally and walked past me. I heard the clanking of metal behind me, and it took all that I had not to turn around.

After about five minutes, he ordered, "Come here." I walked to his shadowed figure, in a darker part of the room. I stopped before the medieval wooden stocks. My eyes widened.

"Put your arms and head inside." Swallowing hard, I obeyed. Maître closed the stocks around me. "Now lift your legs to the benches." I did as instructed, and Maître tied my ankles down with the cuffs. With my legs spread wide on the benches, my ass pointed up toward the gods, I tried to move my arms and head and found that I was trapped. I tried to fight back my rising panic at being so restrained.

"Stop trying to move. The point is to be restrained." Maître moved to the wall, in my line of sight, and retrieved something from the rack. When he turned, it looked scarily like a bat with metal spikes on the end. He leaned over and rubbed my ass with his hand. I could barely breathe. What the hell was he planning to do with that bat?

He must have read the fear in my taut body as he said, "This was not on your list, mon petit chaton. If it is not on the list, then everything else is bon. Do you not remember what I told you last night?"

"Yes, Maître. But I didn't see anything like *that* in my research." I felt his hand skim among my lower back and drop to my right ass cheek.

"Ready?" he said.

I was frozen. I wanted to open my mouth to say something, but I couldn't move my lips. I was too out of my depth in this place. I breathed hard, bracing for pain.

Suddenly, Maître's hand left me and he was in front of me. He bent down until I was staring cautiously into his silver eyes. The corner of his lips hooked up in amusement. I frowned in confusion. "Mon petit chaton," he said and ran his hand through my hair. "Your list was the most amusing thing I have seen in a very long time."

"I...w-what?" I stuttered.

"We," he circled his finger in the air, "are a sex club. A hedonistic heaven built for the pleasure of fucking and orgasms, not pain and sadism. This," he said, lifting the spiked baseball bat so I could see it, "is merely for decoration purposes, *d'accord?* Activities such as these are banned. There are other more...*specific* clubs in New York for those with that preference."

"There were people downstairs..."

"Role-play." He shrugged. "Some light bondage and flogging, but none to cause real pain. Being flogged or caned doesn't have to be a painful experience, rather one to set your senses on fire and bring your pleasure to new heights. Some of the people you saw downstairs were my employees. Ma chérie, they are here to arouse the crowd, to help members feel safe to let go and give themselves over to their carnal needs and wants. Tell me, did they arouse you? Did you get wet watching them scream?"

"It was...*intriguing*. I suppose it would all depend on the person doing it to me."

Maître tilted his head to the side. "What about me?" he said and ran the tip of his finger over my erect nipple. I gasped, cold shivers shaking my body at that miniscule touch of affection.

"Yes, Maître." And it was true. I was so attracted to this mysterious man, I would gladly take it.

He lifted the list. "I shall keep this as a souvenir. Some activities to investigate, I think."

His smirk dropped, the serious Maître resuming control, and he placed the torture device back on the wall. "My intention with you, mon petit chaton, is to have you screaming through the night because I am fucking you, or licking you, or making you fall apart. I have no desire to permanently mark this beautiful olive skin." Maître came to me, and I couldn't help staring at his huge length underneath his silk pajamas.

I jumped, gasping, when Maître's hands smoothed over my behind, one hand on each cheek. "This leather lingerie on you..." He trailed off, his voice dropping an octave. I bit my lip so I didn't moan out loud when he traced every inch of my cheeks and upper thighs with his skillful, yet gentle, hands.

"If it makes you feel better about things, you can have a safe word, mon petit chaton." I felt him move between my spread legs, legs that were wide open for his viewing.

My face blazed in need. Heat smothered my back, and I suddenly felt his erection pressing against me. I sucked in a sharp breath when his chest met my back and his masked cheek met my cheek. It was a heady yet erotic sensation being held in stocks, unable to move, while a man well over six feet tall sprawled across me.

"So, what shall it be? Do you want a safe word? But remember, in NOX, you just have to say stop and I will stop." He pressed a warm kiss to my neck. My bones turned to liquid at the feel of him taking control, at his soft lips caressing my throat.

"No, Maître. No safe word necessary," I said, fighting a moan, and his teeth bit down on my earlobe. He began rolling his hips, creating a delicious kind of friction, then moved down my back until I felt his hot breath at my clit.

"If there's no need for a safe word, then I'll just proceed with fucking you instead."

In seconds, I felt the first swipe of his tongue run from my entrance to my clit. I moaned as he delved back in, his hands pulling my lips apart as he sucked and flicked my clit with his tongue. I moaned, unable to move with the straps on my ankles and my hands and my head fastened in the stocks. My eyes rolled back, and my mouth parted just searching for the breath that Maître was stealing with his hot touch.

As I drowned in the hedonism he'd promised, it occurred to me that I couldn't feel his mask. He'd taken it off. I was tempted to fight the stocks, needing more than anything to see what he looked like, but I was trapped and, more than that, I didn't want him to stop.

I cried out when he slipped two fingers inside me, his tongue never letting up. "I'm coming," I said, the crash of pleasure slapping over me like the hardest of floggers. My body tightened and I collapsed, thankful that the stocks were holding me in place. Maître quickly pulled his tongue away, but before I'd had a chance to recover, he slid inside me with one hard thrust.

I screamed as I clenched around his huge cock. He filled me so much. I gritted my teeth as he started pounding into me like the man had been starved of sex. His hands moved from gripping my hips to pressing against my back. His rhythmic thrusts never faltered once.

"You feel so good," he said, his accent French-kissing the vowels of each word. "Hot and wet and tight."

I cried out as he changed his angle and started relentlessly pounding against my G-spot. I'd never felt anything like this before. This heat, this attraction, this mind-blowing pleasure. I was like a living orchestral crescendo, gradually getting louder and louder until I screamed, bursting apart like a supernova.

Maître Auguste slammed into me one more time, exhaling loudly as he came. His hands massaged over my bare back up to my hair, where he wrapped his hand around the long strands. Using his grip, he rolled his hips until all his pleasure had been wrought.

The feel of Maître's lips kissing my spine caused tremors of bliss to shudder across my skin. My back arched, searching for more of him. As exhausted and drained of pleasure as I was, I wanted more.

I didn't have to wait long.

Maître pulled out of me and reached over me to unfasten the bolts on the stocks. I sagged against the wood, unable to move. Maître gathered me in his arms. When I looked up, his mask and cloak were firmly back in place. He took me to the bed in the center of the room. It was dressed in a red PVC sheet.

He laid me down, moved to the rack on his wall, and took what looked like a blindfold from one of the hooks. Bringing it to the side of the bed, he said, "I'm going to fuck you up close." He knelt on the bed and laid the blindfold beside me. Reaching to the wall behind the bed, he took hold of two metal bars.

"Spreader bars," he said, threading one through the metal hoops in my wrist cuffs. He pulled on the bar and my arms flew apart. He attached the other bar to my ankle cuffs and adjusted it so my legs widened and I was completely open for his viewing.

He placed his finger at my ankle then traced it up my calf, over my knee, and up my thigh, until he plunged it inside me. "Argh!" I hissed, trying to roll my hips, searching for even more. Quickly removing his hand, he took the blindfold that had been sitting patiently beside my head.

"Lift your head." I did as he said and he placed the blindfold over my eyes and everything went black.

"Not afraid of the dark, are you?"

"Not right now."

Maître's fingers crossed over my lips, and I held my breath, wondering if he was about to kiss me. I wanted him to kiss me. I wanted to taste him. It felt like he planned to. Then his fingers moved. I heard the rustling of clothes. The bed dipped again. He'd taken his mask off, and I heard it hit the wooden floor.

Blinking under the blindfold, I tried to make it move enough to see any part of him. Just a glimpse—his cheekbones, his nose, his jaw, *anything*.

"Ma chérie," he said as I felt him climb over me. I felt his hot skin against mine. From foot to face. He had taken everything off. I groaned just imagining how perfect he looked.

I arched so that my nipples scraped against his hard chest. "I wish I could see you," I allowed myself to say.

I moaned in surprise when he ducked down and sucked my nipple into his mouth. "NOX is about playing in the dark, mon petit chaton. About anonymity and the freedom to let go without truly knowing who just made you fall apart." With his mouth back on my breasts, his finger dropped between my legs and caressed my clit. I instantly climbed higher and higher, my lower back aching from the force of the previous orgasms. But I didn't care. Nothing mattered right now; no worries plagued my mind. It was just me and Maître and more pleasure than I'd ever felt before.

Suddenly, just as I was about to crest, Maître moved up my body and placed his hands on either side of the bar separating my hands. The force of his strength pinning me down made warmth gather between my legs.

I managed to take in a breath just as he placed himself at my entrance and slammed inside. I was glad his heavily muscled body kept me down as the wave of pleasure that overcame me caused me to bow off the mattress, testing the bars' strength. My channel squeezed, seeking release, and Maître growled in response.

"Ma chérie," he said, his voice thick and strained. Maître thrust harder and harder into me. I was slowly falling apart. I was willingly giving myself to this man.

Maître pulled out of me, and I moaned at the loss. I heard steady footsteps across the room then felt him on the bed again. The classical music and my breathing created a heady symphony as I waited for what came next. I called out in surprise when Maître used the spreader bar at my feet to turn me over. My breasts pressed against the PVC sheet; then I felt a sharp swat to my behind. I cried out. Not in pain, but...I felt it again. And I wanted more. I wanted more and more.

"Flogging," Maître said, just as another smack lashed my cheeks. It didn't hurt; the subtle sting the soft strands brought carried a feeling of electricity racing up my back, switching on every erogenous zone I had on me.

When Maître flogged me again, he aimed lower, the strands brushing my clit. I groaned at the addictive sensation, desperately wanting it back again. Sweat built on my forehead, and I tried to grip the PVC sheet beneath me just for something to ground me.

"I will bring you pleasure," Maître said. His voice was calm. "Never pain." Maître lashed the flogger down again. I'd barely had enough time to familiarize myself with the static currents buzzing through me when he pushed inside me again, smacking the flogger down on my ass as he did. The twin sensations of pleasure and subtle stinging became so much I thought I would black out.

With every strike and thrust, I melted into the mattress until every fiber in my body tightened, and I screamed so loudly in release that my throat grew hoarse. My ass cheeks were still pulsing and throbbing when Maître gripped my hips and pounded into me three more times before he growled out his release. His grip slid to the spreader bar at my hands as he lay over me, his full body draping over me like a blanket. In the darkness, I lay spent and so sated I feared I would never be able to move again.

Maître breathed hard. I felt his abdominal muscles against my back and never wanted to leave this room. "Are you okay?" he whispered.

"I don't know." Maître huffed out a laugh. The beautiful sound of his humor curled around me, holding me close. Letting go of the bar, he moved down my body. Next I felt his hands rubbing my ass cheeks, massaging the skin. I groaned. His soothing touch felt like heaven.

I sank into the mattress, but eventually Maître moved off me. When he returned, he untied my hands and ankles from the spreader bars, placing them back on the wall behind us. He rolled me onto his chest, wrapping his arms around me. Out of everything, this had startled me the most tonight.

"You did well," he said, running his fingers through my hair. I frowned at the fluttering feeling shifting beneath my sternum again. I hadn't expected the closeness, the softness.

"I'm boneless," I said, seeking warmth from the muscled arms that lay around me.

"Then it has been a successful night."

Several seconds ticked by, "Ave Maria" serenating us through the speakers. I melted against his warm skin. "You're holding me," I said, feeling completely spend and...safe. He made me feel warm and *safe*. "I'm not complaining."

Maître laughed, and I felt the comforting rumble against my cheek, lying on his pec. "This, mon petit chaton, is aftercare."

"Like you get after an operation?"

Maître's hand moved up and down my back. It was hypnotic. "When a siren has been fucked, or punished, or both, their Maître cares for them, makes them feel safe, as you said."

"Mm," I murmured, feeling sleepy. I must have fallen asleep, as

Maître woke me up peppering kisses along my spine. I blinked away my slumber, the bed coming into a hazy view under my veil.

"It's time to go," Maître said, and I sat up. I ached everywhere, but I wouldn't complain. It was a delicious kind of ache.

"Every weekend," he said, kissing the back of my hand like a true gentleman. "You will come to me. Friday and Saturday nights. No going to the main floor. You are mine and mine alone." Exhilaration took me in its hold. Maître wanted me. Wanted me only for himself. "Do you want that?"

"Yes, Maître," I said, as his hand skirted down my arm, across my breasts, and between my legs. His touch was a silent promise of what was to come. I wanted to be just his. The main room was overwhelming. In this chambre...it was a kind of freedom I'd never felt before.

"Bon." He got up from the bed. "You have been good tonight, mon petit chaton." I found myself relishing his praise. "I cannot wait until we play again. Bonne nuit, ma chérie."

Maître left through his private door. The gong sounded through the building, and I went home, still feeling his lips kissing every inch of my skin.

CHAPTER TEN

"I CAN'T BELIEVE you let him do that, Faith!" Amelia said, wide eyed.

I took a sip of my coffee. For weeks I had been under Maître's control, and thus underneath him. "What's a little gentle caning between friends?" I said, shrugging. Things had progressed in Maître's chambre. And every time I stepped away from NOX, I craved my return.

"Whatever floats your boat, I say," Sage agreed.

"You've been tied to spreader bars, put in stocks, tied to a St Andrews Cross—"

"A firm favorite," I interrupted.

"You've been flogged and caned. And now he's training you to not come until he says so?" Amelia said in exasperation.

"Delayed gratification. It's amazing," I said and shook my head. "It's like he's a magician and my body magically cannot release until he says so. It's crazy. And you come so much harder when you hold off. I actually think I might have passed out for a few seconds last time."

"It's impressive, is what it is," Novah remarked.

"Don't you ever just want *normal* sex?" Amelia asked.

I thought about her question. "I wouldn't rule it out, but I love all the kink. Never thought I'd buy into it, but here we are."

"And Maître?" Sage asked.

At the mention of Maître Auguste, I felt tingles along my spine. I knew it wasn't a good thing. He was my sex club master and I his siren. But every time I was with him, I could feel something inside me starting to change, a fondness toward him starting to grow. I would find myself praying his mask would fall off. I wanted to know who was underneath his disguise so much it was a borderline obsession. He fucked like a sex god, but it was the aftercare I craved most. Obviously, he was the first master I'd ever had. I had no idea how other masters treated their subs. But when I laid against his chest, his skin warm and smelling of mahogany and tobacco because of his cologne, I never wanted to move.

"Oh shit," Sage said, whipping to face me. "You like him."

"Of course I like him. I'm sleeping with him."

"No, he's right," Amelia said and placed her hands on my cheeks. She searched my eyes. "Faith, you have feelings for him. This is how you looked during the Oscar Dempsey episode in sophomore year."

I laughed but felt the truth of those words spanking my ass as hard as Maître's cane could. "Not true," I argued.

"Can you fall for your master?" Novah asked. "I mean, you don't even know what he looks like. He could be sitting in the booth next to us right now, and you'd have no clue." She was right of course. It wasn't a just that I *liked* Maître. I was infatuated with him, with his hands and confidence in the bedroom. No man had ever pleasured me like he did. I was completely addicted.

"He's hot. I know he is. A man with that kind of strut and sexual prowess cannot be anything but."

"He said himself that the club is just one big role-play. What if his affection toward you is just sexual? Or what if he's just playing the part really well?" Amelia said.

A pain akin to a blade being plunged into my chest hit me with blunt-force speed. "Look," I said, flicking back my hair. "I don't like him that way. Like you said, it's impossible to know the real man underneath all the theatrics. It's sex, sex I'm writing about for a feature. That's all there is to it."

My three friends were silent at that, which was a feat in itself. We never shut up. "Nove?" I said and gathered my jacket and purse. "Are you ready? Sally's only out until ten and I've got a meeting with her. I think we've stretched out breakfast enough." She stood and grabbed her things. "See you hookers at home," I said to Sage and Amelia. I kissed Sage on his cheek, then Amelia.

"We love you," Amelia said softly, weirdly causing a lump to block my throat. "We just don't want you to get hurt."

"I know," I said and pulled my best friend in for a hug. I could never accuse them all of not caring. "I'll be fine, I promise. Time is quickly running out with Maître anyway. Weeks, that's all."

"Finite weeks can be a lifetime when you're in love. Hell, so can a single day."

"I'm not in love." I smirked. "Okay, maybe a little bit with his epically huge disco stick, but that's it. I swear." I found Novah. "You ready, Red?"

"Let's go." We headed toward the building and Nove said, "Little boy blue blood is back tomorrow isn't he?"

"That's what Theo said yesterday. Said he flies in sometime today." My thoughts immediately went to Harry and our last meeting. *Get in the bloody car, Faith!*

"You think it'll be awkward? You know, since the last time you spoke you soiled his car with rainwater and he read the list."

"Shit, don't remind me," I said. "It'll be fine. We don't speak, it was just unfortunate circumstances that shoved us together that night. Yeah, he might think I'm a dirty little bitch who's into really messed-up sex." I shrugged. "To me, that would only make a person more intriguing, but to a prude like Harry Sinclair, he's probably planning to give me as wide a berth as possible and regular STD tests."

Novah laughed and covered her mouth. I gave her the side eye. "I'm sorry! But you have to admit that our uptight CEO reading about fisting and nipple torture has been a real highlight of the year so far." I decided to ignore her. It didn't last long. As we entered the elevator, Novah asked, "You got your notes ready for Sally?"

I tapped my purse. "In here."

"She'll love them."

"I hope so."

I had worked for a couple of days on the first lot of notes for my feature to show Sally. The big article wouldn't be expected for review for a while yet, but she wanted to make sure I had the right tone. I was proud of it. It had my trademark cut-throat style and elements of humor and wit, and I'd adhered to the strict rules of the NDA.

As soon as my appointment time with Sally rolled around, I knocked on her office door. "Piss off!" she shouted. She never said "come in" or "enter" like a normal person. It was always a synonym of "go away," but normally not so polite. Carla, her PA, nodded at me to go in. Sally was behind her desk, reading something.

"Notes," she said without looking up at me. I handed them over and sat down. My ass had barely skimmed the leather when Sally slammed her hand on the desk and swiveled around in her chair. "Are you shitting me with this, Faith?"

I jumped at her sudden ire. "Erm...in what way?"

"In what way!" Sally stood up, her chair plummeting straight into the wall behind her. She hit my notes with the back of her hand. "A deviant display of the too-rich Manhattan elite." She went on. "Pompous pricks prancing as ponies...purple-eyed bunnies, too-rich singletons who need deeper orgasms?"

"What?" I asked, not understanding what the hell was going on.

"Are you even taking this seriously, Faith? Have you read any of our main features?"

"Of course, I have, I—"

"They delve deep, not sprinkle verbal confetti on a pile of generic shit. Who are these people? What makes them want to do this?"

Sally's gaze skimmed the page and she froze. "You have been the Maître's pet since the first night?" I thought her jaw might fall off in shock.

"Yes."

"Yes? Yes!" She laughed but there was no mirth behind it. In fact, Sally's eyes began to bug out of their sockets so much that I feared her head was about to spontaneously combust. "And you don't think *that's* the story? You've been fucking the owner and the most infamous man in New York, and you're telling me about middle-aged Wall Street assholes with beer guts pretending to be Seabiscuit?" Sally slumped down on her seat. "I've made a mistake," she said, and I felt my hope for the feature begin fading away.

"No, you haven't—"

"You are fucking the famed Maître of NOX, have intimate liaisons with him. Have access to him in ways nobody else has." Sally leaned forward, her strangely angular and strict face hovering before mine. I felt like Sigourney Weaver in *Alien* when it tried to sniff her out, only the alien had slicked-back black hair and hard-edged Prada-framed glasses. "You have the chance to write the biggest exposé of the decade, Faith." Sally's taloned finger tapped on the wooden desk, emphasizing each word she spoke. "Find. Out. Who. He. Is." Sally sat back in her seat and I remained frozen. "*That's* our feature."

"But the NDA..."

Sally batted her hand in dismissal. "We can reveal his identity without explicitly revealing his identity, you understand?"

"Yes," I said, but something in my heart felt off, expired, like milk going bad.

"Now get out."

Gathering my notes, I walked to the elevator in a state of shock. By the time I reached Novah, I slumped down in my chair and whispered, "She wants me to reveal Maître's identity."

Novah's eyes widened. "Oh no, Faith..." she whispered and reached out to take my hand. "She didn't like your notes?"

I let out a sardonic laugh. "Liked? She fucking crucified them,

Nove. Hung, drawn, and quartered and sent to the edges of New York to warn other writers not to be so shit."

I stared unseeing at the carpet beneath my feet. I thought of Maître, his muscled body and his gentle hands, his French accent, which was so suave it made snakes of my clothes—with his words alone he could charm them right off. But more importantly, I thought of the aftercare, when he held me close. When he huffed reluctant laughs at my breathless jokes.

And Sally wanted me to destroy him.

*Anonymity is everything, mon petit chaton...*I heard his voice in my ear. Sally wanted me to rip right through that anonymity. Expose him and, no doubt, destroy his club and all he'd worked for. The thought of doing that to him...

My desk phone rang and I answered it robotically. "Yes?"

"Get your ass down to the rec center. Michael has food poisoning and can't cover the charity event that's taking place. So you're covering it, serving your fucking penance for disappointing me with that shit you brought into my office. One thousand words by tomorrow afternoon about what the charity does and all that sad crap that will make our readers weep. And get there now!" Sally slammed the phone down and I winced.

"Faith?" Novah said.

"I have to go cover a story at a rec center." An email with the address and notes came through from Carla. I printed it off, grabbed my jacket and purse, and tucked my useless notes away in my drawer.

Novah reached out and grabbed my hand. "It'll be okay, I promise." I gave her a tight smile and high-tailed it out of the building, caught a cab, and handed the driver the address. Of course, when it's a warm, sunny day, a cab stops immediately. As I stared out at bustling New York, I thought of exposing Maître, who he was, what he did, his face...and I felt sick.

I took a deep breath. *Faith, you've known the guy for a handful of weeks. Yes, it has been a pretty fucking intense handful of weeks, but that's all it's been. It's a sex club. You are just another siren in a mask.*

But I wasn't. Bunny had told me so. As had Maître himself. He didn't take sirens. But he had taken me.

"Fuck my life!" I shouted.

"You say something, miss?" the old cab driver asked.

"No, sorry." The cab pulled to a halt, and I climbed out onto the sidewalk. It took me a moment to realize we were in Hell's Kitchen. I walked to the rec center I'd come to as a kid, and some of the heaviness in my chest was lifted. My parents lived only two blocks away. I smiled up at the sky. Papa always said that when you were in a bad place, God always delivered to you exactly what you needed to be lifted back up again. As I looked at the rec center, a place that had helped mold who I was today, I wondered if this was it.

As I pushed through the doors, the musty smell of sweating teenagers slapped me in the face. Some things never changed; they were the steadily balanced constants you needed so life didn't get too dizzy.

I heard noises coming from the back gym. As I passed the office, I heard, "Well if it isn't the troublemaker Faith Parisi herself." Instantly smiling, I found Mr. Caprio walking around the desk, the baker boy cap he always wore still firmly attached to his head.

"Mr. Caprio," I said and was immediately wrapped up in a bear hug.

"What the hell are you doing here?"

"I'm here to cover the event today. The fundraiser for..." I looked down at my notepad. "Children's bereavement." My heart fractured at the topic, and I hated myself for not reading the brief on the way here.

"It's more an activity day. The new artificial turf football field has just been opened, and it's the first day the children from the charity have played on it." I nodded as he led me through the familiar hallways that led to the back gym. "The Charity CEO is through here."

We entered the back gym and noise of the highest decibels greeted me. Children were running everywhere, sports of every kind happening on every inch of space.

"Mr. Caprio," I said. "Where's the artificial field?"

"Near the east entrance. But the photographers have already been. We're taking all the press in here now." I nodded but found it strange that the new field would be closed when all of this was for its opening.

"Faith, this is Susan Shaw, the CEO of"—he quickly checked his notes— "Vie." Who was Vie? Was she the woman the charity was named after?

Twenty minutes later, I had a notepad full of information thanks to Susan. I smiled, watching the children playing soccer or tag, and felt my heart break wondering what they had been through. I loved my parents with everything I had. I couldn't imagine losing them. Some of the children before me where as young as five. I couldn't fathom being that young and losing the person you loved most in the entire world, what it could do to an infant soul.

Feeling tears building in my eyes, I waved to Mr. Caprio across the gym and decided to duck out so as not to cause a scene. Knowing the way to the ladies' bathroom, I walked down the old corridors, laughing, remembering my first kiss against a wall or the time my friend Dina drank her first wine cooler in the bathroom and then vomited all over Billy Day as soon as she stepped out.

After I'd finished in the bathroom, I was about to head home when I heard the unmistakable sound of children laughing. "The east entrance," I said, realizing the new field would be just down here. Mr. Caprio had said it was closed, but that had never stopped me before. As I got closer to the door to what used to be the old basketball court, the shouts got louder.

Opening the door, I was met with a flurry of activity. Gone was the old cracked concrete of the basketball court, and in its place was vibrant green artificial grass. Children were running around, throwing what looked like a football. No, it was bigger than a football. It was white, and I quickly realized it was—

"To the left!" A voice shouted. A deep, very proper voice, with a very English accent, one I knew very well.

A flash of white whizzed by me. Harry Sinclair. Harry Sinclair in a white rugby jersey with a red rose on the left breast, gray sweatpants, and sneakers. I froze as I watched him pass the ball, hands suddenly thrust in the air when one of the young boys scored a...goal? Touchdown? Home run? Hell if I knew!

As if he could sense my shocked gaze, he looked over at me, and the wide smile he'd been sporting suddenly slipped from his face.

"Harry! Head's up!" Another boy shouted, pulling his attention away from me. It all happened so fast. The young boy threw the ball and even I, a complete moron at sports, could tell it was never reaching Harry, who was supposed to be the target. Instead, it sailed over Harry's head, bowing high and wide, and smacked straight into my face. To say I toppled to the ground like a sack of last week's potatoes would be an understatement.

In typical Faith fashion, I landed on my ass, clutching at the side of my head, which I felt was about to break free of my skull, and fell to the ground. Feeling it was better not to scare the kids with such a gruesome scene, I began crawling back through the doorway. It was a crawl I had perfected under Maître Auguste's strict instruction.

I had made it to the far wall in the hallway when Harry came barreling through, searching for me, and ran toward me when I waved my free hand.

"I'd heard rugby was a dangerous sport, but Jesus Christ, Harry! A heads-up would have been nice," I said as Harry crouched down to face me. He gently took my wrist and moved my hand off my head. It must have been the knock to the brain; I couldn't take my eyes off him as his blue eyes searched my face and he pressed the wounded area with timid fingers.

"Ow, you sadist!" I snapped, and I hissed at the onslaught of pain.

"It's not bleeding. But you may be concussed."

"Awesome," I said.

"Miss Parisi, has no one ever told you to duck when balls are flying toward your face?"

My head was throbbing, but I was not going to miss that kind of invitation. I held Harry's hand, which was still on my head, and said, "Harry, usually when balls fly at my face, I have my eyes and mouth wide open."

Harry's mouth parted in shock. Then shaking his head, but with a reluctant smile on his lips, he said, "You are incorrigible, Miss Parisi."

I winced when I saw a bright light above me. Panic flooded my bones. "Harry, I can see a light. Is that *the* light? Am I fucking dying right now?" The light seemed to expand, growing ever closer to me.

"Relax," he said.

"I can't! The light! It's coming for me!"

Suddenly two hands pressed onto my cheeks, and the light ebbed when a face blocked it out and hovered before mine. A perfect face. The most handsome of faces. "An angel," I whispered, feeling all kinds of dizzy.

"Jesus Christ," the angel said. I was shocked to find angels had English accents and also took the Lord's name in vain.

"Viscount Sinclair will love that the celestial beings of heaven are English. Why do you have to have an English accent? Does that mean that the British have been justified in feeling superior to everyone else this entire time? We'll never hear the end of it. I always thought an Australian accent would suit angels. *G'day, Mate. You've only gone and fucking died. But don't worry, there's enough shrimp for everyone on this barbie.*"

"Faith. I'm taking you to hospital. I think it's safe to say if you're speaking with such a terrible Australian accent, you have a concussion."

The angel lifted me in his strong arms, and I couldn't stop staring at his seraphic face. Wait, angels were genderless, right? No genitals. No sex.

"Do you not have a dick?" I asked the angel. His blue eyes blinked at me, yet he said nothing. It didn't matter. "Such a perfect face." I stroked his cheek. It was rough under my palm, but I didn't mind. I'd always had a weird thing about liking the feel of sandpaper on my skin.

"Faith, you are speaking aloud. You are saying *everything* aloud."

"Will you sing to me?" I asked. I wanted to hear the angel sing.

"Nobody should be subjected to that torture," the angel said. I wanted to pout, but I couldn't stop stroking his pretty face.

"I've never seen anyone so beautiful." The angel placed me down on something warm. It must have been his cloud. He sat beside me, and I felt like we were floating. As we moved, I felt my eyes begin to close. "Sleep," I said, the warmth around me cocooning me in its embrace. "I'll just have a little nap."

"No. Faith. Stay awake." A sudden blast of cold attacked my face.

"No!" I moaned. "Bring back the cocoon!"

"I need you to stay awake. Can you do that for me?" I struggled to keep my eyes open, but the angel wanted me to stay awake. He was too beautiful to say no to. Then I felt his hand in mine. It was so big and strong, but it felt so right pressed against my palm.

"You're not allowed to let go of my hand ever again, okay?" I said and held it against my face like a pillow. "You smell of mint, sandalwood, and musk." Someone else I knew smelled that way. "Harry!" I shouted. "Harry smells like this too. But he's not kind like you. He looks down on people. And he hates me. Like, *really* hates me."

The angel didn't say anything for a while. Then, "I'm sure that's far from the truth."

I cuddled into the hand again, and suddenly we stopped floating and the angel took back his hand. But then he lifted me up to his hard chest, and we flew. I heard beeping and something cold being pressed on my head. I thought I'd lost my angel and panic set in, but then I felt his hand take hold of mine again. And as I closed my eyes, I knew that I was safe.

CHAPTER ELEVEN

"HOLY SHIT," I groaned, feeling like I had an ill-tempered groundhog burrowing inside my head. I blinked, eyelids like ten-ton weights, and tried to open my eyes. The view of an unfamiliar white-tiled ceiling met me. "What the hell?" I said, as I tried to remember something, *anything* about how I got here. A hospital? I could hear the familiar beeps of machines and smell the strong scent of Lysol and pine disinfectant.

Then I felt something in my hand, something warm. Something that was gripping me tightly, keeping me centered. I rolled my head to the side, and my eyes rounded in shock at seeing Harry Sinclair sitting in an uncomfortable plastic chair. His eyes were closed and his breathing was even, chest rising and falling under his white rugby jersey that had "England Rugby" on the left breast underneath a bright red rose.

I was glad I wasn't hooked up to a life-support machine, as I was pretty sure it would have been belting out the melody of "God Save the Queen."

Harry? What the heck was he doing here?

Then, as if a dam wall had broken, a flood of memories crashed into my already bruised brain—the rec center, the charity, Harry playing rugby with children on the new artificial field...then taking a smack to the face with that fucking ball. After that, the memories became sparse, like scattered pieces of a jigsaw puzzle I was desperately trying to fit back together. Something about an angel. A light? I didn't friggin' know.

But there was a hand. There was the tight grip of a hand that had wielded its way through all the white noise. I looked down at Harry's hand tightly holding mine, even as he slept. And I stared. I was pretty sure I stared for too many minutes to be normal.

As if feeling the weight of my confused gaze, Harry began to stir. His dark hair was mussed, a mass of waves on his head, and his full lips were slightly pursed. Cracking open his bright blue eyes, he immediately sought me out. "Faith," he said, and something in my stomach flipped hearing him call me by my first name again. Harry sat up straighter and leaned toward the bed. "You're awake." I kept flicking curious glances to our hands, but he didn't let go. I wasn't even sure he realized they were still clasped. "Are you okay?"

"Just peachy," I said, wincing again when I lifted my free hand to my head. Just as I hissed at the lump jutting from the side of my skull, as if I were a motherfucking lopsided unicorn, a nurse came through the curtain that wrapped around the bed.

"How are you feeling?" she asked and handed me a pill. "Take this. It'll help with the pain." Moving around to the other side of the bed, she tapped Harry's shoulder. "Do you mind if I give her a quick examination?"

"No, no, not at all." Harry dropped his hand from mine. I watched him for a reaction. Had he even realized he was holding my hand? Was it some traditional English act of chivalry I wasn't savvy to? He groaned slightly and, as he positioned my hand back on the bed, gave my fingers a quick squeeze. His eyes flicked to me, and I saw a slight burst of red on his cheeks. What did that mean? Was he embarrassed? Damn, my head hurt too much for all this thinking. Harry ducked out of the room and shut the curtain behind him.

"Bless that man," the middle-aged nurse said, and she started timing my pulse. "He has not left your side since you came in earlier. He was barking orders at us to be sure you were okay."

I wasn't sure if my pulse started racing too fast because of the head injury or because of what the nurse was telling me. "When we were sure it was just a nasty hit to the head and slight concussion, nothing worse, he sat by your side, held your hand, and never took his eyes off you as you slept." She smiled my way, clearly oblivious to the fact that right now, fuck the head injury, I was pretty sure I was having a coronary. "You have one dedicated man there, girl." The nurse wrapped a blood pressure cuff around my arm. "He's British?"

"Yeah," was all I could say. *He isn't my man* should have followed, but my naughty little tongue didn't quite fess up.

"Love that accent." She shined a light into my eyes. I flinched. The penlight felt like a laser beam burning straight through my retina and piercing my brain with white-hot heat. "Sorry," the nurse said. "You're okay, just will have a headache for a while. We'll give you medication for that." She pressed the button on the side of the bed and raised the head of the bed so I was in a sitting position. "We will monitor you for a bit longer, then you'll be fine to go home."

"Thank you." As she opened the curtain to leave, Harry was on the other side, holding two paper cups. He nodded politely at the nurse as she walked past. He ducked into the booth and placed a steaming cup on the table above my lap.

"Coffee?" I asked, knowing caffeine would be all the remedy I needed right now.

"Tea," Harry said and sat down on the plastic chair.

"You're shitting me, right?"

Harry's mouth twitched, no doubt at the amount of venom in my voice. "I am not, shitting you, as you so eloquently said. It's chamomile, caffeine free. It's tea, Miss Parisi, don't you know it's the cure for everything?"

"Maybe back in the *auld* empire, but here in New York it's a cup of Joe all the way." I shuddered just looking at the light brown water that resembled dirt sitting tauntingly before me. "I may swear like a sailor off his tits on gin, but *'it's chamomile, caffeine free'* may just be the most offensive sentence I've ever heard in my fucking life."

Harry reached over, took the tea, and switched his drink with mine. From what my coffee-trained bloodhound nose could detect, it appeared to be a double-shot grande latte. "There. Have mine. Can't have you so affronted by Britain's best stuff."

"I thought tea cured everything. Why did *you* get coffee?"

"I wasn't sure tea was going to be strong enough for me to face your expected wrath."

I couldn't help but fight a smile. "My expected wrath?"

"I feared I was about to be nailed inside a coffin for the mishap with the rugby ball."

"Mishap? You mean the leather egg that decided to kiss my face with the force of a freight train? That mishap?"

"The rugby ball that was thrown by an *eleven-year-old* who weighed no more than eighty pounds. Yes, that mishap."

"Eleven? Shit, sign that kid up right now for the draft." I took a sip of my coffee, already feeling its healing powers zip through my veins, bringing them back to life. "Do you have the draft in rugby?"

"No."

I sighed and rested my head against the pillow behind me. I knew nothing about sports.

"I am sorry, though," Harry said. "That you were hit."

I rolled my head to look at him. "You were at the rec center, playing rugby."

His face tightened, adopting his usual shuttered-down expression. I didn't know if it was the concussion, but I heard myself saying, "No. Don't do that. Don't go all cold and distant on me again. Don't do the aristocratic stiff-upper-lip thing that only comes off as rude and annoying."

Harry's expression didn't change until he huffed out a laugh and shook his head. "Do you ever not say what is on your mind, Miss Parisi?"

"Faith. Call me Faith, if you call me Miss Parisi once more I'm going to bang my own head off the wall, just so I can be knocked out and not have to hear it again."

"Slightly dramatic."

"But very me."

"Fine," Harry said. "*Faith.*"

"Hallelujah!" I settled back down, swallowing the coffee so fast it left a trail of caffeinated fire down my throat. "And to answer your question, yes, I always say what's on my mind." I shrugged. "I'd rather tell people to their face what I think than say things behind their backs. And I rarely care what people think of me, so I don't care if they don't like it."

"Duly noted."

I laughed at his dry response. I sobered quickly when I asked, "Why were you there today, Harry? I heard you were back in the UK this week."

"I was in England this week. Just came back a little earlier than I said I would." He played with the edge of his coffee cup. He sighed and met my waiting eyes. "I'm the main benefactor for the charity."

"Vie?" I asked.

"Vie."

Then it dawned on me. "You wanted the media coverage for the charity but didn't want to be tied to it?"

"Exactly," he said stiffly. "It's not about me. But I'm also not above using my connections to get it the coverage it deserves."

"Why that charity?" I asked. "Children's bereavement?" Then I remembered something I'd read about him and felt like the biggest asshole in the world. "Oh, Harry, I'm sorry," I said and felt like hitting the egg on my head in self-punishment. "Your mom."

Harry nodded. "Yes." I stayed quiet for once in my damn life. Even I knew when to shut up on occasion.

"I was only twelve when I lost her. It…" He trailed off then sighed. "It was very difficult. To be so young, and alone..." My chest clenched at the brokenness I heard under the forced strength in his voice.

"You still had your father though, right? He helped you through it?" Harry's lips thinned a fraction, and a flicker of coldness washed over his blue eyes.

"Of course."

I laid my hand over his and squeezed. "I'm sorry you lost her."

"Thank you." Then he smiled and shook his head. I was so confused.

"What?"

"I'm just imagining what she would have thought of you."

I grimaced. "That bad, huh?"

"On the contrary," he said, and his expression lightened. It softened and, with it, so did some of the ice around my heart when it came to him. "She would have adored you. She always championed strong, independent women." He leaned forward, voice lowered. "I'll let you in on a secret. She didn't much care for the ladies of the aristocracy. In fact, she would often smile to their faces, then when they were not looking, swiftly show them the middle finger, encouraging me to follow suit."

"Sounds like my kind of lady."

"Yes, quite." A lightness spread in my chest. A tattoo of his brief smile etched into my brain. It was quite the sight. And extremely rare. Like seeing Bigfoot wearing a thong and stiletto heels.

"So, you're teaching rugby to the youth of Hell's Kitchen?"

He nodded. "I felt like they should be shown a true sport, not ones played with an abundance of helmets and padding."

"Careful, or you'll be hunted out of the states by a tailgating mob," I teased. "But why Hell's Kitchen?"

Harry relaxed back in his chair, and I couldn't help but notice the sliver of skin on his flat stomach where his rugby shirt had ridden up. "I remembered reading a piece on them last year and how they were setting up a club for those who had lost parents young. They were asking for donations. I knew I could do better than that." He shrugged, and it was the most casual gesture I'd ever seen from him. This, I understood, he could talk about freely. "I wish I'd had something like that when I was dealing with my grief."

I imagined a young Harry, lost—no doubt in a mansion—his fun and loving mother gone and only his cold father for comfort. King Sinclair would have given as much comfort as an iron lung.

"It's a lovely thing you're doing."

Harry narrowed his eyes at me, and I could tell he was thinking hard about something. "The pitch had been closed off to journalists..." He let the question hang in the air.

"Is that so?" I shrugged innocently. I sighed, caught. "I used to go to that rec center, Harry, okay? When I heard you all down the hallway, I had to find out what was going on." I pointed to my head. "Karma got me back for my nosiness, don't worry."

"It seems so."

"Harry?" I asked, not wanting to hear the answer. "Did I say anything stupid when I was concussed? I can't remember much. Was there something about angels?"

"No," he said and took a long drink of his awful tea.

"I did, didn't I?" I shrieked.

Harry held up his hands in surrender. "What? I can't help it if you believe me the most beautiful seraphim in all of heaven."

"Oh my Jesus Christ. Kill me now." I paused and checked my surroundings. "No, that's it, right? I *did* die, and I'm in Hell."

"Wow," he said, the slang word sounding strange coming from his proper mouth. "Good to know being in my presence would be your idea of Hell." Harry said it as a joke, but I caught the slight echo of sadness on his face, heard the quick inflection of disappointment in his tone.

"Harry, since we met, we have been meteorites crashing together, knocking each other off course. I can't imagine two more unlikely people trying to strike up a friendship." He dropped his eyes to his cup, picking at the label. I felt a cave of sadness burrowing in my stomach.

"It's like you're two people." Harry tensed, eyebrows furrowed. "You can be degrading, prideful, and curt." I pointed at him. "Then you can be like this. The man I saw brief glimpses of in the elevator that night. The man you have been today, showing whispers of smiles at my shitty and inappropriate jokes." He huffed a laugh at that. "This may be way out of line, but I thought you were just a carbon copy of your dad."

At that, Harry's head snapped up and his eyes blazed with fire. I held my breath at his strong reaction, which wasn't wise, as the world seemed to tilt on its axis.

"I'm nothing like my father," he said firmly. His wide shoulders tensed and his jaw was tight.

"I know," I said, and I watched him lose some of the built-up tension. "I'm beginning to realize that now."

Harry turned his head, facing the curtain. I thought this was when he'd get up and leave. Make his excuses. Instead, without facing me, he said, "You must understand that being raised nobility in England, there are expectations and a strong sense of decorum..." He trailed off and ran his hand down his face.

He faced me again and, with a self-deprecating smirk, said, "Not every prison is behind iron bars."

"Harry..." I whispered, feeling something around my heart crumble. A wall? A fence? I didn't know. But whatever it was, at those heart-wrenching words it fell away, leaving my beating flesh open to Harry Sinclair.

"More coffee?" Harry said, jumping to his feet.

"No, I..." The hopeful look on his face made me say, "Yes. Thank you. I can always use more coffee." Relief beamed from him, and he ducked out through the curtain.

What had it cost him to reveal that? And his prison? Was he trapped by the rules and regulations of his social standing, or was his father not a good father at all? From the little I knew of King Sinclair,

I couldn't imagine him being anything but degrading. And if someone had lived with that all his life? Been on the receiving end of censure and never praise. And worse, he had lost the woman who'd shown him what love was at such a young age...

Seeing my cell on the nightstand, I checked to ensure that the coast was clear; then I conducted a quick Google search. After typing in "young Henry Sinclair III," I pressed on "images." In seconds, I was staring at a baby-faced Harry. In most of the pictures, he stood beside King. I searched through pages of pictures and, heartbreakingly, I couldn't find one photo where Harry was smiling.

I looked more closely at his face on one particular photo and felt as though I might cry. He was standing in front of a stone wall of some sort, maybe a house? He was beside his father, but it was Harry's eyes that held me captive. They, of course, were the same cerulean blue, but these eyes were haunted. They were tinged with such sadness and...loneliness that I felt my cheeks grow damp.

Putting down the cell and wiping my history of any Harry-themed evidence, I wiped at my tears, just as he came through the curtain to the booth.

"Faith?" He put the coffees down and rushed to my side. "What's wrong? Is it your head? Are you in pain?"

I tried to think of something but those sorrowful blue eyes. "Erm...I'm...I'm premenstrual, okay?" Harry took a step back, as men do at any mention of period-related issues. "And this," I said, pointing to my head. "I'm not sure I can pull off a giant horn on the side of my head."

Harry fought a smile, which was as welcome as a blindfold on a nudist beach. "I'm sure you've been told this plenty in your life, Faith. But you're beautiful, and I'm pretty sure that beauty wouldn't lessen no matter how many horns you sprouted on your head."

I dried my eyes and blinked up at him, his words landing like arrows in my now Harry-exposed heart. "You think I'm beautiful?"

Spots of red burst onto Harry's cheeks. "Yes," he said, clearing his throat. "Exceptionally." Our gazes were locked and, for once in my life, I had no jokes to crack. In fact, only silence hovered between us.

"Okay, Faith," the nurse said, opening the curtain. "Here's your prescription for your pain meds." She placed a clipboard on my lap. "If you just sign these forms, you're good to go." I forced my attention away from Harry and to the forms. I signed my name robotically.

An orderly came through next with a wheelchair. "Do you have a ride home?" he asked.

"I'll take her," Harry said, standing and gathering my belongings and our coffees. "That okay?" he asked.

"More than."

Then Harry smiled. Not a whisper of one, not a smirk or minute cocky grin. But a true smile. I was glad I was sitting or that sucker would have dropped me straight on my ass.

Exceptionally.

As the orderly led me to the underground parking lot, all I heard in my head was Harry's voice saying *exceptionally.*

Harry brought the car to the curbside. I slid inside onto the passenger seat. "Home?" Harry asked, keeping his eyes straight ahead.

A strange sort of tension had filled the car. Not a bad tension, but one that felt like a weird kind of purgatory. Confusion and unfamiliarity crackled in the air like an old wireless radio trying to find a station. I used to know my place with Harry. I didn't like him. He didn't like me. He was cold and arrogant. I was loud and annoyed him. Now...we were in a no-man's land. One I couldn't find my way out of.

"I'll go to my parents' house," I said as Harry pulled out of the parking lot and onto the street. "It's two blocks from the rec center."

Before we'd left, the nurse had explained to me that I needed someone to watch me for the next twenty-four hours. Amelia and Sage were working late. And I just wanted to go home. I was a twenty-five-year-old woman who wanted her mom to spoil her while she recovered. Sue me. I was high maintenance. I knew that. I couldn't friggin' cope with caring for myself; I'd annoy me too much.

The ride was silent as we cut down the dark streets of Hell's Kitchen. People filled bars and restaurants, spilling out onto the streets. Coming back to Hell's Kitchen was as comforting as grilled cheese and tomato soup. It wrapped its magic around me with a forceful hug and welcomed me home.

"Just here," I said and pointed at the apartment block. Mom and Papa lived on the ground floor. "Thank you," I said. "For today. You didn't have to stay with me and then bring me home. I'm sure you had other places you had to or wanted to be."

"Nowhere," he said again, those intense blue eyes conveying unspoken words. Ones that I was sure I was misinterpreting.

"Okay, well..." Harry opened his door and walked around the hood of his car. He opened my door and held out his hand. As I took it, I said, "Shouldn't you be saying 'Milady' as you do this?"

Harry's nose crinkled and, in my bruised brain state, I thought it was the cutest damn thing I'd ever seen. "Tad too servitorial," Harry said, regal chin in the air. "I normally have a member of my staff do this kind of menial thing." Just when I thought he was cute, maybe not the pompous prick I'd pinned him up to be, his wannabe-royal ass says something to prove me wrong.

I opened my mouth to tear him a new rim; then I saw his mouth twitch and a smirk pull on his lips. "You are such a twat."

"High praise."

Harry linked my arm through his and we traipsed up the stoop. If I closed my eyes, I could believe we were in Georgian Britain and had just departed our carriage to enter the ball. He would be a dashing duke, and me the servant he had fallen in love with and was defying society to be with. And—

"Hey baby, show us your labia!" My eyes opened just as a car full of teenage boys with pimples and braces drove past, fingers on either side of their mouths, flicking their tongues in my direction.

"At least we can be thankful the biology education in Hell's

Kitchen is sound," Harry said so seriously it caused me to burst out laughing. I winced at the sudden rush of pain to my head but didn't care.

"It's definitely better than them shouting *show us your flaps* anyhow."

"How one knows so much crudity is truly astounding," he said, just as the door opened and Mom stared at me in shock.

"Faith?" I must have looked a sight, because then she shrilled, "FAITH! Jesus fucking Christ, what the hell is wrong with you? You look like shit!"

Before Mom pounced on me like an overprotective mother hen, Harry leaned down to my ear and said, "And now I see where you get it from."

I laughed, just as Mom wrapped me in her arms, pulling me away from Harry. Papa came to the door next. *"Mia bambina."*

I heard footsteps on the stone stairs. Pulling free from the octopuses that were my parents, I saw Harry leaving. "Harry," I said, and he looked up. "Thank you."

"Oh, how rude! I didn't even see you there, young man. Did you bring Faith home? What's happened?" Mom said.

"I got hit in the head by a rugby ball," I said. I pointed at Harry. "This is my boss, he helped me to the hospital and brought me home."

"Well, you must come in!" Papa said, his Italian accent matching Harry's English one in strength.

"Thank you. But I am afraid I must go," Harry said. "It was very nice to meet you both." Something inside me fell at that. Fucking hell. I needed to sleep and rest. I was losing my goddamn mind. "Take care, Faith," he said and went to his car. I watched as he drove away, until he was out of sight.

"That was your boss?" Mom said. "Well he's sex on legs, isn't he? If I were a few years younger..."

"Nice, Mom," I said as she walked me into their apartment and deposited me on the couch. "As if my head isn't killing me enough, you have to go and put that disturbing visual in my mind."

"He must come for Sunday dinner," Papa said and sat beside me, lifting my legs and placing them on his lap.

"I'm not inviting my boss to Sunday dinner."

"He helped you, brought you home. We are Italian, Faith. We say thank you with food."

"We do everything with food, it's why my ass is the size of the empire state."

"Men like women with a little meat on their bones, darling," Mom said and handed me a bowl of soup. She always had a bowl of soup of some flavor on the stove. Said it was Scottish thing. That you never knew who might pop around at any moment and need to be fed. "They like something to be able to grab hold of."

"It's true, there's a reason Botticelli's Venus is so loved," Papa said, as the first spoonful of vegetable soup slipped down my throat. "Invite your boss, Faith. He must come."

I finished my soup and went to my old bedroom. As I lay down on my single bed, my cell chimed.

Sorry again about today. Please take care of yourself.

The text was from "Pompous Prick." A laugh slipped from my throat and I felt weightless. The pain drugs were good.

FP: How did you program your name into my phone?

PP: I may or may not have used your fingerprint while you were sleeping to break into your cell.

I saw the dots telling me he was typing something else.

PP: That is all circumstantial of course. Would never stand up in court.

My heart was beating like a bass drum. Hell, it was beating so hard it was doing the drum solo to "In the Air Tonight" by Phil Collins. I needed sleep. And maybe an asylum. I knew I was going insane because I was suddenly finding Harry Sinclair amusing and not imagining his unfortunate death at the hands of my stiletto heel in the place he should have had a heart.

In for a penny...

FP: My parents want you to come to dinner on Sunday as thanks for today. They didn't get a chance to ask you earlier.

I pressed send, quickly followed by instant regret. What the hell was I? Fifteen? Who the heck invited someone to their parents' for dinner anymore?

FP: Okay, scratch that. No need to subject yourself to that kind of torture. Forget I said anything. I'll tell them you had a medical appointment you couldn't get out of.

I sent that. When I read it back, I panicked.

FP: Not like an STD appointment thing. There will be no mention of herpes or anything. I know your namesake was apparently riddled with syphilis, but that's not what I was hinting at by saying that.

I sent that too. *Oh, for fuck's sake!*

FP: Just forget the whole thing. Delete these texts, and while you're at it, my number too. While you're at it, delete this whole day, especially the ball in my face and the angel talk. Terrible, terrible day to have to think of. I—

PP: I'll be there.

I stared at the three-word response like it was a new species of dinosaur that I had just discovered. He'd be there. He was accepting the invite. He was coming.

FP: Okay.

Tucking my cell under my pillow, I stared at my old One Direction poster on the wall, left over from when I was a teenager. "It's your fault, fuckers," I said maliciously to their smiling faces. "You and those accents that I had my first lady wank to." I leaned up and smacked Harry Styles on his perfect hair. "You ruined me. Broke me! I'm Pavlov's dog with all the English shit." My head throbbed at my rather psychotic outburst. Lying back in my bed, I closed my eyes.

Blue eyes.

Heart-stopping smile.

Exceptionally.

CHAPTER TWELVE

I TRIED to catch my breath, Maître's fingers skirting up and down my spine as I lay across his chest. Every time I came here, he showed me more and more pleasure. The ropes that tied my wrists and ankles to the bed were still intact after tonight's debauched offerings.

"I can't move," I whispered, each fiber of my tender muscles torn, just like the white lace panties hanging from a post on the bed. They oddly looked like a flag of surrender.

"That is the point, mon petit chaton." I looked up at Maître and saw the mask move upwards, and I knew he was smiling underneath. He rolled me over onto my back, my arms and legs stretched at the head and foot of the bed. Maître turned me over and kneeled between my open legs. His hand rubbed over my behind. He moved it away before swatting my ass with one firm, hard slap.

"Mm..." I moaned at the delicious sting. I pressed my head into the mattress, smiling as he rained four more highly addictive spanks onto me. When I could barely take any more, he flipped me to my back, once again laying my head on his chest. I cherished these moments. And over the past few visits, he had begun to talk to me.

Not only orders and commands, but actual conversation. It only made me crave him more, if that was even possible.

Maître ran his hand down my body and cupped my still-tender pussy. He would always touch me, caress me, keeping me eternally on the edge of pleasure. He removed his hand from between my legs, and I breathed in his mahogany and tobacco scent. His hands ran through my hair, and I was content to just lie there on his chest with him stroking me.

"Why the club?" I asked sleepily.

"Are you feeling curious tonight, ma chérie? I could put that curiosity to good use."

"Always. But I was just wondering how one goes about starting a sex club." I stared at the expertly tied ropes on my wrists.

"You're thinking of starting one?" The quarter of his lips that was exposed under the mask pursed. I liked him this way. After sex, when he began to talk to me. It was just as exciting to me as the pleasure. Some nights I craved it more. As the weeks had rolled on, I had relaxed around him. I spoke more. He got to see my personality more. And best yet, I saw flickers of his.

I rolled my eyes. "No. Just saying that I found it almost impossible to start a book club at my school, never mind an entire promiscuous empire for the sexually curious."

"A book club?"

"Not just any book club, Maître Auguste. A *banned* book club." I smirked at the sound of Maître laughing under this breath.

"Of course, mon petit chaton could not just do something normal, she must take it to higher heights."

"And higher heights it was. Want to hear what book I was planning on starting with?"

"I'm all ears."

"*Lady Chatterley's Lover.*"

"How erotically apt," Maître said.

"I see your point there." I shrugged. "Maybe I've always had a propensity for the racier side of life and just didn't realize it."

"And how old were you when you started this banned club? Sixteen, seventeen?"

"Twelve." The deep, throaty laugh that spilled from Maître's throat made me a puddle on the bed. "Have you read that book? It's *hot!* A sex-starved upper-class woman having an affair with a lower-class gamekeeper."

"Sounds intriguing."

"It is." Maître leaned down and kissed the side of my neck. My eyes rolled at the feel. "We were talking about the club," I said breathlessly, wanting to know about him.

"*You* were talking about the club, ma chérie," Maître Auguste said, his lips leaving my neck.

Maître was quiet for so long I thought I'd pushed too far. "You want answers, you will earn them," he said. Maître rolled off the bed and came back to me with a bag of what looked like wooden clothespins. I frowned in confusion.

Maître took a clothespin in his hand and ran it up and down my sternum. "These are not for domestic purposes." He lowered one toward my breast.

I cried out, feeling the sting from the clothespin travel straight to my clit.

Maître flicked the clothespin attached to my nipple, and my body jerked at the short burst of pain, which made my skin heat. As if to soothe the second of pain he'd inflicted, he swiped his tongue over my clothespin-free nipple, and I moaned at the feel of his hot tongue swirling around my flesh.

"Some of our everyday lives are not so good," Maître said, and in my lust-fueled mind, I realized he was answering my question. "This club...it frees those who cannot be free. It ignites passion in those who have their wants and needs suppressed."

"You've been suppressed?" I asked, sadness fueling my words. "You don't enjoy your life outside of these walls?"

I couldn't imagine him being anything other than larger than life. He didn't answer with words. Instead Maître pinned a clothespin on my other nipple. I hissed in a breath when he flicked them both back and forth. I yanked on the ropes around my wrists, gritting my teeth against the rising pressure between my legs.

Maître crawled over me, silver eyes hovering right over my veiled face. "Do I like my life? Not always. It is not bad. Yet I am not so free. But as of late, it has improved."

"How?" I whispered.

"He shook his head and reached into the small bag on the end of the bed. He pulled out another pin, but this one was all metal. Inching up my restrained legs, he stopped at the apex of my thighs. He held the pin in the air, making sure I'd seen it, then slowly clamped it on my clit.

My eyes rolled back in my head at the sudden, maddening pressure it brought. Addictive pressure. Mind-blowing pressure. Maître's hands roved over my thighs, the tensing of my muscles causing the pins on my nipples and clit to sway back and forth, biting me with delicious pain.

"How has my life improved, you ask?"

"Yes, Maître," I whispered, biting my lip, trying to focus on the question at hand when my body was begging for release.

"A siren," he said, and I felt my heart almost stutter to a halt. "She came along, lured me in and woke me from mundanity." His words crashed over me like the warm rays of the sun. Before I could say anything in response, he said, "Only a few questions more."

"What don't you like, your job or your home life?" I asked, trying to sway the conversation back to safe territory. I couldn't let my heart be involved in this. I couldn't like him like this. I had to keep it in this chambre only.

Maître reached into his bag, and ran a long, thin chain through his fingers. I stared at the chain, wondering what he would be doing with that. In time to Andrea Bocelli's voice singing through the speakers about dreams, he wrapped the chain around the pins on my nipples and clit until it formed a perfect triangle. The chain pulled on the pins. I felt shivers race like dominoes over my skin, addictive pressure building inside me.

"Some of us are not free to live as we choose," he said. "Some of us are bound by things out of our control. Bound to duties by blood."

"You have to submit to someone else," I realized, the pieces of Maître's mysterious puzzle slotting together. "That's why you need this control." Maître reached into his bag again and pulled out a long, sleek black vibrator. I jumped when he turned it on and the buzzing sound filled the room.

Maître placed the vibrator against the clothespin on my clit. The second it pressed against the metal, I screamed, pulling on the ropes around my wrists. The vibrations traveled like earthquake tremors around the pins on my nipples and clit, a torturous kind of hell that I never wanted to stop.

Maître's eyes were glued on me as I thrashed against the restraints, needing to get away from the pins but, at the same time wanting to drown in the vibrations. Then Maître turned up the vibrator, faster and faster, until I couldn't take anymore.

"Do not come," he ordered and, as I had for weeks, I obeyed his command. My orgasm built and built, but it waited on a hellish precipice for his permission to release. The vibrations were torturous, relentlessly pushing me further and further until I thought I couldn't bear it. But I did take more. I took so much that my neck ached from tension, and if he didn't command me to come soon, I was sure I would fracture apart.

"Come," he suddenly ordered, and I did, breaking apart at the seams. The ropes pulled so tight at my wrists and ankles I was sure I would bruise.

In the numbness that followed my orgasm, I felt Maître taking the pins off my nipples and clit. I throbbed everywhere, my body one rhythmic heartbeat.

When the ropes had been untied from my wrists and ankles, I collapsed on the bed, strong arms wrapping around me and cradling me to a warm body. I tried to catch my breath, but air evaded me.

"You did well," Maître praised. The rush of pride those words brought helped me breathe. I ran my hand down his perfectly cut abdominals and down to the V that led underneath his silk pants.

Sighing, he laid a single kiss on my head. Maître *never* did this. He never kissed me above my neck. Not my head, and never my lips.

Not wanting the connection to end, I nuzzled into his warm skin, closing my eyes. Then I felt a hand thread into mine. It took me a moment to remember we were in NOX and I was with Maître Auguste. But his hand reminded me of Harry and how he'd never let go of me at the hospital.

Harry, whose hand felt just as lovely as this.

Exceptionally...

CHAPTER THIRTEEN

"TOO SLUTTY, OR RAVISHING IN RED?" I asked Sage and Amelia as I walked out of my bedroom the next day in my knee-length scarlet body-con dress. Today was the day of "the big dinner."

"You're getting all fancy for dinner with your parents?" Amelia said, a shit-eating grin pulling on her mouth. "You normally rock up in yoga pants and a hoodie."

"Oh, that reminds me," I said and reached into my bra, pulled out my hand, and showed her the middle finger. "I got this for you." Amelia laughed smugly into her coffee.

I dropped onto the couch beside her and Sage. Sage, being a good buddy and pal, popped a square of milk chocolate into my mouth.

"Better?" he asked.

"No," I groaned and took hold of Sage's hand. "He held it like this." I demonstrated Harry's hand in mine, showing the exact grip and tightness. "And he never let go."

"We know, baby girl," Sage said placatingly and kissed the back of my hand.

"But what does it mean?" I cried and jumped to my feet. I caught my reflection in the mirror over the TV and at least felt happy with my choice of attire. I wore my hair down and in loose waves. I didn't particularly like my hair in one style over another, but Maître loved it down. Demanded it of me. So I assumed it was the better look on me.

And that was the annoying part of this whole thing. I actually cared what Harry thought of me. The man I'd sworn was my archnemesis. But here I was, waiting for him to collect me to go to my parents' home for Sunday dinner. Not even in my wildest dreams had I thought I'd be here.

"Maybe just don't overthink everything, Faith," Amelia said. "Just go with the flow. If something happens, then it happens." She smiled. "I, for one, am *living* for this. You know my favorite trope in romance is enemies to lovers." Her eyes became lost to her fantasy. "It's like you're in a modern regency novel. He's the swarthy viscount and you the pauper scullery maid."

"Oh my god! I thought that as we ascended my parents' steps after the hospital. How I felt like I was in a period drama or something."

"Ascended the steps?" Sage said, lips pursed.

"Hush, heathen! I am still in scullery maid mode." I sighed. "But my fantasy was cut short by the mention of labia."

"By Harry Sinclair?" Amelia shrilled, choking on her coffee.

"Sadly no." My cell hummed on the coffee table.

PP: I'm outside.

My heart started thudding out of rhythm, and I got to my feet. Just as I did, the buzzer to our apartment sounded.

"Chivalrous bastard, isn't he?" Sage said, crestfallen. "You sure he doesn't swing for my team? I could get used to an English gent romancing me."

"Afraid not, my fair-weather friend. But he said he has a cousin."

Sage stood and gripped my shoulders. "We need intel, Faith. We need to know if he is a cock in a hen house, or a cock in a house of cocks."

I blew out a breath. "That was a lot of cock talk, Sage. Even for me."

Sage slapped me on my ass. "Get him, baby girl."

Waving to my friends, I caught the elevator to the ground floor, and as I opened the door, I saw Harry Sinclair leaning against the stone handrail on the steps, looking out onto the busy street. One hand was in his pocket, and the other held a bouquet of red roses. He looked like Richard Gere in *Pretty Woman*. Wait. Would that make me—

Suddenly, too busy not paying attention, I tripped over the entryway and plummeted toward the ground, just in time for Harry to see, and thus dive forward and catch me in his arms.

"I'm not a prostitute!" I shouted as I crashed into his chest. My hand found purchase on his blazer pocket and I heard a loud rip.

"Good to know," Harry said dryly and righted me where I stood. "I would dread to think of the calamity you would cause to paying customers."

"Oh shit," I said seeing that, in my fall, I had also decapitated the roses.

Harry followed my gaze, first to his pocket, then to his roses. "Miss Parisi, you appear to have deflowered me."

My mouth fell open at Harry's unexpected dirty joke. Sidling dramatically to his side, I pressed against his chest, idly noticing his pupils dilating at the contact. "Deflowering, Viscount Sinclair? How terribly naughty of you," I said, imitating his accent.

Lowering his head to mine, making me lose my breath, he said, "You must be rubbing off on me."

Seeing this as too good an opportunity, I said, "Oh, Mr. Sinclair, I can most certainly rub off on—"

"And we're done," Harry said, cutting me off, and stepped away from me. But he was smiling. That friggin' wide, stunning smile he'd shown me at the hospital and the one that was about to make me hit the ground again with the impact it had on my heart. "You're incorrigible."

"So you keep saying. But you teed that one up for me. I had no choice but to take the hit."

Harry tossed the headless flowers into the trash near his car. I caught up with him. I sighed sadly at the deceased flowers. "What is it with you blue-blood Henrys and decapitations?"

"An English rite of passage it would seem." He opened the passenger-side door for me. As I passed, he said, "Although this time I think we can put the blame in your corner, and your bizarre insistence that you are not a lady of the night."

Harry shut the door and I took in my fill as he rounded the hood of the car. He was dressed in dark jeans, a white shirt, and a gray blazer. As always, his top two buttons were undone and a handkerchief sat proudly in his now-ripped pocket. This one was purple. His dark-brown hair fell in soft and effortless waves.

He was beautiful.

Harry ducked into the car. "Sorry about the jacket and the flowers," I said. "They are not the first victims of my klutziness. Pretty sure they won't be my last."

"Not a problem," he said. Then, "Have you had a good weekend?"

Blood drained from my face. *Well, I have, thank you, Harry. Last night I had things done to me with laundry sundries that frankly would make your bleached white sheets pale.*

"It was adequate," I said, once again in my English accent. I winced, wondering why the hell I was ever permitted to open my mouth. It was nerves, I realized. Before, when I was around Harry, I gave zero shits how he perceived me. Now everything was different.

"Faith, I must tell you something that might not be pleasant," he said, seriousness lacing each word.

"What is it?" I clasped my hand over his, which rested on his knee. I saw his nose flare at my touch.

Clearing his throat, he flicked his eyes from the road to me and said, "You have the worst English accent I have ever heard in my entire life."

As his words filtered into my moonstruck brain, I finally dropped open my mouth and shouted, "Harry! You dick! I thought something was actually wrong!"

"There was," he said plainly. "Your god-awful accent. Do you realize Shakespeare and Chaucer are rising from their graves, hands clasped over their ears, highly offended at that sorry attempt at what is arguably the best accent in the world?"

"The best in the world?" I asked, choking on a laugh. "Like hell! The best accent in the world wouldn't say *zebra* so funny."

"We say it correctly," Harry said. Why did he argue so smoothly? He wasn't even raising his voice. Who the hell argued this way?

"Well, don't even get me started on how you all say aluminum."

"Ah, you mean in the proper fashion? We champion the use of vowels, is that was has you so offended?"

"Herbs," I shot back.

"Begin with prominent H."

"Vase," I said, smugly.

"Vase." Harry pronounced it *varze*. "The item we could have used had you not destroyed the roses that went in it."

"Eggplant."

"Aubergine."

"Zucchini."

"Courgette."

Harry smirked at me, looking like the cat who'd gotten the cream. Well, asshole, not on my watch! "Well, fanny is your ass, not your pussy. What do you say to that?"

"Pussy, dear Faith," Harry said, sounding as condescending as ever, "is a cat. Not a lady garden."

That was it. That was what broke me. I roared with laughter, tears spilling from my eyes. "Lady garden? What the hell is that!" As the car came to a stop, I realized my hand was still on his knee. As I laughed, Harry squeezed it harder. "That is literally the worst slang word I have ever heard." I scrunched up my nose. "All I can see in my head is a miniature gardener in a straw hat, mowing up and down a hairy *lawn*. That is not the visual one should be having on a Sunday afternoon."

As my laughter died off, my attention became fixated on my hand on his. Harry's hand had flipped over and his fingers now linked through mine. I wiped my eyes, and then the car suddenly became quiet.

"Are you ready?" Harry asked, breaking the silence. His voice sounded so relaxed and smooth. He was so often uptight and as though he had the weight of the world on his shoulders. I used to believe that to be condescension to those below his elevated social status. Now I believed I knew better. He had just needed someone to see through the hard shell he wore like a repellant.

"I'm ready," I said. "And I should be asking you that question. You're about to have Sunday dinner at the Parisi household." I reluctantly moved my hand from his and patted his shoulder. "Godspeed, young sir."

I got out of the car, and Harry reached into his back seat, pulling out a bouquet of flowers, a wine bag, and something in a bigger gift bag. I raised an eyebrow. "Trying to make a good impression?"

But Harry didn't smile or laugh at my joke. He simply said, "Yes." My heart flipped in my chest, did a split-leap, a back handspring, a somersault, and an expert finish. Harry held out his arm for me. "Shall we?"

I linked my arm through his and, shaking my head, said, "Pussy is a cat." I laughed at that sentence, still replaying our argument in the car.

"Or a kitten," he said as we stopped at the door and I took my key from my pocket. I looked up at Harry. "A little kitten. I could see you as that," he said nonchalantly, and goosebumps broke out all over my body.

Mon petit chaton...my little kitten.

I felt my heartbeat in my throat and heard it echoing like a dance drumbeat in my ears. Harry couldn't know that was what Maître called me. But why would he say that? Out of everything he could have said, why would *that* be it?

I was ripped from my thoughts when Mom opened the door with her usual dramatic flair. "Faith! Harry! Why are you standing out here sweating your pants off? I saw you pull up and you took so long I thought you'd been mugged or something."

"No, as you can see we're in one piece," I said, and Mom ushered Harry inside first. He glanced back at me with a furrowed brow, clearly noticing something was up. As they disappeared into our apartment, I took a deep breath. "All these orgasms of late are fucking my brain as well as my..." I trailed off, laughing again over Harry saying *lady garden*. It was the worst damn thing I'd ever heard. But trust a viscount to use the name of something so *floral* and innocent for a vagina. "Lady garden," I huffed, just as my mother came to the door.

"Why are you still out here, alone, talking to yourself about vaginas, Faith?" She shuddered. "And never say it in that way again. Your granny McIntyre used to say that to me when she came to visit from Scotland. It never sounds right. Ever."

I followed Mom into the apartment. "I got these for you, Mrs. Parisi." Harry handed her the flowers. Mom positively melted.

"Thomasena, please," she said.

"And Mr. Parisi. Faith told me you came from Italy." Harry handed over the wine bag.

When Papa pulled it out, his eyes widened. "The Bella Collina Merlot from Savona Wines." He was speechless. That didn't happen often. "It is too much. It is so rare. I could not accept it."

"Please," Harry insisted. "I had this at home. I thought a man from Italy would enjoy it more than I would." I swore there were tears in Papa's eyes.

"*Grazie mille,*" he whispered, holding the bottle like it was the most precious gold.

"And Thomasena...Faith, of course, told me of your Scottish heritage." He handed her the bigger gift bag. Mom looked inside it and gasped. I leaned over to see what was inside. I laughed, seeing cans of Irn-Bru, haggis, and oatcakes.

"Harry," Mom said, eyes shining now. Oh, Jesus Christ! My vision shimmered at the kindness Harry had bestowed on my parents when all they had been dealt of late was bad luck and sadness. Seeing them this touched was like witnessing a rainbow after a storm.

As I looked at Harry, something inside me shifted. Like a tectonic plate moving under land, forever shifting the earth above, my heart seemed to switch to a new kind of beat. One that finally heard Harry's.

"Thank you for inviting me into your home."

"Fuck, Harry," Mom said, shattering the heavy moment. "You can move in if you keep us in this kind of supply!"

"Harry," Papa said, patting Harry's blazer, which was looking all kinds of shabby with a half-ripped pocket and an incredibly limp pocket square. "Your jacket. I'll fix this for you."

"No, thank you. I will have a tailor attend to it tomorrow." Harry flashed me an amused glance. "Someone fell into me and somehow managed to rip it."

Mom shook her head. "Some people."

As she walked away to put away her presents, I leaned close to Harry. "Are you sure it didn't just buckle under the weight of all those pocket squares?"

"I'll have you know those squares are the epitome of gentry fashion."

I patted his chest, trying to linger longer than necessary when I felt the hard muscle underneath. "I'm sure it is, Harry. Keep telling yourself that."

"Please. Let me look at it," Papa insisted. Harry took off the jacket and immediately folded his shirt sleeves back to his elbows. I had the sudden urge to lick the muscles on his forearms. I had no idea why his forearms had grown into a fetish for me.

Harry watched Papa disappear into his back room. "Your father is sewing my jacket?" he asked, confusion clear on his face. "I have no idea what is happening."

"He's a tailor. That's what he came to America to be." A rush of pride threatened to take me down. "He's the best in all of Manhattan." Harry must have detected an air of sadness around my words because he momentarily took hold of my elbow in a comforting gesture. His gaze implored me to tell him what was wrong. I shook my head. *Not right now*. He must have understood, because he didn't push any further.

But as I lowered my head, he pushed back a strand of hair from my face. "I like your hair like this." My breath trembled as he said those words. "Down. Wavy. Just like this." In that moment, I was glad Mom chose to come back with drinks, or I was sure I would have scaled his six-foot-three frame like King Kong climbing the Empire State Building. That disturbing scene might have been difficult to explain to my parents.

"Prosecco?" Mom asked and I swiftly swiped a glass from the tray. I knocked back the bubbles in record time. "Christ, Faith!" Mom said. "Calm down. We're not at a frat party. I know we're not the richest of people, but I'm sure we can be civilized if we try." Harry coughed into his glass, hiding an amused grin. I narrowed my eyes at him, promising him a painful death.

"Sorry, Harry," Mom said. "I think I dropped her on her head one too many times when she was a baby."

"It is what makes her unique," Harry said, and I couldn't help the smug grin plastered on *my* face.

"Well, at least someone thinks so."

"Mom!" I shrilled.

"I'm just joking, baby. You know that." Mom held me in a one-armed hug, but I saw her shaking her head at Harry, as though she was anything but sorry. "Dinner will be ready in five. Make yourselves comfortable, kids!"

We sat on the couch, and I watched Harry soak in the room. His eyes fixed on the many photo frames on the old wallpapered walls.

Pictures of family past and present, from Scotland to Italy, and every awkward stage I'd gone through growing up.

"Pink hair?" he asked, pointing at my fourteen-year-old self, glaring menacingly at the camera.

"My expressive stage."

"And the septum piercing?"

"Emo stage."

"Wow." I smiled at that word coming out of his mouth again.

"What? You didn't have the quintessential teenage stages in high school?"

"Lord no," he said. "My father would have disowned me." He smiled as he said that but then took a long drink of his prosecco. "I went to Eton. The boarding school. I would have been expelled if I'd even attempted anything of the sort. That and my father would have killed me." When he faced me again, I recognized those eyes. Those eyes that were racked with sadness. They were the same ones that had stared back at me from the picture I'd found of him as a child with his father.

He sat back against the couch, and I mirrored his movements. I found his hand by his side, resting on the couch, and held on. I heard Harry's breathing hitch as our palms kissed. The moment was quiet, but not awkward. Just then, Papa came back into the room, carrying Harry's blazer.

"*Va bene*," he said and held out the blazer for Harry to see. Subtly releasing my hand, Harry stood and took the jacket from Papa. He brushed his hand over the pocket, which looked like new.

"Thank you," Harry said, sounding genuinely grateful. He studied the jacket more closely. "That is excellent work, Mr. Parisi—"

"Lucio."

"Lucio." Harry folded the blazer over his arm. "Where is your shop? I have several suits that need attending to. I would love for you to tailor them."

I ached at the happiness breaking out on Papa's face. It was as bright as the sun outside. "Just down the block from here. Parisi Tailoring."

"Shall I pop down at some point this week?"

"*Perfecto*," Papa said, clasping Harry's hand.

"Dinner's ready!" Mom shouted from the dining room. Papa walked through first.

I held Harry back by his arm. "Thank you," I whispered, fully aware he would see the raw emotion in my face.

"He is good, Faith. Excellent, in fact. I meant it."

"The best," I said, echoing my sentiment from earlier.

"Faith Maria Parisi, get your ass in here this second! I won't have my potatoes going cold!"

"Just so you know, she was actually shouting at us both there, but it wouldn't be polite to rip into you when she just met you."

"Duly noted," Harry said and offered me his arm to walk into the dining room.

I spluttered a laugh. "It's eight feet that way," I said, pointing to the table.

"Bloody hell, Faith. Can you just let me be chivalrous for one damn minute without all the commentary?"

"Yes, sir," I said, impressed by his vigor, and saw the rush of heat in his eyes.

As we walked to the table, I realized I was turned on. I was turned on at Harry's stern words. As I sat down, I tried to pretend like everything was okay and I wasn't about to ravish Harry over the green bean casserole in front of my parents and God.

"Why do you look like you've just bumped uglies, Faith?" Mom said, as direct as always. "Your cheeks are flushed, and I can see your nipples through your dress—"

"Let's eat, shall we!" I reached over to the center of the table to fill my plate.

As I began to fill it high with all the complex carbs, Mom hit my hand. "Faith, let Harry go first. He's the guest, and not my ill-mannered daughter, who acts like she hasn't eaten in weeks."

Harry's lips twitched as he politely, and ever so cautiously, filled his plate with veggies, chicken, casserole, and gravy. I stared at him, confused at how anyone could be so controlled when all this delicious food was positively crying out to be eaten, the flavors invading the nose like tiny Viking marauders, pillaging the senses.

It occurred to me then that Harry rarely did anything that wasn't completely perfect and somewhat measured. Not in a negative fashion, but like he'd had manners and "proper" etiquette completely hammered into him. I wanted to see that careful control shatter. I covered my salacious smirk with the back of my hand, knowing the very place I wanted to see that control break.

"So, Harry? Whereabouts in England are you from?" Mom asked, nodding her head in permission for me to get my food.

"Surrey."

"Harry Sinclair from Surrey," Mom mused. Then her eyes widened and she dropped her fork, the metal clattering to the plate like a thunderclap. "Not *the* Harry Sinclair from Surrey? The one whose father owns HCS..." I could practically see the lightbulb appear over my mother's head.

"Yeah. You knew he was my boss, Mom," I said, trying to keep her calm.

"I didn't realize he was *the* boss. One of the Sinclairs."

Harry shifted in his seat, showing his discomfort. "My father is actually the one in charge of HCS Media right now," he said politely.

"Would you want to take over one day?" Papa asked, and I could have kissed him for making it sound like it wasn't a big deal. Unlike Mom. I was making slashing gestures across my neck to tell her cut out the Sinclair talk.

"I can't wait," Harry said, drawing my attention. He placed his fork down while he spoke. Shit, I felt like I should enroll in a damn finishing school or something just so I could be in his presence and not feel like a caveman. "I studied at Cambridge for my degree in journalism, then went on to Oxford to complete my master's. It's not just in my blood, but it's my passion too."

"I didn't know this," I said, just as enraptured by his answer as my parents.

He looked at me and I saw it. I saw the passion blazing in his eyes. "Yes," he said and took a drink of his water. "I have lots of ideas for HCS Media. Where to take it, how to give back. Masses of journals with notes and ideas on how to truly change the media and publishing industry for the better."

"Wow," I said and Papa nodded.

"Your father," Papa said, "He knows you have these ideas?"

The glacial shell that Harry wore like an ice-filled jacket slowly knitted back into place, his rigid posture rearing its stiff head. "My father is very set in his ways and likes things as they are." He gave us a tight and unhopeful smile. "Maybe one day."

There was a slight awkward pause in the conversation, and Mom broke it. "Faith, I've been meaning to say, I finally read your column last week. Sound advice on the rimming question. And I agree that a pogo stick is never safe to lose one's virginity on." Harry suddenly began choking on his food. I slapped him on the back and was close to bending him over the table and conducting the Heimlich Maneuver when he suddenly started breathing again.

"Jesus, Harry! You okay?" I asked.

"Just went down the wrong way," he said, his voice weak.

"Harry, have you read many of Faith's columns?" Mom asked, when he could breathe again.

"Some," he said, a faint blush building on his cheeks.

"She's fabulous, is she not?" Papa said. "Such a creative way of dealing with such complex problems."

"I couldn't agree more," Harry said and tapped my hand. As he moved his hand away, I felt the searing heat still on my skin like it had been branded.

"She wants features at some point, don't you, Faith?" Mom said and I felt my stomach sink. They didn't know about the big feature of course. As open-minded as they were, I wasn't sure it was something they would like to hear about. *Mom, Papa, for the past several weeks*

I've been placed in stocks and ravished every which way to Sunday by a sexual master in a Phantom of the Opera *mask.*

"She mentioned that," Harry said.

"One day," Papa said, echoing Harry's words, and smiled my way.

"So, how did you both meet?" Harry asked my parents, and the conversation trickled on from there. Over two courses and after-dinner coffee, conversation flowed. In the two hours spent at my parents' house, I had never seen him so relaxed. I'd never seen him smile so much.

"Lucio, I'll be seeing you sometime this week," he said and shook Papa's hand. "I know quite a few businessmen in Manhattan who would pay good money to have their suits tailored to your high standard. I'll send them your way."

"*Grazie*," Papa said, his voice thick with gratitude.

"Okay, let's go," I said to Harry, pressing my hand on his lower back. I had to vacate the apartment quickly or become a broken, emotional mess at the sight of Papa so happy with Harry's promise.

"Lovely to meet you, Harry. I hope you'll come again," Mom said affectionately. I could see by her moon eyes she was already smitten with Harry.

"I'd love that," Harry said, and I felt every ounce of genuineness at those words.

With a wave to my parents, Harry took my arm and linked it through his. His gaze dared me to argue with him over the gesture. I made a show of pretending to fasten my mouth shut with an invisible lock. He tipped his head up to the sky. "Good Lord, I believe today we have witnessed a miracle. Faith Parisi is not offering her usual sarcasm to my chivalry. Thank you." It took all that I was not to make a wisecrack to that, but I refrained.

As we descended the steps, Harry held tightly onto my hand. "Just wanted to make sure you don't trip and fall headfirst on to the sidewalk. You seem to fall a lot in my presence."

I tried to hold my tongue, I truly did, but it was too much to hold back. "Harry Sinclair, I can't help it, your animal magnetism shakes the very ground you walk on, and I just cannot help but fall at your feet."

He released a heavy sigh. "Well, it was good while it lasted."

The sun started to set, casting a pink summer's glow over the city. Harry opened the car door for me, and I stepped inside. That fluttering feeling was back underneath my sternum. It had taken me a while to get there, but I realized what it was when Harry slid into the driver's side and gave me that wide smile he only seemed to offer in my presence.

I liked him.

Holy shit.

I liked him *a lot*.

Harry pulled out onto the street. "You are very lucky, Faith," he said after a few minutes of silence. I was mute, frozen in shock at the truth that was smacking me in the face. I liked Harry. Oh my god, I was *falling* for Harry Sinclair. "To have parents like you have." He swallowed the thickness in his voice. "The way they love you. Care for you. Take an interest in your life and work." Harry's eyes, which were firmly fixed on the road, were glistening.

"Thank you," I said quietly, not wanting to interrupt the soothing stillness that had built up in the car. "I love them so much." I thought of Papa's situation and felt like crying.

"Faith?" Harry said and laid his hand on my thigh. In that moment, it was as warming as a tight embrace. "Is everything okay with your father? His health..."

"His health is fine." I stared out the window at New York. At the hustling and bustling that teemed from every street and nook. Passing people who had problems of their own. Highs and lows and everything in between.

"You can talk to me. If you're upset, I want to help you. I want to listen, if that's what you need."

"You do?" I asked and looked at Harry. I needed to know if he felt anything for me too. If he was falling just as quickly and deeply as I was. "Why?"

Harry's jaw clenched, and the muscles in his forearms tensed when his grip tightened on the wheel. "You must know," he whispered. "I'm not an actor, Faith. With you, I feel I have failed completely in hiding my affection."

I smiled. Because he *had* hidden it. But not lately. Not in certain moments in the elevator. Not in the hospital, and certainly not today. I covered his hand, which was on my thigh. It felt so right, like it had always been.

"He is losing his shop," I said, for once actually saying the words aloud. I had denied them for so long, prayed for an answer, a miracle. But I knew there wasn't one. Papa was going to lose his shop. Maybe more. "Many years ago he took on a partner." I thought of Ludovico and imagined castrating that fucker with a serrated knife. Yeah, I got real dark when it came to people who messed with those I loved. "My papa trusted him. Loved him like a brother."

"What happened?"

I ran my finger over Harry's fingers, which were laid protectively over my knee. "Last year he ran, taking all of Papa's savings from the shop. Everything. He left them with absolutely nothing but rising debt and a trail of empty bank accounts." I shook my head, fighting the anger that was rising inside. "Papa has been fighting to keep the shop, working as much as he can, but with all his money gone..." I quickly wiped a tear that had escaped my eye.

"He has been given a little bit of time to pay the back rent. But he won't be able to make it up. We all know that, we just never dare speak the truth aloud." Lifting Harry's hand, I kissed the back of it. "You lit up his world today with your compliments. With saying you would use him as a tailor and recommend him to your business friends. He would be happy in life if all he had was me and Mom and his shop. Not money or accolades, not a fancy apartment or the best car. It's not who he is. Thank you for making him feel special today. I can't tell you what it means to me too."

"It's the very least I can do." Our hands were clasped, and I stroked his fingers and the back of his hand before bringing it to my lips. Harry's breathing deepened and the ambient calm that had filled the car quickly crackled and became live with electricity.

"Harry," I said, at last, my voice hoarse with need.

"Yes?"

"How far away is your apartment?"

"It's close," he said, his voice equally tight.

"Good."

CHAPTER FOURTEEN

HARRY'S FOOT pressed on the gas, and we zipped like lightning through the New York streets. We entered the Upper East Side, and I kept my face straight forward when we passed NOX. The fantasy of NOX and Maître had no place in my heart tonight. It was Harry that filled every inch. NOX was a mirage. Harry was *real*.

We were only two blocks from NOX when he turned right and we entered an underground parking lot. Harry pulled into the spot reserved for the penthouse. As the car ground to a halt and the engine cut out, we both gathered our breaths. Harry left the car and came around to my side. He held out his hand. I put mine in his, the butterflies in my stomach swooping in hordes, breaking free from their confines and flooding the rest of my body.

Hand in hand, Harry took me to the private elevator to the penthouse. We stepped inside, the doors shut, and the elevator began to rise. Second after strained second passed by, the air in the small space growing hotter and hotter until I thought I would lose my ability to breathe in the stifling heat.

Harry stood beside me, as still and as stoic as a marble statue. This close I could smell the addictive scent of his cologne—the mint, the sandalwood, and the musk. It was driving me insane. I clenched my thighs together, trying to stop the pressure from building as high as the penthouse floor we chased. In my peripheral vision, I saw Harry's chest rise and fall at a heady speed. His hand in mine twitched, his jaw clenched, and when I saw the hardness in his pants, I moaned aloud.

That was all it took. That one rebel sigh from my throat caused Harry to snap. He came barreling toward me, pushing me back against the elevator wall, and he crashed his mouth into mine. In mere seconds, he was everywhere. His scent, his taste, and the press of his hard, warm body smothered my every inch. Gone was the prim and proper Harry Sinclair, and in his place was a man wild and intent on bringing me to my knees. His lips moved against mine, his tongue slipping into my mouth, as his hands searched my body, as they roved over every curve, causing me to moan and roll my head back at the feel of finally being under his ministrations.

The ding of the elevator sounded, but Harry didn't stop kissing me. Instead, he picked me up, wrapping my legs around his waist. My eyes were closed as he guided us through the apartment. I didn't even see what it looked like; I was too busy undoing the buttons of his shirt. One by one, they opened and my hands brushed against his hard-muscled chest. Harry rolled up the skirt of my dress higher and higher until his hands landed on my lace panties.

"Fuck, Faith," he moaned against my lips, and I groaned at hearing a cuss word pour from Harry's mouth. His shirt open, I stroked my palm along his chest, his torso, and down to the bulge in his pants. "Fuck!" Harry said louder, as we crashed onto a soft mattress, my hand still cupping his dick. I didn't even have time to catch my breath before he ripped his shirt off and climbed above me, chest bared and the button and zipper of his jeans open.

"You're ripped," I whispered, and Harry took hold of my dress and yanked it down my arms. He rolled the body-con material down over my stomach and off my legs, leaving me in my black lace panties and bra set.

"Christ, Faith," he said, biting his bottom lip as he stared down at me. "You're perfect. How are you this perfect? Like you were made for me." I didn't get a chance to respond as Harry kissed me again, broke from my mouth, and traced a hot path down my neck to my breasts. A trail of goosebumps shadowed the journey.

Harry reared back his head, his blue eyes appearing black from how blown with lust his pupils had become. With a gentleness that contradicted his wild eyes, Harry pulled down each strap of my bra until my breasts spilled out. Growling at the sight of me, he lowered his head and took a nipple into his mouth.

My hands threaded into his hair. I pulled on the soft strands, and when I did, he sucked harder. I yanked again, the pleasure he was inciting coursing through my veins like lava, setting me on fire. The more I pulled, the more savage he became. As I pulled for a third time, Harry lightly bit my nipple, causing my clit to throb and my back to arch. I rolled my hips, desperate for relief. Not making me wait, Harry pressed his fingers between my legs. I cried out at how good it felt.

"Harry. God, Harry!" I moaned and Harry suddenly sat back.

I reached out and tried to pull him back. I needed more. I needed everything Harry Sinclair could give. I wanted it all. I wanted him to consume me, devour me, own my damn soul.

Harry's talented hands took hold of my panties and ripped them apart at the seams. "Oh, God!" I said as he tossed them over his shoulder, and he slammed his gaze to mine. There was a fraction of a pause. A heaving inhale, then Harry crawled over me, taking my mouth with his. The hardness in his jeans pressed between my legs, and I arched my back at the feel of him. He was huge.

Harry slipped down my neck, kissing my glistening skin. He tortured me with sweet kisses to my throat, my breasts, my stomach. I widened my legs, leaving no doubt of what I wanted and where I wanted him.

Harry moved lower, and I sighed feeling his hot breath between my legs. He placed his hands on the tops of my inner thighs then leaned in. I bowed my back at the first swipe of his tongue. My hands threaded through his hair, ready to guide him where I needed him. But no guidance was needed. Harry knew just where to go, his tongue flicking at my clit, his finger slipping inside my channel. In no time at all I felt my skin prickle and pressure build at the base of my spine with the oncoming orgasm.

"Harry, fuck! I'm gonna come," I said, rushing out the word, just as he moved his finger, pressing on my G-spot and blackening out my world. I screamed my release, moving my hips so Harry's tongue stayed where I needed him until my body jerked, unable to take any more. Harry lifted his head, pressing kiss after kiss to my inner thighs and my hips.

"You're so beautiful," he said, that accent in that raspy voice my undoing. Rolling to my knees, I pulled on his arm and pushed him down to the bed. It was my turn. When I was kneeling above him, I looked down at Harry and took my fill. Cut muscles, broad shoulders, olive skin, and those crystal blue eyes. Perfection.

Then my eyes moved to his crotch and the bulge that was threatening to bust through his jeans. With his button and zipper already undone, I pulled them down his legs, muscled thighs greeting me. I ran my hand over them, the dusting of black hairs tickling my palm.

"Do I have rugby to thank for these?" I said.

"Among other things," Harry replied, eyes flaring as I threw the jeans to the floor. I unclasped my bra and threw it down alongside it. "Christ, Faith," Harry hissed, and I moved my hands to the waistband of his boxer briefs as his palms kneaded my breasts.

"Calvin's," I said and kissed the brand name. "I approve." With Harry's teeth clenched so tightly I thought his jaw might break, I pulled down his boxers, swallowing when his length slapped against his stomach.

"Harry," I whispered and threw his boxers over my shoulder. "You're fucking huge." Harry lifted himself up, placed his hands on my face, and smashed his lips to mine.

"I need inside you," he said, the authority in his voice making me squirm.

"Not before I taste you." I pushed him back to the mattress. His back hit the bed, eyes narrowing.

"You're going to pay for that, Miss Parisi," Harry said. I ignored his heated warning and kissed along his stomach and his defined V. I licked at the mouth-watering muscle then moved along to his hardness. It twitched in anticipation as I grew closer, and I licked the vein that lay on the side. From root to tip, I caressed it with my mouth. Harry's hands clenched at his sides until his fingers threaded through my hair, wrapping it around his hands. The touch felt familiar somehow.

"Faith," he said like he was in pain. "Suck my cock."

"Yes, sir," I said, loving watching his eyes bore into mine as I moved my lips over the tip and took him into my mouth. He was too big to take him all, so I moved my hand to the base of his dick and worked him there too. Harry lifted his hips, but like the gentleman he was, he held off from giving me too much. I lapped my tongue around his tip, taking him as deeply as I could, until Harry guided my face away. "Stop. I need to fuck you. I want to finally come inside you."

"Harry," I murmured and crawled over his ridiculously perfect body. "Keep speaking to me like that. I like this version of you."

Harry grabbed hold of my arms and flipped me over. He reached into his bedside table and pulled out a condom. I watched, mesmerized, as he slipped it on and moved above me. "It's you," he said, in a moment of pure tenderness. "I'm only like this because of you."

"Harry," I whispered, my heart shattering into tiny particles and vanishing into the night.

Harry positioned himself at my entrance and, pressing his lips to mine, pushed inside. I moaned into his mouth; he groaned into mine. I wrapped my arms around his corded neck and my legs around his waist. I cried out when he filled me to the hilt.

"Mm," I moaned when he started moving, hitting every perfect part inside me. My breasts pressed against his chest, creating friction as he rocked back and forth, and my body felt ablaze, lit up from the white-hot sensations coursing through me.

"Harry," I moaned again as he tucked his head in the crook of my neck and increased his speed. He thrust and thrust until I was a body filled with nothing but pleasure. My eyes rolled closed as I held him tighter, starting to feel flickers of the deep orgasm that was building. "Harry," I cried, biting into his shoulder as my legs began to tremble.

He growled at the bite then lifted his head, his eyes locking on mine. That was all it took for me to break apart, fireworks exploding around me. Harry repeatedly slammed into me until I was nothing but putty in his arms.

"Faith, fuck Faith...FUCK!" he shouted then closed his eyes, his teeth gritting together as he came. I stared at him as he orgasmed, sure I'd never seen anything more perfect in my life.

"Fuck!" he groaned again, his voice echoing in the room around us. His body boasted a sheen of sweat, and his dark waves were unkempt from my roaming hands pulling at the strands. His lips were swollen from kissing, and his cheeks were flushed from coming so hard. I moaned when he twitched inside me. I was exhausted yet still craving whatever else he wanted to give.

I fought for breath in the aftermath. Harry lay over me, his weight keeping me safe. Then he pressed his forehead to mine before pulling out of me and rolling to the side. He took me with him, his arm cradling me to him like he couldn't stand to be apart even for a second. My stupid romantic heart liked that. It liked that too much.

I ran my hand up and down his flat stomach, his chest rising and falling, breathless. Lifting myself up on my elbow, I stared down at him. I smiled at him and, laughing, Harry smiled back. "It's always the quiet ones," I said and Harry rolled his eyes. I traced the pattern of the black hairs that dusted over his chest. I kissed along his pecs to the base of his throat. Harry tilted his head back, giving me more access, hissing when my tongue flicked out and tasted his salty skin.

"Where did you come from?" I said, seeing his skin bump as my breath ghosted over his chest. "So aloof, so withdrawn by day." My finger followed the valleys and ridges of his abdominals. "Then so dominant in bed, so fucking *good* in bed."

Harry's fingers traced my spine then dipped lower. Kissing my face, he pushed a finger inside me. My forehead fell against his chest as he fingered me from behind, brushing over my sensitive G-spot, which had barely had time to recover before he was back, punishing it with those talented hands.

Harry's mouth moved to my ear. "I've wanted to fuck you for so long," he said, his deep voice and fingers causing tremors to rack through me. I felt his dick harden at my thigh. I bit my lip, brushing my cheek against his. "I wanked off so many times, imagining you on this bed, in my arms, under me, screaming my name."

"Jesus, Harry," I said, blood heating. Harry kissed the back of my ear. Harry shifted over me, pressing my front to the mattress. It felt like a cloud beneath me; it was so soft. And it smelled of Harry's cologne. I breathed it in as he licked from the top of my spine to the bottom. Harry gripped my hips then pulled me to all fours.

I heard the crackling of another condom wrapper being opened; then I cried out, my forehead falling to the mattress, as Harry slammed into me from behind. I moaned and moaned and moaned as he filled me so impossibly full, moaning as he crawled over me until his chest was slick against my back and his hands covered mine as I gripped the sheet. Harry took hold of my chin and, without breaking his stride, guided my lips to his. His tongue plunged into my mouth in time with his thrusts.

Harry Sinclair was owning me, merging my body with his. He was inserting himself into my heart. Everywhere was Harry Sinclair. Every breath I took, every moan he consumed. I rolled my hips back, the movement setting off a spark in him. Growling, he gently linked his fingers through mine, in stark contrast to how he'd slammed inside me from behind. I was floating. As my pussy began to clench, Harry's cock causing all my synapses to explode, I cried out my release.

Harry grunted, froze, then came with my name on his lips. "Faith!"

I collapsed to the bed, sure I would never be able to move again. Harry lay on top of me, his strong arms keeping his weight from crushing me. But he didn't move. He stayed inside me for as long as he could, his lips peppering kisses along the back of my neck, my hair bunched into his hands.

Turning my head, I said, "You've literally fucked me into the mattress."

Harry huffed a laugh, and the sound of it, him on top of me like this, felt familiar. Too familiar. Before I could think any more of it, he moved to the side and wrapped me in his arms.

We lay in silence for several minutes, just catching our breath. I looked up and saw we were in a huge four-poster bed, the posts gilded. We lay in the center and still had masses of room on either side. My eyes widened seeing the size of the room. I was sure it was as big as my entire apartment. The walls were painted navy with panels, making it look like a manor house. Antique dressers stood under large mirrors. A couch sat beneath the window, which showed the now-darkened sky and the vast Manhattan skyline, with Central Park visible in the distance.

"Harry, the view," I said and lifted my head from his shoulder. I moved from the bed, dragging the top sheet with me, and wrapped it around me as I walked to the huge window. I inhaled and exhaled, for once realizing just how different our lives were.

I felt Harry behind me and leaned back against him, my heart missing a beat as his strong arms wrapped around me. I could feel he was still naked. "This view," I said and saw joggers in the distance running through the park. "It's beautiful."

"I agree," he said, kissing along the side of my neck. I smiled, knowing he wasn't even looking out the window. I turned in his arms and looked up at him. In the glow of the lights outside, he looked like the angel my concussed brain had dreamt him up to be. I wrapped the sheet around him, our bare skin joining in an embrace.

"Can't have the Upper East Side paparazzi catching you naked."

"They'd need one hell of a lens." He pushed my hair back from my face; then he cupped my cheek and kissed me. But this kiss was unhurried, his tongue slowly caressing mine.

As we parted I smiled, saying, "With a dick this size..." I took it in my hand and gave it one gentle stroke. "They wouldn't need a big lens." Harry huffed but thrust into my hand. I felt it hardening again. "I'm pretty sure the astronauts on the space station see this from way up there. It's their wanking material." I cleared my throat, donning the voice of an astronaut. "*Get ready, boys. Harry Sinclair's at his window again.*"

"They can keep looking," Harry said, pulling me in closer. He was rock hard against my thigh. "You're the only one my 'massive cock' wants." My eyes rolled in pleasure at Harry speaking so dirty.

"Say cock again," I said, smiling as Harry lowered his forehead to mine and whispered, "Cock." I groaned and allowed him to push me against the wall beside the window.

"Was that good for you?" he asked, a hint of playfulness in his voice I had never heard before.

"More," I demanded, dropping the sheet and hooking my thigh around his hip. I pressed against his erection. "Give me more. *All* the dirty words."

Amusement rumbled in Harry's chest. Between kisses he said, "Pussy, arse, clit, tits..." He smiled against my mouth and whispered, "Lady garden."

Throwing my head back, I laughed. "No! Not the fucking creepy-ass lady garden!" As I fought to catch my breath, I felt Harry's hand still on my cheek. When I cleared the tears from my eyes, I saw he was watching me, his eyes soft and...happy. They looked *happy*. My heart thudded so fast I thought I might pass out.

Taking his hand in mine, I pulled him from the wall. "Come. Show me your apartment." As we moved by the closet, Harry stopped me and opened the door. He took out two robes. He released my hand and pulled one around my shoulders.

"My naked body too tempting?" I said as he tied the sash around my waist.

"Always," he replied with a kiss on my lips. He slipped on his robe and I felt like crying when his Adonis body disappeared under white terrycloth. "But you're right, we can't have the perverts of Manhattan watching your sinful naked body though the windows with their lenses."

Taking my hand, Harry opened the door and my mouth fell open. His apartment was epic. There was no other word for it. A small hallway led us away from the bedroom to a living room filled with plush, overstuffed furniture that looked out over all of Manhattan, the floor-to-ceiling windows like frames around the most perfect art.

As I walked through the living room, I stopped dead as I caught sight of the kitchen. "Holy shit, Harry," I said and entered the white marbled room. I ran my hands over the granite worktops and all the top-of-the-range appliances. "You cook?"

Harry leaned over the countertop as I ran my hand over the mass of wooden cabinets. "Never."

"What a travesty," I said and, leaving the kitchen, walked down a hallway. "What's this way?"

"My office. Two other bedrooms." Harry opened the door to his office and I gasped. A traditional mahogany desk sat in the center, but all around him were floor-to-ceiling bookshelves. And the ceilings in this penthouse were high.

"Oh. My. God," I whispered as I ran my hands over the many volumes that stared back at me.

"You like to read?" he asked, perching on the corner of his desk. I walked past the library ladder and read the titles: *Lord of the Rings*, *The Hobbit*, *The Chronicles of Narnia*. All my favorites. "Dickens?" I asked, seeing a whole shelf dedicated to his works.

"When I'm in a dour mood," he teased.

I stopped dead and looked at Harry. "Jane Austen?" All her works were present and accounted for.

"Her work has merit," he said, like he was the judge and jury of all literature. I mean, HCS Media *did* have a publishing house, but still. A playful glint remained in his eyes. I couldn't get enough of it.

"Merit?" I laughed and walked to Harry, pulling on the collar of his robe. His arm wrapped around my waist and I melted. "I think her works have more than 'merit'." I pretended to mull over this. "In fact, I'd say you and certain characters of hers share some attributes."

"Is that so?" he said with a single raised eyebrow.

"Arrogant."

"I'm offended." There was no malice in his voice.

"Posh."

"I suppose that could be argued."

"Do you live in a stately home in England? That could be a similarity." Harry froze, and when I looked at him he grimaced. I'd been joking. He, apparently, was not.

"A teensy-tiny one." He held up his index finger and thumb and pressed them together to exaggerate his point.

"Is it really teensy-tiny?"

"Erm...no."

"Like, how many bedrooms?"

Harry sighed. "Seriously, Faith, can we not—"

"How many, Harry?"

"Bedrooms? Twenty-three." I stopped breathing. "That's just in the main house. Then there's the outbuildings."

"Outbuildings," I echoed.

"Guest houses. We have...a few of them on the property."

Right, I said, starting to realize there really was an entire world separating us. I normally wouldn't have given a damn about that, but...twenty-three motherfucking bedrooms!

"It doesn't matter," he said, and I heard the panicked plea in his voice for me not to close off on him. His lips were parted, and he looked at me in such a heated and affectionate way that it made my toes curl.

I ran my hands through his hair, Harry's eyes closing at the comfort. "You can appear prideful."

"On occasion." The tug of amusement was back on the side of his mouth.

"One might say, *prejudiced*."

"No," he argued. "I think that one better fits you." I opened my mouth to protest, but he was probably correct.

"Okay. Well on that note, shall we leave it there?"

"Of course." I leaned down and kissed him, his hands parting my robe and moving to my ass.

I moaned into his mouth but pulled away. "Come," I said and held out my hand for him to take. "I'm going to put that pristine and batshit-crazy expensive kitchen to good use and cook for you."

Harry did as I asked. As we headed for the door, a book stood out from a shelf, one that was not in line with the others, as though it had recently been read and not put back properly. My pulse kicked into a sprint. *Lady Chatterley's Lover*.

"Faith?" Harry asked, wrapping his arms around my shoulders and kissing my cheek. "Are you okay?"

"Fine," I said, so confused it felt like a fog was invading my head. I pushed the fog aside. It was coincidence. It had to be. There was no way Harry...

I turned to look at him. All prim and proper and very British. He was a damn viscount for heaven's sake. There was no way he was in any way tied to NOX. It was impossible. My pulse calming, I took his hand and pulled him to the kitchen.

I opened the cupboards, searching for the right equipment and ingredients. Harry poured us both a glass of wine and sat at the breakfast bar, never taking his eyes away from me. "Ah-ha!" I said, finding the pasta maker and the ingredients I needed. I placed them on the counter where Harry sat. "Why on Earth do you have all this stuff if you don't cook?" I asked, beginning to prepare the bowl with the ingredients for fresh pasta. *Tortelli de Zucca*, my favorite.

"I'm loathe to tell you," Harry said and took a huge gulp of his wine. The more alcohol he consumed, the more relaxed he became.

"What?"

He grimaced. "I have a chef that comes in four times a week while I'm at work. He prepares my meals for me." He pointed to the pasta roller. "That is why all this is here. I asked him what he needed. He gave me a list. I have no idea what most of these are."

"Harry," I said, pausing to place my hand over his. "That is the poshest thing you've ever said."

"You are correct. Although I could hear myself muttering 'where is my favorite pocket square?' the other day and immediately thought that if you were there, I would never have heard the end of it."

I laughed, pouring the flour, sending a cloud of white into the air. I blew it out of my face and was sure it was now in my hair.

"Faith, you are the clumsiest person I have ever met."

"I know," I said, once the cloud had disappeared, and continued cooking. "I like to think it's sexy in a roundabout way."

"Sexy clumsy," Harry agreed and raised his glass.

"Sexy clumsy." I began kneading the dough. "So, you said at my parents' you went to Eton?"

Yes, I was using this as an excuse to find out more about him. He was a damn locked file. I needed to crack it open. Harry's lips twitched; he knew exactly what I was doing. "Harry, you had dinner with my parents. They told you about me and all my colorful ways. Give me something here. We've just fucked like rabbits." I pointed at him with my rolling pin. "One of whom had a massive cock. And although that is a good thing, the other rabbit will be stinging for days, thus deserves some kind of compensation."

"Thus?" Harry said dryly. "You just said 'thus'."

"Answer my questions or pasta shall be denied."

Harry held his hands up in surrender. "Don't threaten that. Please. I'll tell you anything you need to know."

"Eton. Go."

"I was sent there when I was eleven. For high school as you say here in America."

"Did you like it?"

"It wasn't bad." He ran his fingertip around the rim of his wine glass, losing himself in the memories. "I just missed home. I missed…"

"Your mom." Then my stomach sank remembering the hospital

and that he had been twelve when his mother died. "Harry, please tell me you were with her, when..."

He shook his head. "I was at school. My father called the school when she had died. I couldn't speak when I was told. I never got to say goodbye. I knew she'd been having tests, but I wasn't told anything else. I found out later, my father didn't want it to affect my studies."

"He kept you from her?" I whispered, stopping what I was doing.

Harry rubbed a hand over his head. "You have to understand, my mother was the lifeblood my father had been denied growing up. It was an arranged marriage of sorts. He had to marry well, as did she. My mum once told me that they never expected to fall in love. But they did, fast and deep. When she got sick, he went into denial."

Harry took a breath then continued. "I think he felt that if he didn't send for me, then it wasn't really the end for her." Harry lifted his head when I walked to him and sat on his lap. "When I went home for the funeral, the man I knew and loved was gone. And in his place was the man he is now. Cold, distant. Missing half his heart and soul." Harry looked up into my eyes. "I never used to understand how he changed so much..." He swallowed and let that hang in the air between us.

I became dizzy with the amount of affection in his eyes when he looked at me. Harry kissed me. "When I was eighteen I went to university. But I always knew I would go into the family business. I wanted to. It can just be hard at times." I knew he was talking about his father again. I kissed him on the cheek and went to cut up the pumpkin for the filling.

As I sliced into the orange skin, something Harry had said circled in my head. "Harry," I asked and met his eyes. "You mentioned that your father and mother had an arranged marriage of sorts." Harry stilled, paling a little. "I've seen you in magazines, with a woman with blond hair and pretty eyes."

"Louisa," he said stiffly, the old Harry rearing his head.

I dropped the knife. "Are you expected to marry well? As in to money? Another member of the aristocracy?"

Harry stayed still for so long I thought he might never move again. "I'm going to refuse to," he said and rose from his seat. He walked around the counter and lifted me to sit on it. Cupping my face, he said, "There are certain expectations of me. To marry well, to produce heirs, to never step out of line. To not embarrass the family, to not do anything that would rock the status quo of the famed Sinclair dynasty." My heart plummeted with everything he said.

"I write a sex column, Harry. A filthy one. I'm the daughter of an Italian immigrant and a first-generation American, neither of whom have ever known what having money was like." I felt my eyes glisten and hated myself for it. "This," I said pointing from him to me. "Is just sex, right? A story to tell your *mates* back in England. You fucked Miss Bliss and gave her some of her own medicine."

"No, Faith. Most certainly not." I tried to turn my head away from his gaze, but Harry's hands on my cheeks kept it in place. "Has any part of being together felt like nothing? Has any part of it felt like just a fuck?"

"No."

"Because it's not. Look at me, please," he begged when I lowered my eyes. I lifted them and saw with crystal clarity the conviction written on his face. "That won't be my life." Harry kissed my forehead. "I decided a long time ago that I didn't want it. Then you came along, annoying me and getting under my skin. Smiling sarcastically at me, hitting me with your quips, and I knew I was done. And those bloody pencil skirts you wear around the office." I laughed and he smiled. "You made me stop *wanting* it, Faith, and instead made me *crave* it."

"So this is not just sex?" I hedged.

"There's sex," Harry said and pressed his hard length between my legs. "There'll be lots and lots of sex. But..." He kissed the back of my hand. My breath stuttered. Harry Sinclair acting like a real-life

Prince Charming was going to be the death of me. "No. That's not all I want."

I felt reborn. I felt like a firework on the Fourth of July exploding into a million colors in a dark sky. "Stay with me tonight, Faith. Let's eat the pasta, watch crap TV, and go back to bed. Stay with me. Please."

"Okay."

Harry kissed me thoroughly. When he pulled back, he said, "As for my house back in England, you will see it soon."

I frowned. "What?"

"It's HCS Media's hundredth birthday. My father asked each publication's boss to nominate a few people from their staff to be flown to our estate for a midsummer's party to celebrate the milestone birthday. I saw and approved Sally's list last week. She's chosen you as one of the staff members to represent Visage."

"What?" I asked again. Harry pulled me closer to the edge of the counter. I moaned when his hardness pressed between my legs.

"Let me show you around when you come."

"Where will we be staying?"

"On the property. Everything is paid for. My father wanted it to be a real celebration." Harry kissed my neck, my cheek, and then my mouth, and I became lost in his touch. "But I want you in my room, in my bed. With me."

"Yes," I said and closed my eyes.

The pasta was eaten later that night. *Much* later. I stayed with Harry that night, and the following few nights. No one knew outside of us two. And every time I kissed him, I felt myself falling deeper and deeper. And when he lay asleep, my head on his chest and his arm and scent wrapped around me, I knew the truth of what my heart beat. I never spoke those words aloud. But as I closed my eyes and Harry pulled me to his chest, his lips seeking out mine even in slumber, I couldn't deny my feelings anymore.

I, Faith Maria Parisi, had fallen for Harry Sinclair.

And I had fallen for him hard.

CHAPTER FIFTEEN

"SEXY MAMA!" Sage sang as I strutted out of my bedroom like Gigi Hadid on the Paris runway.

"You look like a sexy glitterball," Novah said.

"You all look amazing too. Sage, very suave. Amelia, blue is definitely your color, and Novah, Jessica Rabbit eat your heart out!"

"Drinks!" Novah shouted and poured us each a shot. Tonight was the Manhattan Media Charity Ball. Sage and Amelia were Novah's and my plus ones. We were suited and booted and getting aboard the tipsy train.

"You got your vodka bra on, Faith?" Sage asked. With some crafty stitching passed down from Papa, my vodka bra was pumped and back in action.

"No need, my friend, it's a free bar." I waggled my eyebrows. "My natural C-cups can breathe freely tonight."

"Ah, free bar," Sage said. "The sweetest words that were ever spoken."

"So," Novah asked when we poured another shot down our throats. "Harry will be there."

"Yes. And?" I said innocently.

"Oh, cut the shit, Faith," Sage said and pressed his hand over his heart. "It's like Cinderella, Brooklyn edition."

"Faith, you've spent every night at his place this week. He drops you off at seven a.m. every morning and, truthfully, Sage and I have been watching you two French kiss your goodbyes from the window," Amelia said.

"Perverts," I said, narrowing my eyes on them both.

"You don't tell us anything anymore," Novah said. "We have to find out by our own devices."

"Because I'm not sure what is happening!" I said, blowing out some pent-up frustration. "Yes, I stay at his. We fuck like nymphomaniacs on Viagra. But we haven't talked about life outside his apartment. It's new, and I have no idea where it's going. We're just taking it day by day."

"You're meant to be with Maître again tomorrow night," Sage said. He threw his arm around my shoulders. "What are you gonna do, baby girl?"

"Go," I said and saw shock on my friends' faces. I sighed. "And tell him I've met someone and I can't do the sexual torture with him anymore."

"Oh. My. Fucking. Christ." Novah stood right in front of me. "You like Harry. Like, *like* him like him." I didn't deny it. What was the point? It was true, and these were my best friends. I told them everything.

"Oh, Faith." Amelia hugged me so hard I felt a lump build in my throat. "I'm happy for you. You deserve love. It's all I have ever wanted for you." I kissed her on the cheek when she released me.

"I'm freaking the fuck out," I said, hand on my head, a low-grade freak-out setting in. "He's Henry Sinclair III, a motherfucking viscount of Britain. I'm me, a chick from Hell's Kitchen with a mouth like a sewer. I hate to say this, because you know I, in general, say fuck the man, and anyone who disapproves of any decision I make can eat shit and die. But there are so many things I don't even know about Harry. His entire life back in England, for one. His father, who

I've never even spoken to. All the pressures he's under with his businesses." I felt like I was about to hyperventilate. "He's a billionaire. A fucking *billionaire*. I can't even imagine that amount of money in my head, never mind dating someone who has that much in the bank."

"Faith, come on. This isn't you." Sage took hold of my arms. "You're Faith goddamn Parisi. And if you want Harry, and he wants you, just say 'fuck you' to the naysayers."

"I know," I said, and I shook the doubt from my head. "But even the ballsiest of us can have a little wobble now and then, right?"

"Right," Amelia said, hugging me to her side. "But then we face the world, unapologetic about who we are. Yes?"

"Fuck yeah," Novah said and handed us our final shot.

We knocked it back and headed for The Plaza Hotel. As soon as the cab pulled up to the curb and we entered the foyer, we saw the place was dripping in opulent crystals, and carefully arranged bouquets were perfectly placed around the entrance and in the ballroom itself.

Music poured from the DJ's mammoth speakers, and round tables dressed in white and gold filled the room, allowing a large space for a dance floor. The place was packed with every businessman in Manhattan, it seemed.

"Drinks?" Sage suggested. We made our way to the bar. Sage grabbed us four glasses of champagne (of course). I scanned the ballroom, but it was a sea of black and white tuxes.

"Couldn't he have worn something red and white—like *Where's Waldo?*—so he'd be easier to find?" I said, just as I felt someone move behind me.

"That color palette doesn't really suit my skin tone, I'm afraid." I spun around and Harry was there, right before me, looking all kinds of hot and sexy in a fitted tux that hugged all his best places. He held out his arms. "Tailored courtesy of Lucio Parisi."

My chest warmed and my heart swelled. Damn, I was pathetic. Really friggin' pathetic and really, really in deep shit when it came to this sexy-as-sin viscount.

A devastatingly handsome blond man arrived next to Harry. He passed him a glass of champagne. He smiled when he caught me looking. "Faith, this is Nicholas Sinclair, my cousin."

"And best friend," he added, before shaking my hand. "So, you're the famous Faith. I've heard all about you." He ducked his head closer. "And just between me and you, I'm an avid reader of your column. I'm in the London offices, and I have to say your weekly column is the highlight of my Sunday."

"Why thank you, kind sir," I said, admiring another ridiculously fancy British accent.

I heard Sage cough behind us and fell forward a step when he elbowed me in my back. I fired daggers his way but then painted on a smile. "Harry, these are my best friends. You know Novah, of course." Harry kissed her on the cheek. "This is Amelia, she is my roommate and best friend."

"Lovely to meet you," Harry said, his charm causing Amelia to blush.

"And this is Sage, the third strand to our tripod, our best friend and across-the-hallway neighbor."

"Heard a lot about you," Sage said.

Then it was Nicholas's turn to be introduced. He greeted my friends with beaming smiles, but when he shook Sage's hand, it was like he'd just seen the sun for the first time in his life (which, coming from England, may have been true)

"Sage?" he said. "Like the herb."

"The very one." Sage held up his empty glass. "You need another drink, Nicholas?"

"Always," he replied, and they moved to the bar. The sexual tension radiated off them like heat from a furnace.

"Well," Harry said. "That didn't take long." He laughed and, discreetly taking my hand, squeezed my fingers. "Excuse us, ladies," he said to Amelia and Novah.

Harry pulled me through the crowd and into a deserted alcove at the back of the room. "You look so beautiful," he said and tracked his eyes down my halter-neck silver sequined dress. He admired my hair, falling in waves down my back.

"You look handsome too," I said, and Harry cupped my face and crushed his mouth to mine. He moaned into my mouth.

"Tonight is going to be long," he said and blew out a breath. "You're coming home with me?"

"Oh, go on then. You've twisted my arm."

"If it's too much trouble," Harry said, pretending to be offended at my jest.

"Fuck that. I want your massive cock in my mouth at exactly midnight. I—"

"Henry?" Harry stilled at the sound of his father's voice behind us. King Sinclair rounded the corner and Harry straightened up, fixing his tie.

"Dad."

King stared at Harry; then he slid his eyes to me. He smiled, but I felt the Arctic chill he was throwing my way. "And who is this?" he asked, holding out his hand.

I placed my hand in his and he kissed the back of it, just like Harry often did. But when Harry did it, I swooned like a damn lady. When King kissed me, I felt like wiping it on my dress but felt that response would be inappropriate and crass. Then again, he'd no doubt just heard me saying I wanted his son's huge dick in my mouth, so I wasn't sure how much further I could fall in his eyes.

"Dad, this is Faith Parisi. She works at Visage."

"Really?" he said politely, but the tone was anything but. "Very good. A sound publication." He turned to Harry. "I'm sorry to tear you away, but we have some people to meet, son. Business calls."

"Of course." Harry bowed his head to me like a true gent. "Miss Parisi, it was lovely chatting with you."

"You too," I said, feeling my heart deflate at his lack of affection in front of his father. As Harry walked away, he glanced over his shoulder, apology in his eyes. I guessed he just wasn't ready for the meet-the-dad milestone yet. Taking a deep breath, I moved back into the ballroom and found my friends. I gave them a rundown on King's frosty behavior and grabbed a few more drinks.

Suitably tipsy, we took our seats for the meal. Sage sat beside me, eyes fixed on Nicholas as he cut through the room to sit beside Harry at the head table, where King Sinclair held court.

"I'm in love." Sage tipped his head back dramatically. "That accent. That fucking *accent*." He turned to me. "How did you resist it for so long, Faith? It's like hypnotic or some shit. Forget love potions, they just need to bottle a hot guy speaking with a British accent and it'll have people falling at their feet."

"So what you're trying to say is that you like Nicholas?" I asked sarcastically.

"He's perfect." Sage sighed. "Now we just need him to move to New York, and we can run off into the sunset, get married, and live happily ever after."

"That's all?" Amelia said dryly. "A cake walk!"

"How's Harry?" Sage asked. I filled him in on Alcove-gate.

"Nicholas didn't say much but hinted at the fact that King is pretty hard on Harry." My eyes drifted across the room, only to collide with Harry's. He gave me a secret smile and took a drink of his champagne.

Just as our food began to arrive, a man approached Harry from a table near the champagne fountain. He was the same height and build, but he had light brown hair as opposed to Harry's chocolate waves. God, that viscount was so perfect, I could just eat him up.

Harry got to his feet and embraced the man. From our table I could hear the low hum of their voices, then... "Are they speaking French?" I asked, my glass frozen in midair, hearing the language pass so fluidly from Harry's mouth.

My friends listened closely. "Yeah," Amelia said, and my heart kicked into a sprint so fast I was pretty sure it rivaled an Olympic sprinter.

"I didn't know Harry spoke French," Novah said. "Then again, he went to an expensive boarding school, it was probably part of the curriculum."

I was stuck on Harry speaking in fluent French to this mystery man. "Who is that?"

Novah narrowed her eyes on the man, waiting for him to turn. When he did, taking his place at his table, Novah said, "Ah. I recognize him now. That's Pierre Dubois..." Novah's voice trailed off; then she met my eyes. I'd stopped breathing and was dangerously close to falling off my chair and slamming to the wooden floor. "He's French," Novah said, clearly on the same page as I was.

"Dubois," I said. "Like the bank?" A friggin' massive bank that had offices worldwide.

"Like the bank," Novah said. She shuffled her chair closer. "Faith, you think he's—"

"Maître," I whispered.

Sage and Amelia whipped their heads to Pierre, suddenly invested in Novah's and my conversation.

"He's gorgeous," Amelia said; then she looked at me. "And he seems to be good friends with Harry." She paled. "Oh. He seems to be really good friends with Harry. How awkward."

"Is it hot in here?" I said, destroying a napkin that had been folded into a swan and wafting it before my face, trying to grab some much-needed air. Harry and Pierre were friends. A man who was possibly Maître and Harry, who I had been sleeping with for a week. Friends. Of course they were. Pierre, who I was pretty sure had tied me up in every way imaginable and screwed me in every position in the Kama Sutra and beyond.

"I'm not feeling so good," I said and got to my feet.

"Faith? You okay?" Novah asked.

"I just need some air." I staggered toward the exit, my vision tunneling as I passed by Maître's table. I felt myself swaying to the left, reaching out for something on which to find purchase. And find purchase I did, right on the champagne fountain.

My hand sliced through the central tier, bringing the entire thing crashing to the floor. I slipped on spilt champagne, landing on my ass, as the smashing glasses created a symphony around the room.

Of course this is happening to me right now!

Getting on all fours I tried to pull myself up, but I kept slipping on the wet floor, repeatedly landing on my ass, which, it turned out, was nothing at all like being spanked.

At this point, I felt the most humane thing to do, for myself and everyone else in the room, was to press my face into the small puddle of champagne gathering beside me and drown so I didn't have to face the many people who were watching me humiliate myself right now. And what a bougie way to go out—drowning in Cristal. We were in The Plaza after all. Had to go out in style.

"Are you okay?" a heavily French accent asked. I raised my head, and there he was: Pierre fucking Dubois or, as I knew him, Maître Auguste, offering me his hand. I slipped my hand into his, allowing him to guide me to my feet. Let's be honest, it wasn't the first time he'd seen me on my knees. In fact, he'd seen me on my knees, my back, and my stomach; fastened in stocks; tied up in ropes; and chained to the wall...the list was endless!

"Are you okay?" he repeated, the music in the background partially disguising his voice. I glanced down at his hand. It was the right size for Maître. His height and build were so fucking right for Maître.

I couldn't breathe!

"I need air," I said and rushed from the room. I moved toward the main door, inhaling the bit of humid breeze the Manhattan summer offered. Security gave me side eyes, but damn them. Did they not know I had just seen my sexual master talking to my current lover?

"Mademoiselle, is everything okay?" The hairs on the back of my neck stood up hearing the thick French accent again. I turned slowly, finally seeing him without the cloak and mask, bared to me in his all his Parisian glory. His brown eyes stared back at me. Not silver but deep brown. Perfectly coiffed hair, a strong jaw, and a clear view of those full lips that peeked just a fraction from the porcelain mask he always wore.

"I'm fine," I said, finding my voice, which had decided to go off on vacation just when I needed it most. "I'm used to being *on my knees.*" I waggled my eyebrows, leaning forward, hoping he understood. It was time to cut the shit. I needed him to confess who he was. It occurred to me that he might not know who I was either. So I stepped closer. "One might say I'm *on my knees* as much as a *sexual submissive.*" Okay, it wasn't subtle, but the guy had to understand now.

"Are you sure you are okay?" he said, his accent exactly the same as Maître's. Was he fucking kidding me with this?

"Mon petit chaton!" I said, voice raised. Pierre didn't show a hint of recognition; he just looked freaked out.

"Mademoiselle, I think you may have hurt your head when you fell." I rolled my eyes. But just as I was about to bring up the use of clothespins as sexual toys, Harry came rushing from the ballroom.

"Faith!" He took hold of my face, studying my eyes. "Are you okay? Are you hurt anywhere?"

"Just my pride is bruised," I showed him the ass of my dress. "And I'm wet. *Very* wet." I looked at Pierre then and bored my eyes into his. He exhaled a long breath, taking a large step back.

"I shall leave her with you, Henry." Pierre pronounced Henry like "*En-ri.*" It was him. I knew it was. I stilled as I realized I now knew who the infamous Maître of NOX was. A man who was trapped in a mundane everyday life. He was a banker, how much more boring could a job get than that? He was familial money. Had pressures. Fuck me. Pierre Dubois of the Dubois Bank was Maître Auguste.

"Faith, you are worrying me," Harry said. "You don't look too well. You've kind of turned gray."

"Yeah, I'm not feeling too hot," I said and blew out a long and loud raspberry. I didn't care that I was in The Plaza. This night had turned into one epic-sized clusterfuck, and I just wanted to go home.

Maître had ignored my hints. Harry knew him, which only made it worse, then his father...

"Harry?" King Sinclair appeared at the door. Speak of the devil. He took one look at me, and I knew something was stirring in his brain. "The speeches are about to begin. You need to give HCS Media's." King addressed me. "Miss Parisi, I am sorry you had an accident."

"Me too," I said.

"I'm coming, Dad," Harry said, as sternly as I'd ever heard him speak.

I studied King and understood what Harry had said about his father losing his happiness after his mother died. He was like a shell of man, simply existing, like a shade. Robotically moving through life as a man of his social standing and business success was expected to.

"Dad, give me a bloody minute!" King looked momentarily taken aback by Harry's harshness, but he did as his son said.

"I'll get your friends," Harry said.

"Let them stay. Enjoy themselves." I checked to see that the coast was clear and pressed a soft kiss on his cheek. "I'll get a cab home and go to bed." I could see that Harry wanted to come too. "Go do your speech. Knock 'em dead."

"Can I come to you? Later? To your home? I know we haven't really done that yet, but—"

"Yes," I said immediately. This man was my personal kryptonite. "I'd love that. Text me when you're on your way."

Harry raised his hand and led me to a cab that stopped at the curb. He opened the door, gave the driver my address, and kissed me on my lips. "I'll be there as soon as I can."

As the cab pulled onto the road, I closed my eyes. I had everything I needed for my big feature now. I knew who Maître was. My stomach rolled with nerves wondering what Harry would make of the feature when it was done. He would find out about my time at NOX. But he couldn't be mad. It was before we were even a thing. But for some reason my heart was in knots the entire journey home, aching in my chest, a dull but persistent pain.

It only worsened when Harry climbed into bed with me two hours later, slipping inside me and breaking me apart into nothing but cells that were desperate to join with his. As Harry fell asleep, holding me tightly to his chest, I knew what I had to do the next night.

Then I'd be Harry's. Completely. And that was the most terrifying thing of all.

AN OUTFIT WAS LAID out for me in my private changing room as always. Tonight's selection was a patent leather bra and panties set with removeable cups. I ran my hand over the material and couldn't help but smile. I had grown to love this place. It was exactly as Maître had described it, a haven where people could be free. I'd been free here. Under his commands. He had made me want him, but being with Harry, I'd realized what I thought I liked about Maître wasn't real. I wasn't sure if any of it had been real, or just a really kinky dream that would stay with me for a lifetime.

Being sure to stick to the rules and understanding why anonymity had to be of the upmost importance, I wore my veil and took the elevator to the top floor. As I entered the room, the melodic sounds of Andrea Bocelli immediately serenaded me. I ran my hands over the stocks and smiled fondly at the birdcage and the St Andrew's Cross.

I turned to the throne and stopped just before it. I heard the door at the back open, and Maître walked through. It was strange how knowing who he was underneath had changed the dynamic between us, at least on my side. I had no idea if he even knew who I was or that he'd been talking to me last night. If he did, he was probably about to have me sectioned.

"Mon petit chaton?" he asked, moving in front of me, lowering his silver eyes to my trench coat. "You are not wearing what was picked out for you."

A sense of rightness flushed through me, and I nodded. "Afraid not, Maître." I took a deep breath. "The thing is...I've met someone."

Maître was silent for so long I didn't know if he was offended or relieved. Finally, he bowed his head. "He is a very lucky man." I heard genuine affection in his voice, which helped with entire situation. "And this stops our fun?"

I envisioned bringing Harry here, to this room, and smiled, trying to hold back my laughter at how his eyes would bug out at some of these devices. It was amazing how quickly medieval torture devices could become much-loved items.

"I'm afraid as much as our time here has been eye-opening and enjoyable, and we've shared many, many...many, many, *many* orgasms..." Maître laughed. "But I'm a one-man woman, and I'm afraid where you could stave off my orgasms with one word, my guy has consumed my heart, and that has trumped it all."

"You have found your gamekeeper," Maître said. It took me a moment to understand he was referring to *Lady Chatterley's Lover*.

I huffed a laugh. "Something like that."

Maître came closer, his scent no longer holding the same pull for me that Harry's cologne did. Jesus. I was cock-whipped and I knew it. But I secretly loved it, even though it felt like free falling off a cliff, praying the object of my affection was underneath with a safety net, or at least an oversized fish-net stocking.

He pressed a kiss to my cheek, over my veil. "I will miss you. But I do understand. It is all we want in life, non? To find someone we can be ourselves with. Who loves us for us. No matter what our desires, or what secrets we may keep." I thought that was an odd way to end things, but then again, he *was* French.

"You will no doubt find another willing siren to keep your bed warm." I frowned. "Actually, not keep the bed warm. That PVC sheet chafes, and it's always freezing cold. Maybe think of something that's not so hard on the ass."

"Your feedback is appreciated, ma chérie." He turned to go back to his private room. *"Au revoir,* mon petit chaton. *Bonne chance."* He disappeared into his room and left me alone in his chambre.

I thought about his words, about what he'd said about secrets, and hoped that someday he found someone he didn't have to hide himself from. What girl wouldn't want to know the love of her life owned a friggin' sex dungeon and could fuck like a god? She'd be one lucky lady.

As I descended in the elevator and passed through the changing room for the last time, I felt sad at not seeing Bunny anymore, or Alfred and his assless pants.

I let myself out at the underground parking lot, guessing I had quite a walk ahead of me before I got above ground and could hail a cab. Then my heart squeezed seeing my personal car already waiting for me. I turned to the camera above me and, having no idea if Maître was watching or not, I blew him a kiss of thanks and got into the car.

I was done at NOX.

Maître had lost a submissive, but I had gained Harry. And that, I knew, was irreplaceable.

CHAPTER SIXTEEN

ONE MONTH LATER...

"DAD, NO. DON'T YOU DARE!" My eyes fluttered open, seeing the morning sun creeping in through the curtains. I stretched out my hands and found the bedsheets cold beside me. I groaned into my pillow when I heard Harry's voice in the front room. I thought I'd been dreaming of hearing him speaking, but as he spat out, "Dad. Dad? For Christ's sake!" at a high volume, I knew it was him.

Moving from the bed, I tiptoed to the living room, grabbing my robe off the door. That's right. *My* robe. In a month, Harry and I had gone from close to inseparable. And it had been bliss. Not "Ask Miss Bliss," but actual, real fairies-and-unicorn bliss.

Last night I'd handed in my feature piece to Sally. She was taking the weekend to read it. I felt sick at the thought of her rejecting it. I also dreaded finally having to tell Harry about it all. I had decided to wait until Sally had approved it to come clean. It was an odd thing to have to explain to a lover, but I was hoping he was open-minded enough to understand. Hell, he knew Pierre Dubois; he probably knew exactly what went down there. In my defense, I'd ended it when we got together. And I hadn't regretted a single day since. There may have been no sex toys in our bed, but Harry didn't need them.

As I stepped into the living room, I was rewarded with a fantastic view of Harry's naked back and his pert ass in silk pajama bottoms. His hands were in his pockets and he appeared tense. I approached him, and when I wrapped my arms around him from behind, I felt how rigid he was. I pressed a kiss on his spine, and he eventually breathed out a long sigh and laid his hand over mine. He brought it to his lips, and I laid my cheek against his shoulder blade.

"Everything okay?"

Harry opened and closed his mouth a few times before he finally said, "My dad has flown into New York."

"Okay?" King Sinclair had been back in the UK since the disaster that was the charity ball. I knew Harry hadn't been expecting to see him until the midsummer ball at their estate in a couple of weeks. "Why is he back?"

Harry lowered his head and I felt the tension pulsing off him like sonar. "He wants to meet with me today."

Moving around Harry, I squeezed between him and the window. I stuck out my bottom lip. "But I thought we were going to spend the day together." I looked up at him through my lowered lashes. "I had some really nice things planned for us." I covered my mouth with my hands. "Oops! Did I say nice?"

I dropped to my knees and pulled Harry's length out of his pajamas. I burst out laughing when it began to rise, like a flag being pulled up a flagpole, before my eyes.

When it was fully erect and swaying in my face, I gave it a firm sailor's salute. "At ease, Captain," I said. Obviously, it didn't deflate so I shook my head, tutting. "Are you defying me, Private? I'm gonna have to teach you a lesson."

"Faith, will you please stop speaking to my penis like an errant soldier."

"No can do, Harry. It's getting court-martialed, and that's all there is to it."

"And pray tell, what will his punishment be?" I heard the humor in his voice and loved that I was able to bring him from his dourness.

I winked up at Harry. "A thorough tongue lashing, that's what." On cue, I took Harry into my mouth, moaning at the hiss that poured from his lips and how tightly his hands threaded into my hair. I was relentless.

"Faith," he groaned, slamming his hips forward. My eyes watered as I struggled to take all of him. But I was a good commander in chief and got the job done with a little help from my hands. "Faith, I'm coming," Harry said, and I tasted him on my tongue.

After I pulled away, I pointed at his spent dick. "Let that be a lesson, Private. Now, on your way."

I screamed as Harry reached down and scooped me off the floor, carrying me to the closest wall. In seconds my robe was off, and in less than a minute I was stuffed full of the private who had just disobeyed me. It seemed like he didn't like following rules.

Harry pounded into me so hard the back of my head repeatedly hit the wall. But I wasn't complaining. I came like a firecracker, and Harry quickly followed behind, screwing whatever issue he was having with his father out of his system. I loved it when he got all rough and domineering.

I tried to catch my breath as Harry tucked his head into the crook of my neck, breathing hard. I pressed the edge of my hand on each of his shoulders and said, "I dub thee Sir Headbanger, of stupendous and savage wall sex."

"Do you ever shut up?" Harry said dryly, but I heard the teasing in his voice and lifted his head and smiled.

"Nope!" I cupped his cheeks. I loved the rough stubble rubbing against my palms. I preferred feeling it between my thighs, but unless I straddled his shoulders right now, this would have to do.

"And, pray tell, what authority do you have to knight me?"

I acted affronted. "I, Henry Sinclair the Third, viscount and duke in training, am the queen of Pussytown and you will bow to me or risk having your cock severed from your groin. Do I make myself clear? I will not tolerate treason."

"Understood, your majesty," he said in the poshest voice he could muster, with a slight bow of his head.

"Your majesty. I could get used to you calling me that." I kissed Harry's soft lips. "Now, loyal subject, make me a coffee and tell me, what is happening with the king of my enemy's land?"

"God, please don't dub him *that*, he already has a Messiah Complex as it is." Harry placed me down, and I walked like a newborn foal to the kitchen. I heard Harry snigger behind me.

"Laugh all you want, Harry. But someday I'm going to peg you with a strap-on as big as your eight-inch Private Harry there and see how well you can walk the next day."

"Pegging? Where do you come up with this stuff?" he asked, not really wanting an answer. I slid onto the stool, and Harry began making us coffee in his fancy-ass coffee machine, which used beans from Shangri-La or some other bougie place. In fairness, they tasted like heaven, so I allowed it.

"He feels like he's lost control of me, so he's coming back to assert his authority. That's what's happening."

"He said that?" I asked as he placed the espresso in front of me. I piled my usual four teaspoons of sugar into the glass, until it resembled syrup rather than silky cream.

"No. But that's what he's doing." He caught my eye, and I could see he wanted to tell me something. I felt like he had wanted to for the past few weeks. Harry had moments of sadness, which I knew was due to his lack of family and the pressures from his father. But I felt like there was something else too. Something that held him back from giving himself to me completely. I wished he would talk to me. Then again, I was holding back a secret too.

I'd loved this month, and the longer I failed to tell him about the big feature and NOX, the more difficult it became. I was happy, for once, and I didn't want to burst the bubble we'd created for ourselves.

But Harry seemed tortured, and I wanted him to confide in me. To trust that nothing he could say would push me away.

"Harry, is something wrong?" I asked tentatively.

He turned the swivel seat of the barstool I sat on, so I was between his legs. He stared at me for so long, I thought he was finally going to confess whatever was bothering him.

He lowered his head and whispered, "I won't give you up. I—" He closed his eyes. When they opened again, he said, "I don't want to anger my dad. I don't want to disappoint you. I just don't want to lose you." A blush burst on Harry's cheeks, and lifting his head he rasped, "I'm falling for you, Faith. Do you know that? I'm falling so bloody hard for you."

Sunbeams burst inside me. "I'm falling for you too," I said, as a butterfly decided to swoop inside my heart and add a flutter to its already stupidly fast beat.

"Truly?"

"Truly."

Harry sighed a breath of relief, like my response had given him a much-needed battle shield when he'd thought all hope was lost in his inner war. Who and what he was fighting, I wasn't sure.

"I'm speaking to my dad today," he said, and I felt the conviction of those words fill the air around us.

"Get 'em cowboy," I said, play-punching his arm but feeling nervous for the first time in a long time.

Harry laughed, and I could breathe easy again when I saw the crinkles around his eyes. The ones that only appeared when he dropped his worries and frosty persona and let me inside, not all the way, but we were getting close. Those were *my* crinkles. I'd slapped a copyright on those bad boys and declared them my property.

"Let me meet with him today, and I'll see you tonight. Okay?"

I saluted again. "Yes, sir!"

"Faith, I beg of you. Never join the army. I shudder to think what would happen to the fate of the nation if they resolved things as you just did." Harry kissed me and headed to his room to shower and change.

"There'd be less wars and more love!" I shouted to his retreating back.

Harry stuck his head around the doorway. "And an ungodly amount of STDs and cases of lockjaw."

I picked up an apple from the fruit bowl in front of me and threw it at the door, hearing Harry chuckle as it missed him completely. I drank my coffee and wondered what his father wanted. Something in my gut told me whatever it was, it wasn't good.

But Harry was falling for me. *Me.* And I was most certainly falling for him. I'd given him head, and he'd literally banged me against the wall. We were fine. Everything was going to be fine.

I was sure of it.

"I FEEL like a true *lady* in this," I said to Sage, showing him the hat that sat regally on my head. "I've never had an excuse to wear it. Now I have! All thanks to your colleague getting salmonella and your boss going to marriage mediation." I held up my hand to the blazing summer sun above us. "Bless the gods!"

The minute I'd walked into my apartment that morning, Sage had run at me, telling me to get dressed and gather the troops (Amelia and Novah). He had scored box seats at the Belmont Park Race Track, and we were going to the races. I'd never been to see horse racing once in my life, but it had always looked like fun. And since my all-day sex plans with Harry had been thwarted by King, I was game as hell.

"I don't know why, but in these white gloves I walk with the confidence of Miss Universe." Amelia held out her hands and started to wave like the queen. "I'm thinking about incorporating these into my everyday life. I'm sure the other archeologists won't mind me digging up dirt in such exquisite lace."

"Never, darling," Sage said, linking our arms. Novah linked mine on the other side. "Now giddy up, we have a private box with our names on it."

I opened my mouth for the inevitable joke, but Sage covered my mouth. "Today we act like a lady, Faith. Decorum in the box at all times."

I rolled my eyes at him, and we passed through the gates and to the main stand. Crowds of people stood waiting for the race to begin. In the distance the racing stalls opened, and people came alive, waving their bets in their hands and screaming to their horses to "go" or "run faster" as the thoroughbreds galloped toward the finish line.

"This way." Sage led us into the foyer of the stand, and I groaned as the air conditioning caressed my face. New York summers were one humid, unrelenting bitch.

A host led us to the box owned by Sage's law firm. We were handed glasses of champagne and shown to our seats. The boxes were lined up side by side, the partitions low enough to see the neighboring party but high enough for privacy.

"Let's bet, bitches!" Novah said, just as the door to the box beside us opened. I was busy reading through the names of the horses. "Ha!" Novah said. "I've found your horse, Faith." She pointed to the page about the next race.

"Why, yes, that will do!" I said and we clinked glasses.

I'd never heard such a fabulous name for a horse as Kinky Whip in all my life. "Let's go and place the bets." Novah took my hand. The smile suddenly slipped from her face, and the color faded from her cheeks. "Nove?" I asked.

Amelia hissed out a "Oh, fuck" behind me.

Feeling my stomach clench with dread before I'd even moved, I turned my head, only to have my heart shatter. King Sinclair was taking his seat in the box beside us. Nicholas was there too, along with two other men I didn't know. But what had my friends worried was the sight of Harry taking his seat, and beside him, a tall, leggy blond.

"Lady Louisa Samson," Sage whispered, his tone sounding like the entrance soundtrack of the villain on a movie score. Harry seemed stiff, like the uptight man I'd met years ago. The arrogant duke-to-be who didn't tolerate people who were lesser than he was. But when Louisa whispered in his ear and laid her hand on his chest, right over his pocket square, I lost it. I friggin' lost it when those pale-pink painted talons brushed over his silver handkerchief.

"Hold my purse," I said to Novah, passing her my clutch. I started unthreading my earrings from my ears. "I'm gonna kill the fucker," I said, kicking off my heels and readying to pole vault the partition to show the English rose how we throw down in Hell's Kitchen.

Sage's arms wrapped around my waist when I took a step back to make my running leap. I kicked my legs, anger sending a red mist over my vision.

"Let me go, Sage. Let me *go!*" Our commotion must have alerted the royal booth beside us to something happening, as Louisa looked up from whispering in Harry's ear and frowned at my laser beams boring straight into her. Her hoity lips tightened, and I was about to go full-blown Hulk-Smash on her noble ass. She nudged her head our way. Harry's jaw clenched, and with what looked like tired eyes, he saw what had captured her attention. I froze the second he saw I was there. His lips parted and he jumped to his feet.

"Harry?" Louisa asked in her perfect English voice. She peered at me around his legs. "Do you know her?"

"Yeah, he fu—" Sage's hand covered my mouth, smothering my words. I tried to bite his palm to get him off me. Novah rushed to the door and opened it, and Sage began pulling me through.

"So sorry," Amelia said as Sage and Novah ushered me into the hallway and toward the bar. "I hope you enjoy your day."

Traitor! I wanted to shout at my best friend.

"Amelia, wait," I heard Harry's voice say, then nothing as Sage pulled me out of earshot. We arrived in the bar raising only a few eyebrows.

Sage deposited me on a barstool, and he and Novah created a human shield around me. "Faith, I get it. What we saw looks shady as hell. But this is my workplace's box. Don't make a scene. I'm begging you."

I was out of breath, but at Sage's plea my anger faded, the red mist descended from my eyes, and all that was left in the aftermath was a sharp pain in my chest.

Clearly seeing I'd lost all my fight, Novah tapped the bar. "Double vodka. And keep them coming." The bartender handed me the double shot and I swallowed it just as Amelia approached the bar, quickly followed by Nicholas. Sage jumped up from slouching at the bar.

"Nicholas," he said, flirtation thickening his voice.

"Sage," Nicholas said, sounding just as sweet. Then Nicholas looked at me. "Faith, it's not what you think."

"Isn't it?" I said, getting another double vodka and knocking that back. As that filled my stomach and the subsequent warmth flushed through my veins, I wondered when I'd ever been so mad.

"Tell me," I said and got to my feet. I wobbled in my heels, but Nicholas was there to catch me. "Ha!" I said, snorting out a laugh. "Just like your cousin. Chivalrous to a T. Do they teach you that at school, how to save damsels in distress?" I pushed my hair out of my face and stood up straight. "So, how wasn't it what it looked like? Because to me it appears like Harry is having his crumpet and eating it too."

"No, I swear he's not." Nicholas held out his hand. "Please, just come with me."

"And where are we going?"

"To see Harry."

"In the box?" I said, finally feeling like this had been a mistake. He wanted to see me in front of his father and his bit of English crumpet.

But Nicholas winced. "Not in the box, Faith. He's waiting for you down there, and just wants to explain some things to you."

"Hear him out," Amelia said. She came closer to me. "He looked so upset, Faith, when you left the box—"

"Dragged," I interrupted. "I was *dragged* from the box."

"Hear him out," Amelia said sternly, like a strict Kindergarten teacher, making me shut the hell up.

"Yes, ma'am," I said and followed Nicholas down the hallway, taking a right and stopping at a door. He tapped on it, and even in my more-than-tipsy state, I saw it read "Janitor's Closet." The door opened, and I saw Harry inside, pacing the small white tile floor.

Grabbing my hand, Harry pulled me inside and crushed me to his chest. "It's not what you think," he said, and I momentarily let myself breathe in his scent and feel his heart beating fast in his chest. Just that morning he'd been fucking me against his living room wall. And now we were in the closet, hiding from his father, no doubt.

I pushed myself away from all his cut and buff Harryness, which only fried my brain if I got too close. "Good choice for meeting with your dirty little secret." With a wave of my hand, I indicated the cleaning supplies around us. I leaned against a mop who, from this angle, looked frighteningly like an ex of mine. "So?" I said, my voice glacial. "Have you been with her this entire time?"

Harry's cheeks went red, and anger flared in his baby blues. "Don't be ridiculous, Faith. Of course I haven't."

"It would be convenient, though. Her in the UK, me in New York. A girl in every port, so they say. That's what your kind are like, aren't they? Married, with a million mistresses on the side?"

Harry looked like I'd slapped him. It sent an arrow of regret deep into my heart. But I was too pissed, too tipsy, and far too stubborn to take it back.

"My kind?" he said. I saw the hurt in his expression and knew I had stepped over the mark. "I didn't realize I *had* a kind, Faith."

"The blue bloods." I waved my hand. "The aristocracy. Don't lie to my face and say that isn't what this is about." I pointed at the door. "That you brought your noble girlfriend here today because that's what your daddy wants of you." I took a step toward him. "He doesn't want you with me, Harry. Have you not figured that out by now?"

"Of course I have!" he shouted and gripped the back of his head. I knew that King didn't want us together, of course. But hearing it from Harry's mouth was like taking a bat to the gut. "He will never approve of us, Faith. But I was trying. I was trying to work out how to make him see how I feel for you."

Harry dropped his hands and stared at me, and I wanted to crash into him and kiss him until we forgot all of this. "I know I can get through to him. But then he orchestrated this behind my back, and I'm fucking livid." I reared back, surprised at Harry cussing. It was as rare as a blue moon. "I had no idea they were coming. Nicholas had just flown in on business, and he got the invite at the same time I did. I had no heads-up. Went to breakfast to meet my father, and Louisa was there. He told her I had asked for her to come."

"Then why not walk out and tell him where to go?"

"Because he's all I have!" Harry shouted, and he immediately sounded out of breath. My heart twisted as those words left his mouth.

"Harry..."

"I don't have a doting family like you, Faith. I don't have a mum anymore who can take my side and tell me I'm not wrong for wanting you. I have no siblings. I have Nicholas, but he's always busy like I am..." Harry slumped against the wall. "I have my dad and that's it. My grandparents are dead and Nicholas's parents live in France. All I have is him. I have to get through to him. But I can't do that with Louisa here, and the CFO and CCO of HCS Media. And you can ridicule me all you want for being too English about it, but I won't air our dirty laundry in public."

My bottom lip trembled at how defeated he looked as his shoulders dropped. "I know you probably hate her, but Louisa isn't a bad person, Faith. She's a pawn. She's being used by my father, and her parents are no better than he is. She's as trapped in this as I am. So please, don't fight her."

"I wasn't going to," I lied. I damn well lied through my teeth.

Harry's lips twitched. "Then why was Novah holding your purse and why had your earrings been removed?"

"I don't know what you're talking about." I narrowed my eyes at him. "Have you been drinking?"

"Yes. Copiously. Have you?" he challenged, those friggin' irresistible baby blues igniting with happiness again. If he was telling the truth, he certainly handled his liquor better than I did.

"Not at all. I'm stone cold sober." God, wanting to make an example of me and the little liar I was, chose that moment to give me hiccups. I quickly covered my mouth. Harry huffed a laugh, and I edged toward him warily, not sure if he wanted me close. When I stopped a few inches away, Harry opened his arms and I fell against him. I wrapped my arms around his waist. "I didn't like her touching you," I whispered.

"I didn't either," he confessed and kissed my head. I closed my eyes, his hypnotic breathing calming my frazzled nerves. "Every time there was an obvious innuendo to something someone said around me, I was waiting for the inappropriate punchline, but none came."

Harry guided me away from his chest and cupped my face. It was my absolute favorite thing he did to me, and I was sure I'd be happy if he always held me this way. It would make work and other daily activities tricky, but I was willing to give it a good old college try.

"Faith Parisi, no one is you, and that is all it comes down to for me." Before I could crack a joke, Harry kissed my mouth sweetly, turning my legs to Jell-O, and all the jokes I could muster were forgotten. When we broke away, he said, "Nothing has or will ever happen between Louisa and me. My father leaves tomorrow night. I will speak to him tomorrow. You have to trust me."

"I will...I do," I said and saw something that resembled happiness, then guilt, flash across Harry's face. But when I looked again, he was the same old handsome Harry as always, and I blamed it on the alcohol. "I might go home. I can only imagine the hangover I will have in the morning."

A knock sounded on the door again. "That's Nicholas," Harry said. "Let me play the clown in my father's circus today. But know that I'm trying for us always." He brought our joined hands to his mouth and kissed them.

"Okay." With one last long kiss, Harry moved to the door. He stepped outside, and I followed. I heard the sound of Harry's voice in the hallway.

When I rounded the corner, Louisa was there. She looked at me. Harry held his head high. "Louisa, this is Faith Parisi. She works at one of our New York publications."

"Oh," Louisa said, seemingly in relief, as though it explained why Harry had come after me. She held out her hand. "Nice to meet you, Faith. I adore your hair."

I saw Harry fighting a smile, knowing I would never be able to bitch slap someone who'd complimented my hair. I'm joking, of course I would. But she seemed sweet, and if Harry was telling the truth, she was as unwillingly tangled in this King-manufactured web as he was.

"Nice to meet you too." I looked behind me, feeling awkward. "I'm going to go to the bathroom. I've had a bit too much of the vodka."

"Have a good day, Faith," Louisa said, and Harry walked away with her. He glanced back over his shoulder and gave me a reassuring smile.

Deciding I really did need the bathroom, I headed down the hallway only to stop short when King Sinclair rounded the corner. I narrowly avoided bumping into him which, given my inebriated condition, was a miracle.

"Oh, hello, Miss Parisi," he said, clearly as uncomfortable about our meeting as I was.

"Mr. Sinclair."

King looked over my shoulder. When I followed suit, I saw Harry and Louisa disappearing back into the box. "They look good together, don't they?" he said, pulling my attention back to him. I didn't say anything. I knew he knew about Harry and me. I was well aware there was nothing positive to say right now.

"Harry has always known how his life would go, Miss Parisi. Certain expectations come with the territory when you are born into the nobility and will inherit a title. You must behave in a particular way, be educated through certain channels, and marry well."

He checked the buttons on his suit. "Louisa is from a good family and has known Harry all his life. We always knew it would be a good match, her parents and I. In marriage."

I felt my heart begin to shred, layer by agonizing layer. I wanted to open my mouth and rip this prick a new asshole with my venomous tongue, but something kept me rooted to the spot; something kept me silent, stealing my courage. "Harry is twenty-eight now. He will take over all of HCS Media soon, and then he will marry."

Stepping around me, King stopped right by my side. "You seem like a good girl, Faith. And I genuinely hold no animosity toward you, but what you have with Harry can lead nowhere. You are from two very different worlds, worlds that will inevitably collide, and not in a good way. I want him to be happy, and I know what's best for him. That will not be you."

He waited for me to say something, but I was mute and, mortifyingly, my eyes were filling with tears. "Good day, Miss Parisi. I really do wish you well." With that, King Sinclair walked back to his fancy box with his son and his betrothed.

I know what's best for him. That will not be you.

Turning on my heel, I rushed into the bathroom and wiped my eyes. I dug deep within myself to find my outrage, to find my spark, but it had gone out. I thought back to Harry and me. I thought of his posh English accent compared to my thick New York twang. How he fit in like a hand in a glove at the charity ball, and I smashed into a champagne fountain with the grace of an ox. I compared his spacious penthouse to my converted brownstone apartment in Brooklyn. His ancestral home to my parents' in Hell's Kitchen. I didn't want to face the truth, but King was right. We were from two very different worlds. Louisa had been born for that kind of life.

Wiping my tears, I left the bathroom, only to find my friends waiting for me. Amelia saw my red face and held me in her arms. "I say we take this party home, what do you think?" I nodded, safe with my best friends. I felt Novah holding my hand and Sage's hand on my back. They didn't let me go, and in the apartment, we ate junk food and sprawled out on the couch watching *Drag Race*. It took all I had to convince Amelia that she didn't need to stay with me overnight.

"He loves you, you know?" she said in my doorway. My heart kicked into a sprint. "I get I'm no love expert and, frankly, am terrible at dating, but he loves you. I can see it in the way he looks at you."

"How's that?" I whispered, lump in my throat.

"Adoringly," Amelia said and sighed. "He just adores everything about you. What else could you ask for?" Amelia closed the door and I lay on my bed.

I listened to the rain begin to pour outside, the heavy summer drops bouncing on the fire escape just outside my window. I closed my eyes, but I rolled them open a while later, hearing the sound of someone trying to open my window. A flash of fear cut through me, just as the window slid open. But when a dapper, suited man climbed through, that fear was replaced with a heart so full I thought it might explode.

Harry closed the window then stood at the end of my bed, hair soaking wet and dripping to the floor. Without saying a word, he stripped out of his clothes and climbed on the bed. He gathered me in his arms and held me close. I wasn't sure he would ever let go.

Safe in his arms, his body heat lulling me to sleep, I closed my eyes, cheek to his chest. Just as slumber began to pull me under, Harry whispered, "Faith? I need to tell you something. Something about who I am." I thought I heard trepidation, maybe fear, in his tone, but my drowsiness felt too good to resist after the long day we'd had.

"Another time," I said sleepily, my arm tightening around his waist. Harry's hand stroked though my hair, taking away the last of my fight to stay awake.

"Okay," he said, and I went under, weirdly dreaming Harry added, "I just hope you understand." He sighed. "I just hope you don't hate me."

When I awoke the next day, there was a note on my pillow.

Gone to meet my dad. Didn't want to wake you.
I will see you tomorrow,
Yours, and only yours,
Harry x

Gripping the note, which faintly smelled of his cologne, I pulled it to my chest and fell back to sleep, a contented smile on my lips.

CHAPTER SEVENTEEN

I SHOOK out my hands and took a deep, steadying breath. I pressed the button for the top floor. The elevator doors opened and, thankfully, I was the only one inside.

Sally had called for me. I had no idea if she liked my article or not, but in minutes, I would find out if I was actually going to have a feature published in *Visage* magazine. I remembered Papa, at Sunday dinner, saying *one day* and prayed that my one day had finally arrived.

As I exited the elevator onto the management floor, I looked at Harry's door and wondered if he was okay. He hadn't talked to me yesterday besides the note. But I knew he probably didn't want me going into his office. I didn't know where we stood, and although I believed he liked me as much as I liked him, I knew that wasn't always enough.

I smiled at Carla and she said, "Go straight in, Faith."

I knocked on Sally's door. "Leave me alone!" she shouted, and I let myself in. Sally was in her usual position, sitting on her chair, her feet up on her desk, reading something in her hands.

I took my seat, and I tried to prepare myself for whatever the outcome was. Sally peered at me over the top of her glasses and smiled. I shuddered. In all my time at Visage I had never seen her smile. It resembled a viper about to attack an innocent mouse. "I liked it," she said. I exhaled a pent-up breath.

"Oh thank Christ!" I slumped back in my chair like I'd just run the New York marathon dressed as a giant banana.

Sally opened her drawer and placed a copy of my feature before her on the desk. "So, French, rich, fucks like a dog in heat. I have my suspicions of who it might be. I've narrowed it down to about three people. Can I give you my guesses and wait for your reaction?" I shook my head. Sally leaned in closer, practically salivating for gossip. "Come on, Faith. Who is it? Just between us girls."

"Sorry. I can't say," I said and locked my mouth with an invisible lock. "NDA rules."

She slapped the desk. "Dammit! But I'm on to them."

"I can't believe you like it."

"It's got it all, Faith. Sex, fun, intrigue, hotness. It was exactly what I was looking for."

"So...I have the big feature?" I dared ask, wondering how she could ever refuse.

Sally smiled again. "No. Sorry."

It took me a few seconds for that response to sink in. "W-what," I stuttered. "Why?" I felt my hope break apart along with my heart.

"This is not on me, sweetheart," she said and put her legs back on the desk, halfway done with me. "This came from the big guns."

I laughed without humor. "King," I said, his name tasting sour on my tongue. "King Sinclair stopped this, didn't he?"

Sally pulled down her glasses to perch on her nose. "Not King, Faith. *Harry*. He was the one who kyboshed your feature."

"What?" I said, blood draining from my face. She was wrong. She must be wrong.

"Read it this morning, first thing. Threw that fucker out along with last night's trash." Sally went back to reading whatever she'd had in her hands. "We're done, Faith." I stood on shaky legs. "For what it's worth," Sally called over her shoulder. "It deserved the spot."

"Thank you," I said, unable to be excited even about rare praise from Sally. I shut her door and immediately saw Harry's office. I didn't overthink it; instead I marched in that direction like a pissed-off steam train.

"Faith?" Theo said as I stormed by. "Do you have an appointment?" Poor Theo didn't even get a reply from me. I was about to become a one-woman wrecking machine.

I pushed the door open, slammed it behind me, and rounded the corner to see Harry perched over his desk, head in his hands. "How could you?" I said, my voice not as loud and strong as I had hoped it would be.

Harry snapped his head up. His navy-blue tie was discarded on his desk, and his shirt collar was open. I barely registered that he looked stressed, hair in disarray, I was too fueled by betrayal and on a one-way ticket to kick-ass central. Harry got to his feet, his tall frame towering over me on the other side of his desk.

"It was before you," I said, but deep down I had known all this time that my time at NOX was going to ruin us. "It was before you and I even kissed. Hell, it was before I could even stand to *talk* to you!" I paced in front of him. "You knew how much I wanted that feature, and you cut it? To what? Protect your friends? I played the NDA game, Harry. There are no names involved. It was vague enough to protect those in charge. It was a motherfucking masterpiece and you, of all people, are the one to destroy it? *You,* Harry. *Why?*"

He said nothing, so I continued. "I knew I should have told you, at least about being a member of NOX, but things were going so well, and I didn't want to tell you about Maître. I didn't want you to know about my sleeping with him." Harry was a marble statue, just staring at me. It infuriated me. "Is that why you're pulling it? Because you're jealous? Because it makes zero sense to me otherwise! Tell me, WHY?"

Harry laughed without mirth. His shook his head and took a step back so he stood in front of a picture of, I assumed, him and his mother at some pleasant-looking country estate with rolling hills in the background.

"Why?" he said, his voice hoarse. He looked rough, like he'd had no sleep for several days. Harry's head hit the wall beside the photo. His eyes filled with sadness. "I didn't know it was for a feature, Faith. I thought you were there because you wanted to be."

"What?" I said, so damn confused I was starting to believe I was in a parallel universe. One where everyone talked in riddles.

"I tried to give you hints. I..." Harry ran his hands over his face. He was gray in pallor, and he had stubble on his normally clean-shaven cheeks. "I couldn't tell you. I thought I could fuck you out of my system as him, then walk away and get you out of my head after all these years. *Finally*." I started breathing faster. "But then the elevator happened. And you *talked* to me. Like a human being and not something you despised."

"Harry—?"

"I tried to tell you, I promise I did. In the beginning..." He paused, and I saw him smile a little. "Of us. When I dared hope we could go somewhere. But I never found the words. And the more time went on, the deeper we fell, *I* fell, I couldn't stand the thought of you hating me."

"Harry! What the hell are you talking about?"

"I tried to send you hints." He walked around the desk. "Vie," he said, naming his mother's charity, with perfect French pronunciation.

"Your mom's name? The one the charity is named after?"

"Faith, her name was Aline."

"Then...?"

"*La vie* means life in French." I opened my mouth to ask more questions. I was lost in the swirling fog of questions in my head. "The book," he said, coming even closer to me. Until he was right there, an inch away, his expression haunted and his voice raspy. "I prayed you would find out, but then at the same time I wished that you wouldn't." I inhaled his scent trying to let it calm me. But this time, it didn't work. "I told you I was trapped. Told you I was in a prison..." One by one the hairs on the back of my neck started to stand on end. A thought, so crazy it couldn't be true, entered my head with the force of a tsunami.

I needed to think. I needed to fucking think! I moved away from Harry and to the picture frames hanging on his wall. My pulse was racing so fast I felt dizzy. He didn't want my article published, my article on NOX, but mostly on Maître. I had been requested the first night at NOX to meet Maître. I had assumed it was because of my obvious cold feet in the main room and because of my accident with the sex swings.

I swallowed, trying to wet my dry throat. Then there was *Lady Chatterley's Lover* in Harry's library. And *Faith? I need to tell you something. Something about who I am.* Harry's words from Saturday night circled in my head. I lifted my eyes, unable to process the evidence that was repeatedly slapping me in the face, when the photo he had leaned against came into view. I froze, felt my veins ice over. Harry's mother. I read the caption on the frame of the photograph. *Aline Auguste-Sinclair and her son, Harry. St Tropez, France.*

Auguste.

I closed my eyes. "Harry?"

"Yes?" he said, quietly.

"Where was your mother from?" When he took too long to answer, I said, "Was it France? Was your mother from France?"

"*Oui.*" His silky French accent sailed over me like the finest of Hermes scarves. That voice...that voice who *was* him...I thought of all the nights I'd shared with Maître. The stern master who, in time, had slowly softened. The man who had brought me such pleasure I was truly a slave to his desires.

I turned my head and finally opened my eyes. They collided with Harry's. "Maître. You're Maître Auguste." It wasn't a question. I knew the answer without his confirmation. Harry nodded and I felt tears rise in my eyes. "You lied to me," I said, my voice catching with my hurt. "All this time, you were *lying* to me."

"Faith, please. Just listen to me—"

"And the feature?" I laughed. It was that or I would give in to my hurt and cry. I wouldn't fucking cry. I mustn't. "You dropped the feature because it exposed your club, didn't you?" Harry stepped forward. "Do not dare come any closer, Harry. Don't you dare!"

Harry stopped on the spot and raked his fingers through his hair. "I was careless with you, Faith. I was falling for you as both Maître and Harry, and I was in too deep. I told you things I shouldn't have. I did things with you that weren't the norm at the club." I could see him struggling to explain it all. I didn't care. I needed him to. I needed him to explain every little thing that had led us to this shitshow.

"But I didn't think of Pierre. That night, at the charity gala, I had no idea you would sway your suspicions to him instead of me. When I read your article, although it wasn't completely obvious, it leaned to the likes of him and potential others. There's a small pool of French businessmen of our age in Manhattan. I couldn't let you ruin them like that."

"Or ruin your club," I snapped.

"That too." I felt like I'd been punched. Harry held out his hands in surrender. "Faith, it is my business. But more than that, it is people's *lives*. People I know and care for, others I don't know at all. But they shouldn't have their private activities sprawled over the weekend paper for all to read, developing suspicions about who might be there. It is not only my job to keep them protected, but also my moral obligation."

"Obligation," I echoed. "That's the truth of all of this, Harry. Let's not beat around the bush." Walking closer to him, close enough so I could read his expression, I asked, "Does your father know about this side business of yours?" Harry's jaw clenched. I lifted my hands and dropped them back to my sides in frustration. "He doesn't, does he? That's why the feature has been canned, isn't it? Because your father doesn't know about NOX, and you're terrified of him finding out and sullying the great Sinclair name!"

"Faith," Harry said, his voice harder now. I could see in his narrowed eyes he was getting angry. *Good.* Best he caught up with me so we could really thrash this out. "You know nothing of my life, the title I will inherit. You know nothing of the circles I was born into, *still* have to live in. And more than that, what it could do to HCS Media, my family's reputation."

"So you destroy my dreams instead? Destroy my work to save yours." Harry's face crumpled. Instinctively I wanted to run to him, to hold him and comfort the little boy lost I now knew he was deep inside. The one who craved family and love more than anything in the world. But he'd lied to me. He was Maître. My Harry was Maître.

"You lied," I said again. "Out of everything, that's what hurts the most."

"You did too." Fire lit within me as he said those words. "You didn't tell me about NOX. You didn't tell me about the feature. You lied to me too, Faith. It wasn't just me. Don't just lay all the blame at my feet. I will gladly take the lion's share, but you are not innocent here."

"Then this has all been for nothing," I said, voice raspy. "You lied, I lied and, ironically, we both got completely fucked in the end!"

I set off to move past him, and Harry got in my path, palms showing. "Please, Faith. I need to explain. I need more of your time to explain it all. Why I have NOX, why I hide in plain sight as Maître. Please just let me—" Harry's desk phone rang, cutting him off. He ignored it until it stopped. "Faith, just give me that. Give me a chance to explain. I know I've fucked up, but please let me try—"

His desk phone rang again. Harry gritted his teeth, pissed off, but moved to his desk, lifted the phone, and spat, "What?" I didn't hear what was said on the other side, but he tensed, grew motionless. "I'm on my way."

Harry slammed the phone down and grabbed his jacket. He hovered awkwardly beside me. "I have to go," he whispered. "I'm so sorry, Faith, but I have to go." He hesitated, but then he pressed a swift kiss to my cheek. It was soft and gentle and felt filled with goodbye. Harry raced out the door and left me standing in his office, angry and confused. The tears did fall this time. They ran down my cheeks like rivers chasing the sea.

Harry was Maître.

He had stopped my feature.

And he had left—with no explanation.

I wrapped my arms around my chest when I suddenly felt cold. Forcing my feet to move, I walked out of Harry's office.

"Faith? Are you okay?" Theo asked.

I nodded numbly and, this time, forewent the elevator and took the ten flights of stairs down to the exit. I didn't care about my purse or any of my belongings. I just needed to leave this building. With every step I took, I replayed Harry's words: *You lied to me too, Faith. It wasn't just me.* And he was right. I had. I had been so scared to tell him about NOX and the feature. He had lied about Maître and claimed he was too afraid to tell me. I wanted to call him and ask him why he'd fled. But I was so pissed at him.

I hailed a cab, lucky that I kept fifty dollars in my bra for emergencies. "Where to?" he asked.

"Hell's Kitchen," I said and closed my eyes and let the tears fall. My skin shivered. It was hot and humid outside, but I couldn't get warm. What would happen from here? How would I ever come back from this? This whole time, we had built a fantasy around us. Lived in our safe bubble. That bubble had well and truly burst. It had *always* been destined to burst. We were two very different people from two very different worlds.

And Harry was right; I had no idea what it was like to live in his world. To one day inherit a title and rub shoulders with royalty, the peerage, and people who would judge both him and me simply for falling in love. King had told me so at the races. And I'd known. Deep down I'd known it was true.

Inevitable.

Harry and I were impossible.

I glanced out the window, seeing familiar streets come into view. My hands slammed against the window as we passed Papa's shop. "No," I whispered, my heart breaking for the second time that day, seeing a small sign reading "Out of Business" on the door. When the cab pulled up to my parents' apartment, I felt what was left of my heart crack. My stomach dropped, and I felt all hope turn to vapor and be carried away on the breeze.

I handed the cab driver my cash and stepped out onto the street that I had grown up on. I looked at the apartment that held all my childhood and fondest memories. The wooden doors that had welcomed me home day after day. And on the wall of the small apartment that I adored so much was a "For Sale" sign.

After climbing the stone steps, feeling like they were a veritable Mount Everest, I opened the door and let myself into my parents' home. Mom and Papa were sitting on the couch in silence, holding each other's hands. Mom jumped to her feet. I didn't speak a word, just let the tears fall and fell into her arms.

"We have to, Faith," she said. "We need to pay off the debts. There's no more time. We must do what's right."

I looked up through my blurred vision and held my hand out for Papa. His eyes glistened as he wrapped his arms around us. "You love the shop," I said brokenly.

"It is a shop, mia bambina. You and your mama are my heart. That is all I care about." I knew that wasn't true, but he would never show me his pain, even though I knew he was racked with it. And with that, I fell apart. As Mom and Papa held me, I broke down on their shoulders.

"Shh, baby," Mom said, stroking my hair. "Are you okay?" I shook my head. She pulled my head away from her shoulder to search my face. Her eyes softened when she asked, "Harry?" I nodded, and she wrapped me back into her embrace. "It's okay, Faith. Whatever it is, it will work out. I promise." Mom kissed me on my head and said, "Soup? Let's have some soup. Everything is better after soup."

So we ate tomato soup. Afterwards, I climbed into my childhood bed, thought of Harry, and let my heart break some more.

"WHAT'S THIS MEETING FOR?" I asked Novah as we were ushered to the conference room three days later. I walked like a zombie, with Novah holding my hand for support. My friends knew Harry and I had fought, he had left, and he hadn't come back. No phone calls. No texts. Nothing at all. They didn't know he was Maître, though. Despite everything, I didn't want to hurt him like that. And telling even one person his secret could be his downfall.

When everyone was gathered, Sally came into the room and said, "Three days ago, King Sinclair had a heart attack." Shock took hold of me, and every muscle in my body tensed. Harry. My god, Harry...*the phone call.*

Novah squeezed my hand as Sally continued. "It was a close call, but he received emergency surgery and is now in stable condition." I exhaled, thanking God that Harry hadn't lost his father too. "King is expected to make a full recovery. Harry flew out to be by his side as soon as he heard."

I closed my eyes. *Harry...*

I recalled his face when he got the call...I should have realized something was wrong. That it was *really* bad. But I was too wrapped up in *my* pain, in *my* hurt. In that moment, I hated myself.

"But the good news," Sally said, looking at me, Michael, and Sarah. "The midsummer celebration is still happening." The four of us were scheduled to go to England next week to represent Visage at HCS Media's birthday masquerade ball. The other invitees smiled at Sally in excitement, and with that, the meeting was over.

As everyone left the room, I stayed in my seat. "You okay?" Novah asked.

"Christ, Nove. His dad had a heart attack. He didn't say anything to me."

"Maybe he didn't know if he could. From what you said, you had quite the argument." That only made me feel worse. I wasn't there for him when he needed me most. Even after all we had done to one another, I would never have turned my back on him during this.

"I can't go next week," I said. Novah just held my hand. She was such a good friend. "I can't go to his home. Not after all of this. It wouldn't be right."

"That's your choice, sweets. Remember, your heart was hurt here too. You're allowed to take care of yourself too. If that means not going, it means not going."

"Thank you."

"I have a meeting with Hannah," Novah said regretfully, referring to the fashion editor. "I have to go. Are you going to be okay?"

"Yeah," I whispered. Novah kissed my head and left me alone in the boardroom. As I stared at the doorway, in my mind I saw Harry walking through it, months ago, announcing his takeover as CEO. I'd been so mad he had moved here permanently. Now I'd give anything for him to walk in, to hold him and tell him everything would be okay with his dad.

Opening my cell, I let my hand hover over the text button. With a deep breath, I found the contact for "Pompous Prick" and sent him a simple message:

FP: I'm so sorry about your dad. We've just been told. I'm happy to hear he is going to make a full recovery.

I paused, rereading the words, then added:

I'm thinking of you.

I pressed send. When nothing came back through, I tucked my cell away and went back to work. Five o'clock came and I took the subway home. Sage and Amelia joined me on the couch to watch TV.

I climbed into bed, watching the rain splatter on the window. As I closed my eyes, I finally heard my cell beep. I reached over, and my heart stopped when I saw a text from Harry. It was one sentence. One sentence that meant so much:

PP: Please come.

I understood what he was asking. Next week. Please go to his home in Surrey, England. I pressed my cheek to the pillow and hugged my cell to my chest. He wanted me to come to his home. After everything we had said to each other, he still wanted me there.

My Harry.

My Maître.

The man who owned my heart.

CHAPTER EIGHTEEN

SURREY, England

"HOLY. MOTHER. OF. SHIT," I said as the car drove down the main road on the Sinclair Estate. We had already passed through a stone archway not too dissimilar to the Arc de Triomphe. Then came the tree-lined road, framing miles and miles of perfectly manicured lawns. Lawns that housed deer. Real actual deer.

Then this. Harry's House wasn't a *house*. It was a goddamn palace. Made of stone and sprawling wider than the eye could see from a car window.

"First a first-class plane ticket, then this. Am I dreaming? I think I'm dreaming," Sarah, from the copyright department, said.

Michael from features whistled low. "I read it has one thousand acres. *One thousand*. I live in a six-hundred-square-foot apartment in Queens."

"It has twenty-three bedrooms," I found myself saying, which was a struggle considering I had yet to lift my jaw off the floor.

"I don't even know twenty-three *people*," Sarah said.

The car came to a stop at a grand set of stone stairs leading to elaborate wooden doors. Staff dressed in gray suits and tails were waiting. A man who appeared to be in his forties opened the door.

"Welcome to The Sinclair Estate." I was the last to get out. Before my feet had even touched the sandy gravel, a staff member was there to take my hand. Numbly, I followed Sarah and Michael from the car.

"Thank you," I said, just as another member of the house approached me with my luggage.

"Miss Faith Parisi?"

"Yep, that's me."

"This way, please. I will show you to your room." I followed the staff member up the stone stairs, looking behind me only to be met by the most picturesque view I'd ever seen. Green. Lots and lots of shades of green.

The sun was shining in the sky, birds were singing a sweet symphony, and the entire place smelled like freshly cut grass and blooming summer flowers. It was a world away from the familiar scents of car exhaust fumes and the falafel stand a block away from where I lived.

"Miss? Everything okay?" the staff member asked.

"What's your name?" I asked, not able to stand referring to someone as "staff member" for a second longer.

"Timothy."

"Then Timothy, I'm great. Just...this..." I indicated the many acres before us.

Timothy smiled. "This is nothing," he said, leaning close. "Wait until you see the gardens at the back and the view the main terrace offers. You'll be speechless."

"Well, Timothy, it takes a lot to shut me up, so that would be quite the feat."

"You'll see," he said then moved through the open doors to the foyer. I stopped in the doorway, almost getting back shafted by Sally, who had ridden in another car.

"Move!"

I ducked to the side to let Sally past, tipping my head back and drinking in my first glimpse of the Sinclair Estate's interior. A large marble statue of a man stood in the center, dark wooden columns surrounded the room, and plaster busts of Sinclairs of old graced the alcoves.

Timothy was polite enough to let me have my fill and admire the huge fireplace on one of the walls. When I'd stared at the painted ceiling and walked around the antique stone floor, he led me to another doorway. It took me a moment to see that most of the New York Journal and Visage staff were going off to the right.

"Are we not going with them?" I asked.

"No, Miss. They are being given rooms in one of the guest houses in the gardens. You are to stay in the main house." I stopped breathing at that. Not wanting to alarm Timothy by passing out, I forced my lungs to work and followed him to an ornate wooden staircase with black iron banisters with delicate filigrees.

As I climbed the perfectly vacuumed red-carpeted stairs, I looked all around me. The walls were white paneled, the same filigree patterns swirling in plaster. Old-fashioned couches and chaise lounges were perfectly placed on each landing area. Huge windows peered out onto what Timothy told me were some of the gardens. *Some.* As in *many.* I saw topiary bushes sculpted into swans and rabbits and others perfectly shaped into cones. Small hedges swirled around them like ripples of water.

He lives here. Harry actually lives *here.* I couldn't even comprehend being raised in such a place. I now better understood why King believed us so incompatible. To know Harry was a viscount and from the British aristocracy was one thing, an abstract bit of knowledge, one that may have been hinted at by his massive apartment on the Upper East Side. But being here, in this house on one thousand acres of nothing short of English countryside perfection, made it very real —very, very real—who Harry was and his place in this society.

I felt I was walking through an art gallery as we made our way down a hallway with paintings older than America on the green wallpapered walls. Timothy had told me it was the original wallpaper from when the house was built centuries ago. Not everything was original, but some furnishings they'd managed to preserve.

Timothy stopped by a large wooden door. "This is your room for the next few days, Miss Parisi," he said and opened it. A few more doors were to my right. To my left was a door at the end of the hallway. It had a grander finish than mine. The wood had touches of gold painted on the same filigree pattern that seemed to run through the house. "Miss?" Timothy said and held out his hand for me to enter first.

"Holy fucking shit," I said, eyes wide when I realized this would be my room while I was here. A huge four-poster bed sat in the center, draped ornately in blue curtains that fell to the floor and would completely box in the bed if pulled out of their ties. It had a golden dome over it like a cathedral roof. The wallpaper was sky blue, and white columns stood at either side of the bed. I couldn't help it; I let out a loud laugh. The sound of my voice echoed off the high ceiling.

"And this is your bathroom," Timothy said. After running my hand over a plush cream couch and a mahogany desk, I walked into the bathroom. It was just as impressive as the bedroom, with a large claw-foot tub, porcelain sinks that I was sure were older than George Washington, and a toilet that looked like a throne. I would never have believed anyone could look regal while emptying their bowels, but I was quickly rethinking that notion.

As we entered the bedroom again, Timothy said, "Your itinerary is on the desk. The festivities will begin with champagne and strawberries at sunset on the terrace." Timothy pointed to another pamphlet. "A map for while you are here."

"It's crazy to need a map for a house."

"You'll get used to it," Timothy said and went to the door.

"Wait, Timothy, I haven't given you your tip."

"We don't do that in England, Miss. Please, enjoy your stay. The forecast is for sunshine the entire time you are here. It should make for an unforgettable experience."

Timothy shut the door, and I shook my head in disbelief. "No tip?" I whispered. "Am I in heaven?"

I reached into my carry-on and luckily found the code for the Wi-Fi on the welcome pack HCS Media had put together. At least a house of this age had modern conveniences as well as all the history. I even spotted a big walk-in shower in the bathroom. But my heart was fixed on the bathtub. After the long flight, I needed a soak.

I walked to the window and gasped at what greeted me. A stone terrace. This one looked private. It wasn't as big as I'd expected, which led me to believe it wasn't the one we would be having champagne and strawberries on tonight.

Champagne and strawberries. Jesus Christ.

I pressed the video call app on my cell, and it opened to the waiting faces of Amelia and Sage. "Faith!" they shouted, the sound of their familiar voices making me instantly feel calmer. Because I wasn't. I was in Harry's home. I would soon see him, and I had no idea how it would go. I didn't know if he hated me for everything that had happened. I hadn't heard from him since the text where he'd asked me to come. To say I was nervous about seeing him was an understatement.

"Hey guys!" I said and flipped the camera to give them a quick tour of the bedroom and bathroom.

"You have to be shitting me!" Sage said.

"It's like a palace," Amelia said wistfully.

"Wait for this," I said and showed them the view from the window.

"Faith," Amelia said, and I swore she was getting teary. "It's the most beautiful thing I've ever seen. Is that a lake in the distance?"

"Yes," I said, admiring the bridge that had been built over it. It looked like something from a fairy tale, with pink, purple and blue flowers decorating the old gray stone.

I turned the camera again and sat at the desk. I glanced at the itinerary. "There's welcome drinks tonight. Then the choice of archery or horse riding tomorrow. A tour of the grounds and some free time the day after. Then the masquerade midsummer ball." I dropped the itinerary, which had been printed on the fanciest stationary I'd ever seen.

"Have you seen him yet?" Sage asked carefully.

"No." I sighed and tipped my head back. "Maybe I won't until the ball. I don't know if he wants to talk, or if he just didn't want me to miss the recognition I'd received from Visage."

"Faith, you can't honestly think that," Amelia said. "Of course he wants to see you."

"Only time will tell." I rifled through my suitcase, which looked like a miniature model amongst all the opulent room dressings. "I need a nap to try and kick this jet lag, a long soak in the bath. Then the fun will begin."

"We're stupidly jealous, you know that, right?" Sage said affectionately.

"I know."

"Say hello to Nicholas for me. He's going to be at the ball."

"I will." I kissed my fingers and waved at my friends. As I hung up, I climbed into the plush bed, staring up at the golden ceiling. I felt like I was lying on a cloud. As my eyes closed, I imagined what Harry would look like when I saw him again. My heart swelled just picturing that dark hair, his blue eyes, and the smile he held just for me.

He lived in a palace.

Harry, the one-day duke.

And I was in it.

In England.

If this was a dream, I never wanted to wake up.

THE WHITE LINEN dress hung off my shoulders, the sleeves

hugging my upper arms. The hem fell to my knees, flowing out enough to be casual, but hugging my figure enough to show off my curves and absolutely dressy enough for champagne.

As I passed a wall-size mirror (the walls in the Sinclair Estate, it should be noted, were rather large), I made sure my long hair was styled nicely in loose waves and my earrings were correctly in place. I had kept my makeup light but with deep pink lipstick. As I stared at my reflection, I blew out a nervous raspberry.

"Miss," a voice said, making me jump.

"Timothy!" I said, hand over my heart. "I didn't see you there."

"Too busy sticking your tongue out at your reflection?" he teased. I immediately liked him even more than I had that morning.

"I was." I pointed at myself in the mirror. "She's one sassy bitch."

"Call me warned." He gestured toward a wall of glass doors. "The terrace is just through those doors. Most of the guests are already here."

"Thank you, Timothy." Being careful not to lose my footing on the uneven stone floor beneath me, I walked through the doors and gasped. I actually gasped, loudly and dramatically. The view...I blinked a few times, trying to be sure I wasn't imagining what lay before me. The stone terrace was vast and ornate. Stone balustrades created a balcony of the terrace. Sweeping curved staircases on both sides of the terrace led down to perfectly manicured gardens. Colorful and vibrant plants in large Romanesque pots sat on stone columns on the gravel paths. Green topiary domes and small hedge mazes swirled around the garden like miniature mazes. Another stone balustrade was at the end of the garden, offering the perfect place to view the stunning property beyond.

The setting sun reflected off the lake, and the flower-dense fairy-tale bridge lay over it. It looked like a watercolor painting. To the right were what I suspected Harry had called the guest houses. They were mansions themselves. Nothing compared to the main house, but they were impressive nevertheless.

There was so much to take in, my head throbbed at the vastness.

THOROUGHLY WHIPPED

The live string orchestra playing in the corner only added to the dreamlike quality of the mansion and grounds, and that fact that I, Faith Parisi, was really *here*. Then my skin bumped realizing they were playing the beautiful sound of Andrea Bocelli. The same music that used to play in Maître's chambre.

A server dressed in a black-and-white suit with a matching bow tie pulled me from my reverie. "Miss, champagne?"

"Thank you," I said, taking a glass. A waving hand pulled my attention to the back of the terrace. Sarah. I walked down the steps to the main floor of the terrace and joined my colleagues.

"Can you believe this place?" Sarah said, looking beautiful in purple. "Why is Harry in New York? If I owned this place, I'd never leave." My stomach dropped a little at that. But she was right. It was as close to heaven as you could get on Earth. Why would he ever leave here?

"Has anyone even seen him?" Michael asked. "I heard King left the hospital a few days after surgery and is already almost back to normal. It's amazing how quickly you can recover from a heart attack these days."

"That's good," I said and took a sip of my champagne. King was out of the hospital and feeling better. The relief that brought almost made me emotional. Damn jet lag.

"Look out, here's the man himself." Michael nudged his chin in the direction of the glass doors. "Harry."

I froze. No matter how much I had tried to prepare myself for this moment, I wasn't. My heart was beating so fast that I thought it might make me pass out. I closed my eyes and counted back from four to try to calm down. When I was hitting the negative numbers, I realized it wasn't working for shit. Then I heard his laugh, and a strange sense of calm filled my lungs, making it so I could breathe. And this was his true laugh, not the one he used when he was trapped behind the prison of his title. He sounded happy. Harry...he sounded perfect.

Making myself turn around, I found him on the other side of the

209

terrace greeting the guests. My heart fluttered. His smile was wide and genuine, and the crinkles around his eyes were out in full force.

The past week without him and the residual pain from our argument seemed to fade like the champagne bubbles I held in my hand. He was here. Before me again, looking the happiest I had ever seen him. I was rooted to the ground, as if my feet had been buried by the groundsman like the potted flowers around us.

"You're drooling." Sally stood beside me. I rolled my eyes at my boss, decked out in an all-black suit. "Don't worry, if I liked men I'd be drooling too."

"Sally, do you realize it's summer?" I said, tipping my head at her suit and boots.

"This is from my summer collection, Faith. Do get caught up on fashion." Sally moved to a neighboring table, and I waited for Harry to come over. He was wearing a lightweight white linen shirt with, of course, his sleeves rolled up to his elbows. He wore khakis, and his wavy hair moved in a slight breeze. It would have been so much easier to hate him if he didn't look so beautiful.

As if sensing I was waiting, he lifted his head and his blue gaze quickly sought out mine. Immediately locked in a stare, Harry's expression softened and the smile he gave me left me breathless. He tapped the man he was speaking to on the arm and walked our way.

"Hello, welcome to the Sinclair Estate," he said, his accent instantly washing over me. He tore his eyes off mine momentarily while he shook hands with Sarah and Michael. I didn't catch any of their small talk, too busy reacquainting myself with the view of Harry's muscled forearms, his olive skin, courtesy of his mom, and his clean-shaven square jaw.

Then he was looking back at me, holding out his hand. "Miss Parisi," he said, his touch sending electricity through my body. Harry's fingers squeezed mine.

"Harry." My voice shook slightly. Sarah and Michael moved to speak to someone they knew at the next table.

Harry saw them go and stepped closer to me. I saw the wariness in his guarded expression, the uncertainty as to where we now stood with one another. "How are you?"

His scent and voice wrapped around me and pulled me close. "I'm good," I said and took a deep breath. "Your dad...is he feeling better?"

"He is," he said, and I couldn't get past the new air around him. He was lighter somehow, more amiable. Gone was the Harry wrapped up in arrogance, and in his place was a relaxed and friendly doppelganger. "He's doing very well." Harry pointed up at the main house. "Resting in his wing. He'll no doubt be unable to resist making an appearance at some point. Even though he should, technically, still be taking it easy."

It took me a moment to realize that our hands were still clasped, fingers loosely intertwined. I looked down at our joined hands and felt that subtle shifting sensation underneath my sternum again.

"Do you like the house?" Harry asked, his voice quiet, husky, and tentative. He appeared to be holding his breath waiting for my answer.

I laughed. "Harry, this isn't a house, it's..." I trailed off, taking in the view. Sighing at the beauty of it, I finished, "It's paradise."

His smile was so wide it lit up the air around us. I was pretty sure I'd died and gone to heaven. I could now see why my concussed brain, that day at the rec center, had believed him to be an angel. He looked like one now.

"Good," he said and pulled back his hand. "I'm glad you think that way."

"Harry?" A male voice behind us said. "Sorry to interrupt, mate, but we need you over here a second." Harry nodded, but his body language made it clear he wanted to stay.

"It was nice to see you again, Harry," I said, hoping he would read between the lines. That I was no longer angry. That the minute I saw him again, everything that had happened between us had fallen away.

"You too. You look..." A blush coated his cheeks, "You look

perfect." Then he was pulled away from me to a group of English men who gathered around a table. I inhaled the smell of fresh grass and took another offered glass of champagne and a strawberry.

I joined Sarah and Michael, mixing with the guests. As the night fell, and I felt like I had met everyone representing HCS Media from Paris to Hong Kong, I made my way down the stone stairs to the garden and along the graveled path, bordered with green and bursts of vibrantly colored flowers. The sky was pink and the orchestra played "Time to Say Goodbye" as I wandered aimlessly, absorbing the view. I knew I would never see anything like this again.

Stopping at the stone balustrade, I watched the rising moon glitter off the lake and the trees sway lightly in the summer breeze.

"Beautiful," I whispered.

"I was thinking the same thing." Harry was behind me, two glasses in his hands. His shirt collar was open as usual, showing me a glimpse of his toned chest. "Peace offering," he said and held out the glass. Placing my empty one on the pillar next to me, I took it and Harry moved beside me to look out upon his land.

"You own all of this," I said in disbelief. "This is your *actual* home."

"It's okay," he said, shrugging. "But I've seen better." I shook my head at his sarcastic joke and bumped his shoulder. Harry dropped his smirk and, clearing his throat, said, "I'm sorry, Faith. I'm so bloody sorry. For everything."

I shook my head. "Don't." I leaned over the balustrade, resting my arms on the cool ancient stone. "But for my part, I'm sorry too."

We were silent as the orchestra hit their dramatic crescendo. He turned to me. "Spend the day with me tomorrow."

"But I have a day of archery and horse riding. You would pull me away from that?"

"I believe I would, yes," he said dryly, fighting a smile.

"Then I must do what the king of the castle demands!" I said, mock exasperated.

"Prince," Harry said. "Prince of the castle would be more fitting."

"Well, I'm certainly not a princess."

"Not yet," Harry said, causing my heart to flip in my chest. I met his gaze and saw only seriousness in his eyes. I swallowed at the implication of his words and took another long, very deep, very copious drink of my champagne. "Spend the day with me, Faith. Then have dinner with me tomorrow night. We have a lot to talk about..." He hesitated. "If you'll let me."

Straightening from the balustrade, I faced Harry. My lord. Was there ever a man as perfect as he was? God had been very generous when it came to creating Harry Sinclair.

"Then until tomorrow," I said and Harry smiled again, showing me those devastating eye crinkles. "I'd better get my beauty sleep. I need to sleep off my jet lag so I can enjoy all the fun activities you have to bestow on me in the morning."

"I was really only going to give you the grand tour. A personal grand tour."

"Harry, have you seen where you live? It would take a year to cover this place."

"Ah, but I know all the best bits." He tapped the side of his nose with his index finger. "Insider knowledge." He leaned forward and kissed my cheek. It took everything within me not to slam him into the balustrade and crash my mouth to his. But restrain I did.

As I walked on the gravel path toward the house, I shouted, "'Til the morrow!" and waved my champagne napkin in the air like a lace handkerchief. My heel slipped into a crack and I wobbled, almost hitting the ground.

Managing to right myself on a statue of a naked man, clutching his small penis, I stopped Harry from coming to my rescue with a gesture. "I'm okay!" I called out, pulling my heel from the crack and back onto the safety of the gravel. Harry shook his head at my clumsiness.

I pointed my thumb at the statue's manhood. "You could have given him a few more inches," I said to Harry. "Poor guy has been out here all this time, humiliated. For heaven's sake, do the right thing!"

Harry laughed, his Adam's apple bobbing up and down. Why was that so damn sexy? "Goodnight, Faith."

"So I'm Faith again?" I asked as I reached the steps.

"You never weren't Faith to me."

I went back to my room, a new lightness in my step. Who *was* this Harry? This happy and joyful Harry? I wasn't sure if I had truly met him before tonight. But I couldn't wait to know him more. Tomorrow, I was spending the day and evening with him.

As I hit the mattress, exhaustion quickly pulled me under. But for the first time in a week I slept well, and I was glad, because the deeper I slept, the quicker tomorrow would come.

CHAPTER NINETEEN

"MR. SINCLAIR IS WAITING in his sitting room for you to take breakfast with him, Miss," Timothy said the next morning when I exited my room and found him walking the hallway.

"*His* sitting room?"

"Yes, Miss. Everyone who lives here gets one."

"Wow," I said, marveling at the fact that some people were rich enough to get their own of each and everything. Even a lounge. I followed Timothy just two doors down from my room to another wooden door. When he opened it, Harry sat at a small table in the cove of a large window. He was in his usual attire of a white shirt and khakis, but this time he also wore a navy cardigan with a thick collar and a pair of black loafers. Of course he even made a cardigan and loafers look good.

Timothy shut the door, leaving us alone, and Harry got to his feet. He came over to me and took my hand. He ran his thumb over my fingers and leaned in to kiss me on my cheek. When he pulled away, I asked, "Is that all I'm getting?"

Harry's cheek twitched in amusement. "Good morning, Faith," he said. "And yes. That's all you're getting for now."

"Yes, Maître," I said, and Harry's face fell with shock.

I tried not to laugh at his reaction but couldn't help it. Harry shook his head, a blush coating his cheeks. I'd decided to copyright that blush too. It was adorable. "I've said it once, and I'll say it again. But you're—"

"Incorrigible," I finished for him. "Yeah, yeah, I know."

"Breakfast?" he asked, clearly trying to get the conversation away from his moonlight job as a sexual master and back to his idyllic life in the Sinclair Estate. Harry pulled out a chair beside him at the table.

"Crumpets and toast and all the jams and butter," I said. "And tea, lots of tea."

"And coffee for Miss Parisi." He handed me a full cafetière, a pot of sugar and cream. "I haven't forgotten your aversion to England's national beverage."

"You get extra points for that, just so you know." I poured myself a strong coffee, the smell of which nearly gave me an orgasm.

"I'm flattered," Harry said and bit into a slice of toast.

"So? What's the plan for today?" I buttered a crumpet and my eyes rolled back into my head when it hit my mouth. "Mm," I said, "how did I not know these tasted so good? I wouldn't have made them the butt of my jokes if I had."

Harry watched my every move as I sucked my fingers into my mouth to get the last of the melted butter. "You know I'm good at sucking, Harry. So get those sex eyes away from me. I'm eating. And not even you and all your perfection can stand between me and starchy carbs."

I wiped my hands on my fancy cloth napkin, while Harry smirked into his tea. "I thought we'd start with the house then go down to the gardens." He finished his tea. "Then we can have dinner in the dining room tonight."

"Just the two of us?" I asked.

"Yes, if that's okay?" He seemed nervous I'd actually say no.

"Better than." I quickly polished off two more crumpets and two cups of coffee.

"Are you ready?" Harry stood, offering me his hand. I got to my feet, and his eyes tracked down my purple dress, with three-quarter length sleeves, which stopped at the tops of my knees. "You look stunning," he said, and I knew he meant it, seeing the way his pupils dilated.

I had put my hair back in a high ponytail and thrown white Converses on my feet. They didn't quite match the elegance of this house and grounds, but then neither did I, so I didn't let it bother me.

I lifted my foot to show Harry the sneakers. "Figured I'd better wear something less dangerous than heels for the grand tour today."

"For that," he said, kissing the back of my hand like he just had to touch me, "I am eternally grateful." Harry offered me his elbow. I linked my arm through. "Shall we?"

"Let's." He led me to the hallway and, again, I marveled at all the vintage decoration and furnishings. "I still can't believe you were brought up here." A sad thought occurred to me. "Were you ever lonely?"

Harry's arm tensed a little, betraying his answer. "Yes. Especially after my mum died." He shrugged. "Nicholas was here a lot. His ancestral home is not too far away. But it wasn't like having a brother or sister living in the house."

"This place would have terrified me as a kid. My crazy imagination would have created so many ghosts that roamed the halls."

Harry pointed at a room. It was open and a woman was inside cleaning it. "I believed the boogie man lived under the bed in that room." When we came to a landing that forked into two hallways, he pointed to the one we weren't going down, thank God. "And the gray lady roams that corridor. Just floats along in all her sixteenth-century regalia, mourning her lost love and waiting to snatch children from their beds and possess them."

"Christ, Harry. I have to sleep up here tonight!"

He laughed. "You go to any stately home in England, and I guarantee there will be many a story of gray ladies and soldiers who died in battle, defending the Lord who lived there, back for their vengeance." He shrugged. "I've never seen one."

Something pulled my ponytail and I whipped my head around, screaming just a little bit, only to see Harry placing his free hand back by his side. "Prick," I muttered, but I still checked around us just in case.

"Pompous Prick, Faith. At least address me by my proper title."

"You're right. How could I forget."

"Here," Harry said, arriving at the first room. Large cream double doors greeted us. "The biggest room in all the house." Harry opened the doors, and my mouth dropped open when a massive gallery room, filled top to toe with pictures, oil paintings, and statues, was bared to my eyes. "The gallery. In it are all the dukes who have come before. Their wives and children."

"And their dogs?" I asked, seeing a grand picture of a regal-looking wolfhound.

"Some of my ancestors really, really loved their dogs." Harry brought me to a picture of a tall, handsome man in a red coat and breeches. He was staring seriously at the painter. In fact, all of the dukes' poses were almost identical. "The very first duke in our line."

"He looks a little like you," I said, drifting past the other portraits. The women were beautiful and wore exquisite dresses.

We stopped at a duke with sandy blond hair. "He caused quite the scandal in the nineteenth century," Harry said.

"Why? Did he not like tea?" I grimaced.

"Goodness no, nothing that bad," Harry said, his voice horrified. He smirked. "He ran off with his wife's handmaid."

"No," I said, staring wide eyed at the man in the picture.

"Love," Harry said, a hint of admiration in his voice. "He fell in love with her. More than. He was utterly besotted with her. Had been for years. One day, he eloped with her."

"What happened?"

"His brother found him in Brighton and brought him home."

"He lost the love of his life?"

"No." Harry laughed at my confused expression. "He moved her into the guest house and lived out the rest of his days with her."

"Erm...? *What?*"

"It was the nineteenth century, Faith. He was a duke and frankly could do whatever the hell he liked."

"His poor wife."

Harry nodded. "But it's the most common tale of men, and women too, who are made to marry for duty, not for love."

Silence stretched between us and the portrait of the duke who'd given his heart to a peasant. "Is..." I took a breath. "Is there a chance that maybe one day that can be remedied?" I winced, hating myself for even going there. I had loved this time with Harry this morning, seeing his world. I didn't want to spoil it. But—

"I think so," he said, interrupting my thoughts. He put his hands in his pockets. "I think for the first time, there is hope."

Hope. *Yes*, I thought. *It's hope that's now racing through my veins at a hundred miles an hour.*

I moved to the next portrait, Harry beside me. I passed by King, looking handsome in his youth. Then, "Your mom." A beautiful, tall, slim woman posed by a window for her portrait. Her dark-brown hair was swept up into an updo. Aline Auguste-Sinclair wore long white gloves and a purple dress, and she had Harry's cerulean blue eyes. "She's beautiful," I said, finding my eyes filling with tears. One fell down my cheek. I felt the loss of her presence. For Harry's sake, even for King's, but also for mine. I would have loved to have met her.

Harry swept my tears away with his thumbs. Then I moved to the next picture and couldn't help but smile. My lungs seized, my heart skipped a beat, and I fixed my eyes on the handsome viscount before me. Beside me. "Harry," I whispered. He was standing in the gardens, the fairy-tale bridge behind him in all its colorful glory. He was dressed in a navy suit, his handsome face illuminating the picture. "It's incredible."

"It's something, all right," he said, huffing in amusement.

"No, it *is*," I said, not allowing him to knock this. "It really is magnificent."

"Thank you," he said. Then, "If you like it, then so do I."

Beaming up at him, I asked, "So what's next?"

Harry took me to the east wing of the house. It was so far away a light sweat had broken out on my forehead. "No wonder you look like that," I said, moving my finger up and down. "You have to be fit to live here."

"This is worth it." Harry opened the doors and all I saw were books. And not like those in his New York apartment. It was that on crack. That times a million. A room filled from top to bottom with books, books, and even more books.

"Fourteen thousand," Harry replied when I asked him how many books were in here. There was a desk in the center, then four sofas to relax on and read.

"I'd never leave this room if I lived here." I ran my hand along the spines. Some of them had to be over three hundred years old.

After practically dragging me from the library, Harry showed me bedrooms where Queen Victoria and Queen Anne had stayed. I saw the music room, which had a piano in the corner. It was there I found out Harry could play. If I hadn't already been smitten with him, I would have been when he reluctantly played for me.

Next he took us to the old servants' quarters, and into something called a vegetable scullery.

"There was once a room just to prepare vegetables?"

"Yes."

"Just to peel potatoes and the like?"

"Yes."

"Let me get this straight." I widened my arms. "This entire space was for vegetables?"

"Yes, Faith. I won't say it again."

We then entered the pastry room.

"Okay," I said, "this room was just to prepare pastry?"

"Yes."

"This *entire* room?"

Harry rolled his eyes, took me by my elbow and led me from that room and into one with bells. A bell for each room, where the duke or duchess (and anyone else staying there) could ring a bell and a servant would come running.

Harry quickly took me out of the servants' quarters too when I began lecturing him on the issue I had with civility.

"It's all so surreal," I said as we walked down a hidden path to the lake. In the distance I saw the rest of the guests engaged in archery. From where we were, I could see someone who looked like Sally completely ignoring the target, instead taking aim at passing birds.

"I wanted you to see." He led me to a wooden bridge on a private part of the lake. We sat down on the embankment. The sun was shining and warming my face. Harry took off his cardigan and rolled up his sleeves.

"In New York..." He ran his hand down his face. "I appear a businessman, which of course I am." He gestured to the fields of trees around us. "But I am also more." He bowed his head, hiding his face from me. "I suppose I run from this sometimes. Hide who I am so people don't think something of me that I'm not." He looked up at me. I saw a plea for understanding in his expression. "But this will all be mine one day. God..." He took a deep breath. "It was not too long ago..." He was referring to his father's heart attack. I reached for his hand. "After our argument, and then my father's heart attack, it has put things into perspective for me."

"It has?"

Harry nodded and stared down at our clasped hands. "I cannot deny who I am. And more than that, I think, when all the layers are stripped away, I actually *like* who I am."

"Then that makes two of us."

Harry kissed my hand and lowered it to his leg. "I am proud I'm going to be a duke one day, Faith. I am proud to be of this Sinclair line. But I told my father there had to be changes." His voice switched from soft to stern. "After us...after everything...I knew things had to be different. And I had to be the one to make it happen."

"You did?" I was too afraid to ask what those changes were.

"Come," Harry said, getting to his feet. "I have more to show you. Then we'll have lunch in the gazebo."

"Who are you?" I laughed, feeing like I was in a dream.

He pulled me closer and cupped my cheeks just like I loved. "Harry. Just Harry." I waited for a kiss, but it didn't come.

Harry held my hand and led me to the stables. By the time evening rolled around, I had seen all of Harry's favorite rooms and sights on his land. He left me at my room with a promise to see me at dinner.

I wore a long red dress and heels. And I kept my hair down, just how he liked it. I wore my favorite red lipstick and walked to the great dining hall. I had caught a quick glimpse earlier in the day, but as the doors opened, I couldn't believe my eyes. It was adorned with paintings, tapestries, and sculptures, and in the center of the room there was a table so big it looked like it could have held a banquet for a hundred people. It almost blocked my view of Harry, at the fireplace, turned away from me with his hands behind his back. He faced me, his lips parting, when he saw me in my dress.

I held out my arms. "You like?"

"Very much," he said with a tight throat. He kissed my cheek, and I admired him too.

"Very handsome," I said and took a drink he had waiting for me. "Wine," I said with relief. "As much as I love champagne, I couldn't take another drop. I'm a wine cooler and beer kind of girl, you know?"

"Shall we?" Harry held out his hand and led me toward the table. On the way, I went over on my heel, the wine spilling on the carpet.

"Shit!" I turned to Harry. "Please tell me that wasn't some priceless antique."

Harry shrugged. "Just a few centuries old, that's all." He leaned in closer, and I almost fucking whimpered at his addictive scent and how it made my thighs clench. "It has survived two world wars and the house fire of 1819, but I'm afraid it has succumbed to the klutziness of one Faith Maria Parisi."

"Harry!" I said, distressed, my hands on my head. "Is it really that old?"

"No. Just over one hundred. But honestly, in this place, that's practically brand new." We approached the table. Harry pointed to the other end. "You are seated down there, and me up here." He pointed to another seat. I counted the chairs in between. There were thirty.

"Are you serious?" I asked.

"No," Harry said with a completely straight face.

When his lips hooked up into a small smile, I shook my head. "Oh, you're full of the jokes tonight."

"For now." He led me to the place he had declared was his and pulled out the chair beside him for me. "Let's eat, and then we can talk."

A cave burrowed in my gut. Since I had arrived here yesterday, everything between us had been perfect. But no matter how hard we tried, we couldn't get rid of the elephant in the room. I needed him to explain about Maître and NOX and everything in between, and I needed to apologize for my part too.

"So, what are we having?" I asked, trying to push the heavy stuff aside until after dinner.

"Roasted quail with cabbage."

"Lovely!" I said, immediately dying inside. I was famished and needed real friggin' food. But when the dishes came, and the dome was lifted —"Tortelli de Zucca," I said, seeing my favorite dish on my plate.

"I thought we'd leave the quail for another night."

I covered Harry's hand with my own and squeezed. "I knew you were a good man underneath."

We ate and made small talk. When the coffee had been drunk and the dishes cleared away, Harry led me to the now-lit fire and poured me a glass of whiskey. I sat beside him on the couch.

Silence stretched between us until Harry said, "Faith. Please allow me to explain. Explain everything."

"Okay," I said, the warm glow from the fire not staving off the chill in my bones.

Harry leaned forward, elbows on his knees, his whiskey dangling from his hand. "You must understand that the way I was—arrogant, rude, and cold—came after I lost my mother. I'm not saying this to ignite sympathy. I am saying it because it's true." He took a small sip of his whiskey. "My father and I, over the past week, since his heart attack, have had many discussions."

"You have?"

He nodded. "We had a lot of things that needed to be said. *I* had a lot of things that needed to be said. He needed to know what he had done to me that changed me. That had made me...act out after Mum died." I took a sip of my whiskey too, letting the warmth slide down my throat.

"When I was at university, I was a little wild," he confessed. "Spent much of my time drunk and sleeping around. I was Hyde, studious by day and a total bloody mess at night. And that's what I became used to being."

I couldn't imagine Harry this way. But then I'd never lost a parent, so I couldn't imagine how that would have affected me. "I was in New York one summer with my father." He smiled, but it was wan. "A friend of mine invited me to the Hamptons. I went, of course. When we were there, he told me of a party that was happening that night. A sex party, only everyone wore masks. It was completely anonymous. People in the Hamptons needed it to be anonymous. They had reputations to uphold, positions of power to protect."

Harry gazed into the fire, going back to that time. "I couldn't believe my eyes," he said. "It was freedom. Being in that mask felt..." He frowned. "I'd spent my entire life under a microscope. People watching my every move. *Don't do this, Harry. That will harm our business, Harry. That isn't how a viscount behaves, Harry.* I was sick of it. Sick of living with a ghost of a father, sick of living without my mother. Sick of living for others and not myself."

"Harry..." I whispered, feeling weight pressing on my chest at the sadness in his voice.

"I had told a friend about the party. He lived in Manhattan." Harry swilled the ice around in his whiskey. "He told me I should organize something similar on the Upper East Side. Charge people to attend, get them to sign NDAs, and insist on everyone wearing masks and cloaks to protect themselves." Harry shrugged. "So I did. And not only was it popular, it was a roaring success. And I'd done it without any input from my father." As crazy as it sounded, I felt a flash of pride for Harry at that.

"At first, I rented houses, moved the club to a new location each week. By then I'd named it NOX. Eventually we made enough for me to invest in a permanent place."

"The townhouse in Manhattan?"

Harry nodded. "Yes." He laughed. "I had a waiting list as long as the Brooklyn Bridge. But by then, my wild times had come to an end, and I saw NOX as a real, viable business. But also as a way out for people like me. People who felt like they were in a prison of sorts in their everyday lives." Harry downed his whiskey then poured another, topping up mine too.

"Thank you."

Harry sat back on the couch. "By the time we were established, although my wild streak had long since died, I had gained a reputation."

"Maître," I said.

"Maître." Harry shook his head. "From that first night in the Hamptons, I had used that fucking French accent. I could, *can*, speak French fluently, of course. It was all I ever spoke to my mum. And I don't know..." He trailed off, at a loss for words.

"It offered you more protection."

Harry met my eyes. "Exactly," he said with a self-deprecating smile. "It was stupid really, but donning that mask and cloak and that damn accent made me someone else. For a little while, I wasn't Henry Sinclair III, heir to a dukedom. I was Maître Auguste, and being him felt really bloody good. I kept to myself. No one knew me and my business thrived."

Harry took my hand, like he needed the strength, needed my support. "I was no longer indulging in my former wild ways, Faith. But—and it could be argued this was worse—I had become a hard and cold man instead. You were right when you claimed I was pompous and arrogant. I was. And I was fine being that way. In my social circles it was common, and even revered." He held my hand more tightly. "And then I met you." His lip curled fondly. "And you crashed into me like a wrecking ball." Harry kissed my hand, my fingers. "I had never, in all my life, met anyone like you."

"Same here," I said, feeling like I had a balloon attached to each of my shoulders, lifting me high off the ground.

"That first day, in the meeting room for the interns..." I winced, remembering that day all too well. Harry sighed. "I had just begun getting some help."

"Help?"

Harry rubbed his fingers over his heart. "After all the drinking and shagging around stopped." He stared at the flames in the fire, lost in the past. "After I calmed down and tried to focus on my life, my future, most of the time I felt numb. When I wasn't numb, I was angry or sad."

"Why?"

"Mum," he said, the single word filled with so much love it made my heart clench. "I hadn't realized it, but I was still in shock. Even as a man approaching his mid-twenties, the shock, the trauma from losing my mum so young, festered within me like a mortal wound that would not heal." He paused and gathered his composure. "Her death...our not saying goodbye...had broken a part of me, taken away a piece of my heart that, honestly, I don't think I'll ever get back."

"Harry," I said, my voice catching with sadness.

"I have always been introverted. I would look at people like you, full of life and joy, talking freely with others, and wonder how it came so easy. How you could brighten up the room by your mere presence."

"You think that of me?"

Harry met my eyes. "Yes."

"The day before we first met, I'd had a rather intense session with my therapist." Harry sighed. "It had affected me greatly, talking of my mum and dad and those years after her death. I had a headache and felt so bloody angry at the world. Angry that I wasn't sure who I was as a man, as a person, and sad that I had wasted so many years filling the absence in my heart with mindless and superficial relationships."

Harry's lips lifted in a smirk. "Then I met you, so full of life and exuding happiness. The other interns moved to you like you were a magnet and they couldn't resist your pull." He frowned. "I had never seen anyone so…so…*alive* as you were. Alive, and…beautiful. So exceptionally beautiful."

Exceptionally.

"Harry—"

"I liked you. Despite myself, and how wrong for a man of my station my peers and father would say you were, I liked you. And that tormented me more than anything. I would see you in the office, all vibrant and confident, men and women falling at your feet…I didn't know what to do with you. With how I felt about you. I refused to believe it was attraction and convinced myself it was distain." He laughed, and I couldn't help but smile too. "Then you said 'yes, sir.' No matter what I said to you, you would always smile and answer with 'yes, sir' and it broke me."

"I knew it got under your skin," I confessed.

"That it did," Harry said. "In fact, it almost drove me insane." He raked his hand through his dark waves. "Even when I returned to England over the summer, then began working in publishing in Manhattan part time, I would often think of you. The woman who had gotten to me like no other." He huffed a laugh. *"Henry Sinclair the Third is nothing but an overprivileged cockface. An overprivileged cockface who needs nothing but a good spanking and a thorough fucking."*

Harry laughed loudly, and I melted at the happy sound. "Those words tortured me, Faith. Circled my mind for years." He quickly sobered. "I tried to tell myself I didn't care that you disliked me, that you were nothing to me, didn't even know me. But even if I convinced my mind that it was true, the dull ache in my heart exposed me for the liar I was.

"When my father told me he wanted me to take over his New York office a few years later, I immediately said yes."

"To get away from the pressures of being here?"

Harry held my eyes with his own. "That. I had NOX there, which I could be closer to, I could escape the stifling society scene here in England for a bit...and, I now realize, because I knew you'd be there too."

I reared back in shock. "What?"

"Call it masochism, call it self-punishment, but I wanted to take over the New York office, and despite how much I fought it, I wanted to see you again."

"You hated me," I whispered.

"I tried to convince myself I did." He shrugged. "Turns out it was something else entirely." I didn't have any words. "But I was intent on keeping you at arms length. I knew you thought me cold and arrogant, were repelled by my unpleasant character. So I played the part. If you hated me, I could never let myself believe there could be anything more between us. It was my only line of defense."

"You did a stellar job," I joked. Harry chuckled. "I would never have guessed this man lived underneath the façade." Harry nodded.

After a deep breath, he said, "That night, at the nightclub, when we bumped into each other."

"The night I got invited to NOX?"

"That wasn't me," he said. "As much as you were under my skin, I would never have tempted myself that way. By having you in my club."

"Then who—"

"Christoph. He's a scout for NOX, for the sirens." Harry held up his hands. "I was there with Nicholas. He had flown in for a visit, and we were meeting some of his friends. I had no idea Christoph had scouted you, I swear. It wasn't until I was in my office on the top floor that first night that I knew."

"How?"

"I saw you on the camera coming in through the main entrance." Harry coughed. "I couldn't believe my eyes. The woman who got to me like no other was entering my club. Coming to be a siren." Harry blushed, and his eyes filled with apology. "I couldn't do it, Faith. I couldn't see you with other men." I felt out of breath at his confession. "I sat at my desk trying to think of ways to get you evicted. But then I watched you navigate your way through the main room. I saw that you were nervous. The loud and vibrant Faith I knew was intimated and, I thought, a little scared." He shook his head. "It killed me to see you that way."

"I was overwhelmed," I whispered. "I thought I could do it, then saw everyone and froze."

He smiled and laughed. "Then, in typical Faith fashion, you took out the sex swing room in one fell swoop." I laughed too, just remembering that calamity. "I saw Gavin bring you to the back room, and saw your defeated posture." His shoulders sagged. "I wanted to comfort you. I wanted to tell you that you needn't be embarrassed. I needed to know you were okay."

"That's why you called me up to your room?" Familiar butterflies were back in my stomach.

Harry nodded. "I warred with myself over what I wanted to do, what I ultimately *did* do. I wanted to assure you that you didn't need to embarrassed, and I planned to send you on your way. But when you saw me, that nervousness you'd displayed downstairs faded away. You seemed *interested* in me, relaxed in my presence...and curious." Harry ran his hand down his face. "Curious about me and what I could do. All rational thought left my head after that. I convinced myself that, as Maître, I could get you out of my system then get on with my life. But it only made me like you more." The last sentence was said so softly it made my eyes glisten.

"Then the unbelievable happened. I talked to you. *Me*. As Harry. In the elevator. And it wasn't completely strained. You didn't seem filled with hate toward me." Harry took a long swallow of his whiskey, like he was working up to something. "But more than that, I liked the person I became around you. You tunneled through the protective shield of arrogance and rudeness I'd adopted around you. And as we continued to be thrown together, I started to remember. I started to remember the Harry I had been before my mother died and my father stopped caring about life. I remembered that I could laugh and crack jokes and not be dour and miserable, just existing, each day like the next."

Harry shuffled closer to me. My heart beat so fast with the proximity. "Each time we were together as Harry and Faith, I gained a piece of the old Harry back. You, Faith. *You* brought me back. With your innuendos and inappropriate jokes."

"Harry..." I whispered. "But Maître..."

"I never believed, in a million years, someone like you would like me. As Maître I got to have the intimate side of you. But then, impossibly, things began shifting. I felt them changing between us as Harry and Faith."

"I remember."

"And the deeper we got, the more I knew that if I told you I was Maître I would lose you. That I would break any semblance of trust we shared, and I would lose you." Harry looked so sorry and forlorn. "As bad as that sounds, I couldn't bear to lose you. You changed me, Faith." He frowned at that. "No, not changed me. You brought me back to life. You, the feisty brunette from Hell's Kitchen who writes a sex advice column, brought me back to life."

"Harry," I said and, finally, after all this time, I pressed my lips to his. He kissed me back. It was soft, it was beautiful, and it was filled with an abundance of gratitude.

When he pulled back, he said, "You must know that everything I said to you as Harry was the truth. I omitted that I was Maître, but everything else was real, Faith. So bloody real."

I placed my hand on his face. "You are both, Harry. Both men are you. And I fell for them both."

"Faith..." he whispered.

"But your father," I said, shattering the moment. "He made it clear he will never allow this. Us."

Harry dropped his forehead to mine. "And I have made it clear to him that if he tries to get in my way again, in any part of my life, but especially with you, I'll walk away. I'll refuse the title, the businesses, everything. Faith, I told him not to make me choose between you and him."

"You did?" I said, feeling my heart in my throat. "Why?"

Harry pulled back his head so I could see his face, so I could meet his eyes and hear him say, "Because I told him I'd choose you. I told him I'd always choose you."

Tears fell from my eyes and I crashed my mouth into his. This time Harry kissed me back with the same level of longing and desperation that lived within me. My hands ran through his hair, and I tasted whiskey on his lips and tongue. I was consumed by him, and I wanted nothing more than to have him above me. But Harry pulled back and said, "I'll walk you back to your room."

"Wha—?" I said, lips swollen and confused.

"Faith, you need to think about everything that has happened." He glanced at the couch beneath us. "And I'm not going to take you for the first time on an old couch in my dining room."

"Why not?" I argued. "You've fucked me in stocks and in a giant birdcage for fuck's sake. I'd say an antique couch in a stately home is an upgrade from those."

"Faith—"

"I forgive you, okay?" I said, desperately trying to undo his zipper. "Do you forgive me too? If so, let's get to the make-up sex."

Harry moved my hands away. "Of course." He sighed and stood

up. "But now that you know who I am, *all* parts of me, I want to do this right."

"Right spright, I'm ready now!" I spread my arms wide. "Ravish me, Harry. My Harry-starved libido and I are more than ready."

Harry bent down until his chest hovered over me. His lips closed in on mine, but rather than kissing me, he said, "Not tonight, Faith."

"Ahh!" I cried in frustration. "I thought you weren't a sadist?"

"Maybe I am, a little," he said and offered me that bastard hand again. "I'll walk you back to your room."

As he led me through the hallways, despite my big case of lady blue balls, I couldn't help but be charmed by Harry being all chivalrous and polite. As we came to my door, he brushed my hair back from my face, the gesture so familiar I practically swooned. "I showed you my home today, Faith, so you not only know who I am, but also what baggage comes with being with me."

"I'd hardly class this as baggage," I said, scoffing.

"But it is. No matter how luxurious it appears, it is baggage nonetheless. *Heavy* baggage, that lasts a lifetime and requires things in your life you may not like, duties you may not care for. It would put you under the microscope too. More so because many people would not approve of us, despite us not caring." I saw how much he meant those words and quickly sobered. I may joke about things, but he was right.

"Okay," I said. Going onto my tiptoes, I kissed his mouth. "I promise I'll think about things. I'll see you tomorrow?"

"I have to go into London first thing to check on the offices in my father's absence. I must attend a meeting that could not be rescheduled. But I'll see you at the midsummer masquerade ball tomorrow night."

"Do I get a hint on your mask?" I teased.

Harry leaned close and, just before he kissed my cheek, said, "You'll have no problem recognizing me, let's just leave it at that." He brushed his lips against my cheek. "Goodnight, Faith. I'll see you tomorrow."

"Goodnight, Harry."

Finding the doorknob, I slipped into my room, Harry fading from view as I shut the door behind me. I collapsed against the wall and worked on steadying my breathing. Once my composure had been gathered, I walked to the window and sat on the cushioned sill. I stared out at the starry night, birds still chirping in the trees. In the lingering summer's light, I could still see most of the property, and I truly thought about what Harry had said.

Baggage.

I told him I'd choose you. I told him I'd always choose you.

I let my forehead fall on the glass pane. I stared at the glittering lake and remembered it all, from the first time we met to what led us here today.

You brought me back to life.

I smiled, remembering those words. "You showed me what life was, Harry," I whispered to the quiet room. "You showed me what it was to live."

CHAPTER TWENTY

THE SUN HADN'T EVEN REACHED the sky when I awoke. I wanted to blame it on the jet lag, but the truth was it was Harry. It was Harry and last night, this house, his title, and everything that came with it. I had tried to imagine what being in this life would be like. What it would be like to an outsider, not from the same social circles. The looks Harry and I would be given by his peers, the judgment.

I had never cared what people thought of me. But I cared what they said about Harry. I had imagined too many times how I would react if someone slighted him in my presence, *because* of my presence. I wouldn't be able to hold my tongue. I knew I wouldn't. Would Harry be disappointed by that? Would I let him down if I let my mouth fly to protect him? Us? I didn't know.

I let myself out the side door that led to the terrace. The morning was fresh and cool, and I wrapped my sweater more tightly around me. As I crossed the terrace and descended the steps to the gardens, a mist hovered over the grass, basking the property in a gothic white glow. I'd never seen anything like it. I held my hands down beside me, trying to see if I could feel the mist between my fingers. I couldn't, of course, but it made me feel like I was walking through clouds. Birds sang in the trees, and I stared up at the high treetops, heading for the one place that had mesmerized me since the day I got here.

I arrived at the fairy-tale bridge, walked to its center, and looked at the house. Even having spent the last few days here could not take away its majesty. I was sure if I lived here a lifetime, I would still be in awe daily.

The old stone of the bridge was rough under my hands, the flowers' petals kissed with the morning dew. As my fingertips traced the years of use, I wondered just how many people, over the centuries, had stood here as I was doing now. If they'd leaned over the wall and stared down at the lake, contemplating the world and their place in it. If they'd stood on these very worn slabs beneath my feet and thought about the one who held their heart.

I stayed that way until the sun was high in the sky, the mist had gone, and the day had warmed. I saw the house waking, staff members readying for the ball tonight, and guests taking breakfast on the terrace.

Deciding to head back, I crossed the bridge to the other side. When I looked up, I stopped dead in my tracks. "Hello, Miss Parisi."

King Sinclair sat on a bench at the foot of the bridge. "Mr. Sinclair," I said. "How are you?"

"Please, join me," he said.

Preparing myself for his censure, I sat on the wooden bench. The bridge looked even more magical from this angle. "You like the bridge?" he asked. As I faced him, I saw he was very pale and, in very little time, had lost quite a bit of weight.

"It's incredible," I said. "I haven't been able to take my eyes off it the whole time I've been here. I didn't sleep well last night, so I decided to come and see it at first light." I glanced at the house. "Your property really is something special."

"Thank you." We fell into silence. I braced myself, waiting for another "talk" about my being no good for Harry. But instead he said, "My son is in love with you." I stopped breathing, I was pretty sure my heart had stopped beating, and I could have been convinced I was dreaming as those words slipped from King Sinclair's mouth. I wrapped my sweater more tightly around me, a soft layer of self-protection.

King smiled, pointing at the bridge. "It was Aline's favorite part of our estate too." Tears filled my eyes at the sudden change in King's voice when he talked of his wife. It softened, and anyone could hear how much he had loved her. "If I couldn't find her in the house, I knew she'd be out here."

"I'm sorry you lost her," I said, wanting to take his hand and comfort him. As much as he had acted badly toward Harry and me, it didn't take a genius to know he was racked with pain. He may have recently had a heart attack, but that organ had been shattered long ago.

"She was the best part of me—until we had Harry, of course, but even then, she was this light I hadn't known I needed. I was always prone to seeing the darker side of life, and she would illuminate the world until it didn't look so bleak after all."

He turned his head and stared out at the tree line just beyond the bridge. "When she got sick, I thought, God wouldn't be this cruel to take her from me and my boy." King smiled. I think it was the first time it had ever appeared genuine. "She adored Harry. He could never do wrong in her eyes. That boy could have burned down the house, and she would have argued he was just trying to keep us warm."

I found myself laughing, yet simultaneously felt my heart breaking. His smile slipped from his face. "I buried my head in the sand and refused to believe we were losing her. I..." His breathing stuttered. "I didn't even call for Harry in the end. He missed telling his mum goodbye because I just couldn't face reality."

"He would forgive you for that, if he hasn't already."

"Yes. He told me that when I confessed it was my biggest regret." King tapped his chest, over his heart. "When I came through the surgery."

"It would have destroyed him if you'd died too," I said and saw King's eyes glisten.

"In that moment, as I was coming out of the surgery alive, Harry's optimism reminded me of my wife, of the reason I fell so in love with her. It was the best trait of hers he could ever have inherited. Better than my dour nature."

"Your wife was beautiful."

"She was. But it was her spirit that hooked me in so deeply. Her rebellious nature. In a world full of black and white, she was a solitary streak of color." I had to bite my lip to stop it from trembling. I'd never known King could speak so purely about someone he loved. But that was the point, of course. I didn't really know him at all.

"I always thought of her as a walking watercolor painting, brightening the world wherever she went. When she died, all the color faded from the world. It faded from me too."

"You lost the love of your life. It's the worst thing a person can endure," I said, believing every word.

"It is, but failing as a father is tied for that title." I tensed and held my breath for what King would say next. He angled his body slightly my way and said, "I failed to be the father Harry needed when he was younger and until now. But I won't do that again."

My mind raced and my hands began to shake. "I almost died, and I will tell you that coming out of the other side makes you realize just how precious life is, and that it is to be lived." King went quiet for a moment, contemplating. "And I haven't done much living for too many years." I looked at the flowers around us, the lavender scent from the field calming my nerves. "Harry doesn't know it yet, but I'm retiring."

"What?" I whispered, shocked.

"Harry is better in the business world now than I am. It has changed, is rolling with the times, and Harry is good at what he does. Excellent, in fact. It's time he took the mantle."

I tried to process that information. But more than that, I tried to understand what that promotion would mean for us. "It's a lot to take that kind of responsibility on." I nodded, somewhat numb and, if I was being honest, a little afraid. "He will need someone to support him. Someone to help him through rough waters."

I sighed. Louisa. He was referring to Louisa.

"My son has chosen *you*, Faith." I whipped my head to King, eyes wide and mouth parting, but no words would come. King chuckled. Actually friggin' chuckled. "He spoke to me quite frankly when I came to after the surgery." He shook his head in disbelief. "Never in my life have I seen my son so full of conviction as when he spoke of you. Of when he told me how disappointed he was in me for interfering and for not trusting him to know what is best for him. For his life. And more than that, his happiness."

King took hold of a walking cane and moved to get up. "He has chosen you, Faith. And I won't lose him. He's all I have that's good in the world, and I won't lose him because I think I know what's best." I just stared at King. "I'm retiring from the business, maybe I should retire from trying to govern Harry's life too. The world is evolving, tradition is dying, the old stuffy ways of society are gradually giving way to the new. It's time for me to let go." It was too much; this fluttering in my heart and warmth in my blood was all too much.

"But Faith, if you decide to be with my son, stay by his side. You have to know that there will be those in our circles who will talk. Who will ignore you because you are different. Who might offend you because you weren't bred for the station you've been thrust into. Sometimes you will find yourself in a viper's nest."

Finally finding my voice, I smiled and said, "Luckily, I have fangs, Mr. Sinclair. Big, venomous fangs." King laughed and got to his feet.

I went to help him, but he held up his hand. "It's just a precaution," he said, referring to his cane. "I really am feeling better. Even better than before." I remained sitting, and he said, "You know, my wife would have loved you."

He laughed like he was laughing alongside her, here, with us right now. "She would have loved this. Loved that Harry had chosen to break away and make his own rules. Loved that he pushed back against me. And loved that he would fall for a woman who could cut down all of English society with a lash of her tongue."

King nodded, like he was agreeing with an internal thought. "Yes, she would have loved you as a daughter-in-law very much. You are so like her, or so Harry tells me. She certainly was quick to put me in my place. I think that's what I miss most about her—our verbal sparring. I didn't realize how much I enjoyed it until she died and everything went silent." King nodded goodbye, and I watched him slowly walk away.

"Mr. Sinclair?" I called, and he turned around.

I shrugged. "I'm not bragging or anything, but I've been known to throw some epic verbal throwdowns in my day, *if* you ever find yourself wanting a challenge again."

The flicker of a smirk that pulled on his lips mirrored Harry's expression when he was amused. "And you may just be a worthy adversary for me, Miss Parisi. A very worthy adversary for me indeed." He took a step and said, "And call me King."

"In that case, call me Faith." I winked to exaggerate my point. King smiled more widely and, shaking his head, disappeared down the pathway toward the house.

I stared out at the rippling lake in wide-eyed wonder. What the hell was happening? King had given us his blessing. He was giving Harry the reins to HCS Media.

I laid my head back on the wooden bench and tried to let it all sink in. I closed my eyes and let the English morning sun kiss my face. A strange kind of static rushed through my body. Could I do all of this with Harry? Where would we even live? Nerves threatened to overwhelm me, but then I thought of one thing King had said, and it chased them all away.

My son is in love with you.

I replayed it, once, twice, three times, just to allow it to sink in.

My son is in love with you, my son is in love with you, my son is in love with you...

And beside the bridge I loved so much, sure his mum was here in spirit, I whispered, "I love him too, Aline. I love him so much."

As those words disappeared into the bright sky, I returned to the house and began readying for that night. Running the bath, I let the vanilla-scented bubbles envelope me and saw Harry's smiling face in my mind. "I love you too," I said, as though he had heard me. "Harry, I love you too."

THE LANTERNS CREATED a galaxy of stars as I walked toward the ballroom, an orchestra playing classical music and opera singers singing in Italian, luring me closer. Papa would have loved this, all the drama.

I walked with careful feet as I approached the archway that led to the top of the staircase. From here, I saw people dancing, gowns and masks firmly in place. A nervous chill raced up my spine as I passed two men on either side of the archway and let my gaze run all over the room. It was a Shakespearean fantasy. Lights of all colors draped over the ceiling in crisscross shapes.

Giant sculptures of flowers of various hues created an indoor garden, and oversized fairy wings fluttered from the ceiling, up and down, like they were moving, flying across the sky. The floor was a mass of pink flowers, not real but illuminated by a projector hidden somewhere in the ceiling. A large crescent moon and thousands of stars hung from the walls and roof. It was like being trapped in a dream.

I brushed my hand down the skirt of my dress; then I saw him. Cutting through the crowd, Harry, in a black suit and white shirt and tie, looking as tall and handsome as any man could, stopped at the bottom of the stairs. A laugh slipped from my lips at the mask he wore.

Phantom of the Opera.

I saw him smile under the familiar white porcelain mask and

wondered how I ever could have not realized it was him. It seemed so obvious to me now. I descended the steps, seeing Harry's eyes—his true blue, not silver contacts—watching my every move.

I wore a floor-length black lace halter dress with a plunging neckline. A slit was cut up to my right thigh, and my hair hung down to the middle of my back in loose waves. My mask was the same black lace as my dress and fashioned in the shape of a cat's face.

As I reached the bottom step, Harry held out his hand and I slipped mine into it. "Faith," he said, awe thickening his voice. Stepping to the ballroom floor, he kissed the back of my hand.

"Maître Harry." I lowered my head slightly, like a good siren. Harry growled playfully and pulled me to his chest.

"I like the sound of that way too bloody much."

My temperature spiked at his husky voice. "So do I."

Harry studied my mask and said, in that perfect French accent, "Mon petit chaton." He playfully tapped the small pointed ears.

That name purring from his lips instantly made me clench my thighs together. "Meow," I said, winking, and Harry threw his head back, laughing.

"Menace," Harry said and held my hand. Shocked, I looked down at our clasped hands and the people dancing and conversing around us. He was holding my hand. In public. Where anyone could see. It wasn't just his employees here tonight; there were people from English society too. Many, *many* people. But as Harry walked with me through the crowd, curious glances firing our way, I realized he didn't care.

Neither did I.

Harry handed me a glass of champagne. "I have never seen you look as beautiful as you do now, Faith."

"Because half my face is covered?" I teased.

Harry took the champagne from my hands, ignoring my quip. "Dance with me."

Sheer horror filled my bones. "Erm…" I looked at the waltzing couples and Harry's expectant stare. "Not sure I can dance like that.

In case you forgot, I am clumsy. Like the clumsiest klutz that there ever, ever was."

Clearly not taking no for an answer, Harry pulled me to the dance floor. I passed Sally, Michael, and Sarah, who all stood gaping at Harry's hand in mine. As we hit the dance floor, the music changed. I recognized it instantly. It was slower than what had been playing, and Harry pulled me to his chest, wrapping his arms around me.

Under the crescent moon and stars, he guided me around the dance floor, Ed Sheeran and Andrea Bocelli's song about being perfect accompanying our every move.

"Andrea Bocelli," I whispered into Harry's ear. "It will forever remind me of you." Harry as "Maître" had played Andrea Bocelli every night I'd been with him. Harry had played his music in his apartment. How had I ever not known?

"I never thought I'd have this," Harry said. I became trapped in his blue gaze, and the onlookers fell away. "I never thought you would be with me this way."

Cupping my hands on the back of his head, I lowered it and brought his lips to mine. Harry shifted his mask to the side, showing his face so he could kiss me longer, deeper, slower. He tasted of mint and champagne, and I melted against him. We were here. No secrets. Hearts bared and no obstacles in our way. My heart thudded hard in my chest, and the music, which was so perfect for *us*, swept us away.

Harry's arms were tight around my waist, and I felt it. He hadn't said the words yet. But with every kiss, with every caress of his tongue, and with every flex of his hands on my back, he told me he loved me. I tried to show him I loved him too with my hands in his hair as I smiled against his mouth. As the song ended and our lips broke apart, I met Harry's eyes and couldn't look away. The music moved on to another song, but I just stood there holding him, and he held me too.

"I'm so happy you came here," Harry whispered. Then he smiled a breathtakingly crooked smile. "And I am so very happy that damn elevator broke down." I laughed, and Harry took my hand. "Let's get a drink." As we were moving through the crowd, someone took hold of my free hand.

When I saw a blond man in a black traditional mask, I recognized him immediately. "May I cut in?" Nicholas asked.

"One dance, then she's mine again," Harry said sternly, causing me to moan out loud at the level of dominance in his voice. I tried to smother it with a cough, but when Nicholas covered his mouth to hide his amusement, I knew it had been in vain.

As we hit the dance floor, a faster, more upbeat song played, and Nicholas spun me around the dance floor like a ballerina in a jewelry box. "How's Sage?" he asked, not at all subtle about his feelings for my friend.

"He's good." Nicholas nodded, and I asked, "Nicholas Sinclair, what are your intentions for my best friend?"

Sage leaned closer and said, "Naughty ones. Very, very naughty ones."

"Then you'll do fine," I said and let him spin me again.

Nicholas looked over my shoulder and said, "What have you done to my cousin and where can I buy it?" I turned to see Harry drinking champagne at the bar, looking our way, completely ignoring the people who had gathered around him to converse.

"I have no idea what you mean," I said, unable to stop looking at Harry.

"Oh, bloody hell." Nicholas took me from the dance floor and deposited me at Harry's feet. "It's no fun when your partner is mooning over someone else the entire time." Nicholas winked at me, grabbed another woman he knew, and dragged her to the dance floor.

Harry pulled me against his chest. We danced some more, ignoring the questions and eagle-eyed guests. The champagne was buzzing through my veins, the fake stars were glittering, and Harry hadn't let me go all night.

As a slow song began to play, I went to my toes and said, "Make love to me." Harry raised his head from the crook of my neck and met my eyes. "Take me from here and make love to me," I said again.

Harry slipped his hand into mine and led me through the crowd and to the stairway. We headed to my room. When we walked past it to the door at the end of the hallway, he turned the knob. With a blush on his cheeks, he confessed, "My room."

"Next to mine."

Shrugging, he said, "I had to have you close." Throwing off my mask and his, I crushed my lips to Harry's and we moved into his bedroom, locking the door behind us. Harry kicked off his shoes and guided me to the bed. He placed me gently on the mattress, and I could already feel that this moment was different. There were no jokes, no playful quips. This was him and me, our true selves, together at last.

Without breaking eye contact, Harry slipped off his jacket, followed by his shirt. I shivered seeing his sculpted chest and torso again, and I didn't look away—not even once—when he pulled down his pants and climbed on the bed.

Harry kissed me. He kissed and kissed me until my lips were swollen and I was completely drowning in him. His mouth moved to my neck, and I lifted my hair as his fingers found the tie of my dress. The thin material fell away from my breasts and pooled at my hips. His mouth laid kiss after kiss down my neck, along my breasts, and down my stomach. My breathing was stuttered and my body felt on fire, scorched by every brush of his lips on my skin.

Harry pulled my dress from my legs, my panties following afterwards. He crawled back above me, both of us exposed and raw and free. "I love you," he said, a tremor in his voice. Like he was fearful of being refused.

"Harry," I whispered and cupped his face. "I love you too. So much I can barely stand it."

He kissed me again; he kissed me and kissed me until I was breathless. His hand moved down my body, as light as a feather. I parted my legs and threw my head back as he touched me. I moaned, the sound echoing around the room. I felt Harry's hardness on my hip and, with my hands on his back, guided him between my thighs. His lips broke from mine and, staring into my eyes, he slowly pushed inside me. I arched my back, my breasts brushing his chest.

Harry's mouth moved to my neck, and I tipped my head back as his arms threaded around me and held me as close to him as possible. He rocked back and forth inside me, not a single word being spoken. I had never had it like this, never had it so slow and passionate and intense. I realized it was because, before this, before Harry, I had never made love. Because I had never been in love like this.

Love. I *loved* him. So much it was terrifying.

"Faith." Harry's hands moved to the top of my behind. He increased his speed, his thrusts coming faster and faster, a sheen of sweat gathering on our heated skin. I held him close, my arms cradling his head, as I felt my orgasm building, higher and higher. Then my body stilled, filled with pleasure so intense that my eyes shut and I cried out, limbs weightless, my bones nothing but air. Harry tensed then, with a low groan, came inside me. I clutched his hair as he gently rocked back and forth, until he expelled a loud exhale and dropped his forehead to mine.

He licked his lips and whispered, "I love you, Faith. I love you so goddamn much." His breathing was heavy as he fought for air.

"I love you too," I said again, the admission filling a part of me I didn't even know was missing. Harry rolled off me and gathered me in his arms. I took in the rich reds and golds and the impressive four-poster bed we lay in. "So this is what it would be like?" I said, my voice barely above a whisper.

"What?" he said quietly, so as not to break the delicate peace around us.

"Being with you." I soaked in the heat from his chest and his arm around my waist. "Making love to you...waking up with you...loving you from here on out."

"Yes," Harry said, and I closed my eyes. "It could be exactly like this." I could still hear the orchestra from the ballroom, and I let the sound of violins and cellos lure me to sleep. As darkness claimed me, Harry pressed a kiss to my head and held me even tighter. "I want it exactly like this."

When I awoke, the sun flooding in through the windows, it was to another note on the pillow Harry had slept on.

Faith,
There are no words to explain what these past few days and, most certainly, last night, meant to me.
I wish for you to be with me. I wish for you to be by my side for the rest of my life. But I understand the enormity of those wishes. The world I live in, as I have already expressed, is not to be taken lightly. As I woke up this morning, I was the happiest I have ever been in my life.
Having you in my arms, your knowing everything there is to know about me, was freedom. True freedom. No masks, no disguises, just us.
To me, that is perfection.
I know you fly out this morning to New York. I will follow this evening. Please think about everything I have said. Please take as much time as you need, I will not push you. You know my sentiment. I love you like no other, and that truth will remain until the day I die.

I turned the paper over, and my heart stopped.

Publish the feature, Faith. I have given Sally instructions to publish whatever you wish as the Visage big feature. It was wrong of me to destroy your dream. I only ask that you direct the attention toward me, now that you know the truth. You deserve this, Faith. You are an excellent writer.
I love you eternally,
Yours and only yours,
Harry x

A tear splashed on the page, smudging the ink. Leaving the bed, and clutching my letter to my chest, I put on last night's dress and went to my room. I packed, thinking over everything.

As we boarded the plane, and it leveled off, I knew what I must do. I pulled out my laptop and opened a new blank document. I wrote all the way back to New York, tears in my eyes and love in my heart.

As the plane grounded in JFK, I felt changed and the new feature felt right. I read Harry's note again, keeping it in my bra and close to my heart all the way home.

Having you in my arms, your knowing everything there is to know about me, was freedom. True freedom. No masks, no disguises, just us. To me, that is perfection...

Perfection. I was pretty sure that's exactly what Harry Sinclair was.

At least he was perfect for me.

CHAPTER TWENTY-ONE

I CHECKED MY CELL AGAIN. There was still nothing from Harry. I'd spent the morning and most of the afternoon drafting and redrafting the feature. It was going to press tonight. As soon as Sally had signed off on it, I'd sent a copy to Harry.

I'd heard nothing back.

Amelia was at work. Sage and Novah were too. Needing to get out of the house, I jumped to my feet and headed to the subway. As the train stopped in Hell's Kitchen, I walked in the baking heat to my parents'. I checked my cell again and again like a neurotic girlfriend.

Why wasn't he answering? Had he not read it yet? Or had he, and hated it? Tucking my cell back in my purse, I tipped my head back and shouted, "I'm too jet lagged and too fucking hot and bothered for this shit!"

With no divine sign, or even a response from Harry, letting me know his thoughts, I turned the corner to my parents' home and my stomach fell to the ground. "No," I whispered and ran to the steps. The sign that had said "For Sale" now said "Sold." "No, no, no, no!" I said on a crescendo, bellowing, "NO!" as I burst through my parents' door. Mom was walking into the living room with a tray of coffees. Papa was at the table, holding two letters in his hands. "You've sold it?" I asked, my voice catching with sadness. "I can't believe you've sold it."

Mom and Dad shared a look I couldn't decipher. "What?" I pushed. "What's going on?"

"We don't know," Papa said, holding the letters. "I shut the shop because it couldn't pay the rent. And we received a cash offer for the apartment. We said yes, of course. It was even over what we had asked for it." He rubbed his head, stressed. Or maybe confused, I wasn't sure. "Then these came today." Papa held up the letters. I moved across the room like my ass was on fire and opened them.

"Deeds?" I asked, reading the addresses on the documents. "Papa, these are in your and Mom's names." My heart started racing seeing the address of Papa's shop on the paper too. But not just his shop, the entire building. The entire fucking overpriced New York building.

"There must be some mistake," Mom said. "Who would buy our house and then give us the deed? And who would buy the entire building for your papa, and gift us that too. Nothing makes sense! We've called the lawyer who dealt with it. They told us there was no mistake. Even pushed the sale through in a couple of weeks instead of the usual allotted time."

Mom laid her hand on Papa's shoulder. He placed his hand over hers. There was a static feeling zipping through my veins, telling me to see something. Reading the letter again, I froze when I saw the initials of the buyer...

H.A.S.

"Oh my shitting Christ," I whispered and my hands shook. "Oh my fucking god!" I said louder and Mom rushed to my side.

"What, Faith, what?" Mom asked, trying to keep me steady.

"Harry," I whispered, and I saw my mom's expression change from confusion to understanding. H.A.S...Henry Auguste Sinclair...

"It was Harry," I said, choking on the emotion clogging my throat. "He saved your house." I looked to Papa, who had turned white. "He bought you a building. An entire fucking building!"

"Why?" Mom whispered, her trembling hand covering her mouth.

"He loves her," Papa said, getting to his feet. His gaze locked on mine. "He loves you, doesn't he, mia bambina?"

"Yes," I replied, feeling my heart expand so big in my chest I thought it might break through my ribs. "He loves me," I whispered.

Papa put his hands on my arms. "And you, Faith. Do you love him?"

"Yes," I said, tears spilling from my eyes and down my face. "Yes, so damn much I can hardly bear it."

"Faith," Mom said and wrapped her arms around me.

"I need to go." I was already backing away toward the door. "I need to find him." I raced from the door, only stopping long enough to give back the deeds. The deeds to their home. Papa's building. Harry. Harry saved their home and business.

My Harry.

I waved my hands in the air, trying to flag down a cab. When one finally stopped, I gave him the address to Harry's apartment building. It was too late for him to be at work; he had to be at home. I bounced in my seat when the chaotic New York traffic was bumper to bumper. The cab driver beeped the horn and I rolled down the window, screaming, "Get the fuck out of our way, assholes!"

"You wanna ride with me every day, lady?" the cab driver said, but I couldn't stop my mind from racing. Harry had bought my parents' house and business premises for an ungodly amount of money. Because he loved me. Because he *loved* me.

I burst out crying in the back seat, loud sobbing mixed with laughter of pure disbelief. The cab driver, who'd been inviting me to join his business a second ago, was now looking at me as though I had escaped an insane asylum and was about to wreak havoc in his city.

The driver, looking mightily pleased we had reached our destination, unlocked the doors and I burst onto the street. I ran to the glass doors and to the concierge desk in Harry's building. "I need to see Harry Sinclair," I said, repeatedly hitting the top of the desk. The concierge looked at me the same way the driver had. Pure fear in his gaze.

"Miss, are you okay?" he asked.

"I need to see Harry Sinclair. Can you please call to see if he's in?" The concierge did as I said, and I turned to the mirrored wall beside me. My mouth dropped open seeing my mascara running down my face.

Grabbing a tissue from the concierge's desk, I ran to the mirror and began wiping my cheeks, but I was unable to do anything about the red in my eyes and the flush on my cheeks.

"Mr. Sinclair is not in," the concierge said.

Spinning around, I said. "Are you sure?" I wasn't entirely convinced he didn't think I was a stalker.

"Mr. Sinclair is not in," he repeated.

Digging out my cell, I tried to call Harry's number, but it went to voicemail. Just as I hung up, I noticed the time. "Of course!" I whispered to myself before returning to the street to hail another cab. When none stopped, I took a deep breath. "It's only a couple of blocks. How hard can it be to run there?"

I started running, quickly realizing I was severely unfit. But I didn't stop. I didn't stop until I was outside a familiar townhouse. I leaned over, gasping for breath. My throat and chest were raw with the deep inhales and exhales I had to endure to return my pounding heart to a normal speed. I could feel my thick and naturally wavy hair beginning to frizz in the humidity and imagined I looked quite the picture. But I didn't care. I needed to see him. I just desperately needed to see him.

Realizing I had to go through the underground lot, I stared at the long street before me, knowing I had another mountain to climb.

Putting my Converses to good use, I started running again. I ran to the entrance of the parking lot and down the long underground road that led to the basement of the townhouse. By the time I had reached the private elevator, I was close to passing out. But I reached into my purse and found my NOX card, which I had forgotten to take out of my wallet.

Thank. Fucking. God.

I swiped the card in the elevator, the doors opened, and I stepped inside, groaning with pleasure at the air conditioning kissing my flushed skin. I viewed my reflection in the mirror, almost scaring myself. I combed my frizzy hair with my fingers and made sure my face was free from streaks of mascara.

When the doors opened, I pushed through to Maître's room. As I stepped inside, everything was quiet. I was used to music and Andrea Bocelli serenading me with "Ave Maria."

Then I saw a sliver of light under the door to the room Maître had always come out of. Heart filling with hope and love and all the mushy stuff that dreams are made of, I burst through the door.

Harry looked up in shock, his cell to his ear. He was dressed in a suit, his jacket off, his collar unbuttoned, and his sleeves rolled up to his elbows.

"Faith," he said, whispering my name like a prayer. "I was just trying to call you. My cell was dead, and I just read—"

I ran at him. I didn't give him time to finish that sentence before my arms were around his waist and my cheek was to his chest. He was strong and muscled and smelled of mint and sandalwood and musk...and he was mine. He was actually mine.

"Thank you," I said, my voice breaking. I closed my eyes. "I don't know how to repay you for what you've done...done for my parents."

Harry tensed, and I lifted my head. His jaw clenched, his eyes wary. I placed my hand on his cheek, and he covered it with his palm. "I know it was you. I know it was you." I swallowed the emotion climbing up my throat. "Thank you. I...just thank you."

My eyes watered, and Harry pushed a falling tear away with his thumb. "Faith, I..." He exhaled and, fighting his own emotion, said, "I did it for you. Everything I have ever done, it has all been for you."

Pulling his head down, I kissed him. Through trembling lips and salty tears, I kissed him and kissed him and kissed him until I could barely breathe. When I broke away, Harry cradled my face. "I have just finished reading your feature." His voice was hoarse with emotion. "Did you mean it? You love me? A forever kind of love?"

"Yes," I said and gave him biggest fucking smile. "I meant every word."

Harry closed his eyes and quoted, "*I went to NOX a willing slave, ready for my eyes to be opened to the world of sin and pleasure. What I didn't know was that it would lead me to the great love of my life. My soulmate. My master. My Maître of Manhattan.*"

Harry dropped his forehead to mine. "*What I didn't know is that I would leave my inhibitions at the door, but not my heart.*" Harry smiled and radiated happiness, and I thought I might die seeing the joy on his face. "*Because although the world may have heard of the infamous Maître as the king of the sexual underground, to me, he reigns as the king of my heart, the commander of my soul, and the keeper of my eternal love...*"

"And I am his queen," I finished for him.

"Are you?" Harry asked nervously.

"Yes, yes, and even more yes."

"You mean it?" Harry said, expression guarded. "Have you had enough time to truly think about how your life will change, how..."

I took a step back and made sure Harry's eyes were firmly fixed on me. Knowing I had his full attention, I said, "I'm just a really, really, *really* terrible sub, standing in front of her master, asking him to spank her for the rest of their lives." Fighting a smile, I asked, "Is that enough of an answer for you?"

I watched the twitch of Harry's cheek, the hook of his lip, and suddenly I was being swept into his arms, my legs wrapping around his waist, being carried to the four-poster bed in the chambre. As my back hit the fucking god-awful PVC covered mattress, Harry climbed over me.

"You signed it Anonymous," he said, referring to my article. "You signed it Anonymous." He repeated it twice like he couldn't believe what I had done.

"It seemed fitting."

He searched my eyes, all humor gone. "But it was your dream to have that feature, to be recognized for your writing."

I shrugged and wrapped my arms around his neck. "Dreams change."

"Or sometimes they don't," he said, pressing kisses to my cheeks and lips. "Sometimes you have a bloody crazy dream that you think can never come true, then suddenly it does, and it's right in front of you asking you to spank them for the rest of your lives."

Loud laughter spilled from my throat. "We're so fucking romantic it makes me sick." When my laughter died down, I started taking off his clothes. Harry watched me with blazing heat in his eyes. When he was naked, I bit my lip and stripped down to nothing too.

"I'm naked, Maître. What do you want to do with me?"

Groaning, Harry picked me up and carried me across the room to the St Andrew's Cross. Without breaking eye contact, he cuffed my wrists and ankles to the cross. Excitement and exhilaration tingled through my body as always. But this was different. As Harry's bright blue gaze, which I adored so much, devoured me, everything about this moment was different. He was Maître; he was dominant and in control as always. But here, right now, with no masks or cloaks or veils, he was also my Harry. My Harry Auguste Sinclair, the man who I loved more than life itself.

I moaned, feeling every synapse in my body flaring to life as Harry kissed my calf, then peppered kiss after kiss on every inch of my skin. When his lips pressed against mine, I sobbed in happiness. Maître had never kissed me, had never even come close. But now Maître was smothering my lips, tattooing me with his taste, and placing himself permanently in my soul.

"Faith," he moaned, placing himself between my legs. Hands sliding down my waist, then back north to cup my face, he pushed inside. As our heavy breathing filled the room, I submitted to his touch, to his body, and to his love. Harry kissed me as I moaned into his mouth, feeling the telltale pressure building at the base of my spine.

"Harry," I whispered against his lips, feeling a stray tear slip from my eye. It was so much, him and me and the future that now lay before us.

"I love you," he murmured, and I splintered apart. My wrists and ankles pulled against the restraints. Then Harry stilled and, calling out my name, came, his forehead falling to the crook of my neck. We were hot and breathless in the aftermath.

One by one, Harry untied the cuffs fastening me to the cross. When I was free, he carried me to the bed, lying down and guiding me to his chest. When I had gathered strength, I ran my finger down his sternum, smiling as his glistening skin bumped at my touch.

Harry kissed my forehead and ran his hands through my hair, completely contented. "It's different," I said, disturbing the pleasant silence of the room. I tipped my head so I could see Harry. He met my eyes. "This," I continued. "Being in here with you, making love with you like that." His addictive scent wrapped around me, holding me close. "Before it was fun, it was exciting, now..." I trailed off.

"Now?" he said, voice husky.

"I have always loved this. This side of you, of *us*." I saw the stocks and the floggers and canes on the walls. "But just then, trusting you so fully, and having your eyes on me..." I shook my head. "Love," I said, realizing I was rambling. "It made it different." I kissed Harry's cheek, then his lips.

Becoming lost to his taste, I managed to pull away, his hands cradling my face, and said, "It made it so much more. You and me, like this, in here, in love and no secrets between us..." I smiled. "It made it perfect."

Harry rolled on top of me and kissed me. He kissed me until my lips felt bruised. "I'll never get enough of you," he said against my mouth. "In any way. In here tied up, at home in our bed, anywhere, Faith. I just want you."

"You have me."

Harry watched me with so much love in his eyes it made my heart skip a beat. He gathered me in his arms again, like he would never let me go. He moved my hair from my face and said, "My father is giving me HCS Media."

"I know." He didn't even seem surprised by that; it confirmed something.

"I will have to split my time between New York and England."

Bringing his face closer to mine, I said, "I like England, so I approve of this way of living." I pretended to think. "Now if only we had a twenty-three-bedroom palace we could occupy whilst we are there. Anything less grand simply will not do."

"It's a stately home, not a palace. There is a difference."

"Tomato-tom*a*to," I sang.

"But your column," Harry said, being as ridiculously chivalrous as always.

"What about it? The good thing about writing is you can do it anywhere. And Harry, I know you're an expert and everything, but there are sexually frustrated people all over the world needing Miss Bliss's help. By taking us global, I'm doing the world a service, actually. I'm a goddamn superhero to the horizontally challenged." I mock sighed. "If only we had more estates to escape to, we could take on the world."

Harry hesitated. "Well, we have my mother's estate in France that I inherited." I stilled and realized he wasn't joking. "Then there's my villa in Monaco, my penthouse in London, and of course my penthouse here—"

I smothered Harry's mouth with a kiss to cut him off before I had an anxiety attack at how friggin' rich he was and he needed to bend me over to calm me down. When we pulled away, his cerulean eyes were the brightest I had ever seen them. "And the prospect of being a duchess one day doesn't scare you?"

As he said the word *duchess* my stomach clenched a little. I mean *me*, a duchess. But when I looked at that handsome face and saw the smile on those lips, it really didn't faze me. "As long as you're okay with taking a peasant girl for a wife someday, I can be too."

"Society may frown upon us, and we may only be invited to the lesser royals' weddings," he said dryly, never losing that playful sparkle in his eyes.

I fought back laughter. "I always felt like they seemed more fun anyhow."

Harry laughed too and shook his head in disbelief. "I can't believe I get to have you." He stroked his finger down my cheek, "I can't believe I get to love you and you love me back."

I ran my hand down his chest, lovingly, softly, then cupped his length. "And I can't believe I get to have this servicing me for the rest of my days, and nights, and afternoons, and mornings, of course…" Harry pursed his lips, his head shaking in mock exasperation. "Forget the Sinclair Estate, we could build an entire palace on the girth of this."

"Faith," Harry said in his serious, most British voice, "have you quite finished?"

"Not even close." I placed my hand on his cheek. "You have me and I have you, you love me and I love you, forever and ever amen, times infinity and yadda yadda motherfucking yadda." I clasped my hands over my head near the headboard. "Now tie me to the bed and spank me with your flogger. I've got another orgasm building with your name on it."

"Just *one* more orgasm, mon petit chaton?" he said seductively, causing my nipples to stand on end as his perfectly spoken French hit all my good spots.

Deliciously naked, and in all his noble pompousness and olive-skinned gorgeousness, Harry took my favorite flogger from the wall and walked slowly back to the bed. "Is that a challenge?"

"Always," I said and felt the room temperature rise.

Harry tied me to the bed with silk scarves and gave me a long, loving kiss on my lips. Then he stood beside me, smile fading, dominance pulsing off him in waves, and my beloved maître took over.

"Challenge accepted."

EPILOGUE

THE SINCLAIR ESTATE, Surrey, England

TWO YEARS LATER...

"WE'LL SEE you in two weeks!" Mom said as she and Papa jumped in the town car that would take them to the airport. They were off to Parma, Italy, Papa's hometown. It was the third time they'd been there this year. The rental income from the building Harry had bought them was giving them the ability to travel like they had dreamed. Even if they hadn't had the building revenue, I knew Harry would have made it possible anyhow. He was the kindest, most giving man on the planet.

I waved at them from the drive and took a deep breath. When I turned, Harry was approaching me with his dimpled smile. His forearms were bare, sleeves rolled up to his elbows, and he was wearing khaki shorts and loafers.

I glanced down at my wedding ring, glinting in the summer sun.

We'd been married last year on this estate. And like we had planned, we split our time between England and New York. Harry had taken to running HCS Media as well as we'd always known he would—flawlessly. And I still wrote "Ask Miss Bliss." She was my sarcastic wench of an alter ego, and I refused to give her up. But I also wrote features. I couldn't have been happier.

"Lady Sinclair," Harry greeted, wrapped me in his arms and kissed me. I was a 'lady' now. An actual title owning *lady*, which was the most hilarious thing on the planet. I moaned into his mouth, dizzy when he pulled away. "Did they get away okay?"

"They did," I said and led him to our favorite place on the estate, our fairy-tale bridge. "And tomorrow the troops descend from New York for two whole weeks of carnage."

Amelia, Novah, Sage, and Nicholas were coming. Nicholas now ran the New York office, and from what I could gather, gave the orders to Sage in the bedroom too.

I laid my head on Harry's chest and waved to King Sinclair, getting in his ridiculously expensive sports car and driving away, off on another adventure. Or a day at the bowling club, I was never sure. "You're looking particularly gorgeous today," Harry said and curled a strand of my hair around his finger. "In fact, you're glowing."

"Must be from the thorough ravishing you gave me last night. I can barely move my legs today. I think you broke my pelvis with Private Harry."

"For the love of all that is right and holy, please can you *stop* calling my member Private Harry."

"Well, I have to say that Private Harry is better than *member*. What are you, eighty?"

"I'm reserved," Harry argued.

"Reserved!" I snorted. "Tell that to my permanently red ass, which you've systematically spanked the shit out of for over two years."

Harry's lips twitched in amusement; then he gave me a hard look of admonishment. "Anonymity is key, Lady Sinclair. One must keep these things behind closed doors."

I eyed him incredulously. "If 'behind closed doors' means a chain of sex clubs that now spans the world, bringing awful masks and annoying cloaks to the rich and perpetually wet, if you mean *that* 'behind closed doors,' then I understand."

Harry growled and dropped a kiss to my temple, and I had a sudden attack of nerves over what I was about to tell him. As we walked over the bridge, looking back at the house, I let contentment wash over me and took Harry's hand.

"Faith?" he asked, eyebrows furrowed. "What's wrong?"

Taking a deep breath, I said, "Nothing's wrong. I mean, quite the opposite. If you take away the sickness and sore nipples, that is—oh, and the fact that every smell makes me want to rip off my nose—"

"Faith?" Harry held my hands more tightly.

"I'm pregnant," I blurted out. I watched Harry closely for his reaction. Shock quickly morphed into pure, unadulterated happiness, a beaming smile spreading over his face, making my husband look all kinds of impossibly beautiful.

Harry scooped me up in his arms and spun me around, laughing into my neck. Even now I could hardly believe he was mine. My own slightly sadistic, sexually deviant Prince Charming.

When he placed me back on my feet, he kissed me deeply and dropped his forehead to mine. "I can't believe it," he whispered, voice thick with emotion. "Faith. I..." He stumbled over his words. "I can't believe it. I'm...I'm so happy."

"As am I," I said and let him kiss me again. When Harry broke away, he kept his hands on me like I was suddenly made of glass. He led us to a patch of lawn near the bridge. He sat down, gently guiding me down too and I lay down beside him, head upon his lap and his hand stroking my hair.

Then Harry's hand left dropped to my slightly rounded stomach in awe. "A baby..." he said, voice filled with awe. "I wonder what it'll be?" I almost cried at the new kind of wonder in his voice. "Boy or a girl? I wonder who they will look like." I wanted them to look like him. Or at least inherit those blue eyes I was still obsessed with. I snorted in amusement, and Harry frowned. "What?"

"I'm more concerned about when they're older and ask us how we met."

"At work," Harry said. "Easy."

I shrugged playfully. "I don't know, I mean I was thinking of going with the story that I was your sexual submissive and you my firm and well-endowed master." I put on my best voice. "Well darling, your daddy locked me in some stocks, and after a good round of mind-blowing cunnilingus, he pounded the fuck out of me, and it was then I knew I was in love."

"Well, there's years of therapy we have to look forward to."

I sat up and faced Harry, and with my hand on his cheek and those eyes I adored locked on mine, I said, "Then how about this." I felt a bit of my heart melt and turn to mush, because I had Harry and this life and all the love in the world and I was allowed to be mushy if I wanted to be. "Love didn't come easily to me at first, but the more I got to know your daddy, *all* sides of him..." I waggled my eyebrows at him suggestively, and Harry playfully rolled his eyes. "I couldn't resist him."

"Perfect," he said and took my hand. He ran his thumb over my wedding ring and nodded resolutely. "That's perfect. No more needs to be said. Nothing further needs to be explained. Less is more in this case, love. Less is more."

"And the more I got to know him," I continued, ignoring his attempt to shut me up but thanking God that I had this man, and now our baby, in my life, "the harder and deeper I fell."

I kissed Harry and said against his lips, "And in no time at all, he brought me to my knees, and I became totally," *kiss*, "absolutely," *kiss*, "and thoroughly," *kiss*, "whipped."

Fin

PLAYLIST

S & M — Rihanna
Blow — Kesha
Turn Me On (Feat. Nicki Minaj) — David Guetta
Sweat (Remix) — Snoop Dogg, David Guetta, Giorgio Tuinfort, Frederic Riesterer
Scream — Timbaland, Keri Wilson, Nicole Scherzinger
Give Me Everything (Feat. Ne-Yo, Afrojack & Nayer) — Pitbull
Scream — Usher
Higher Love (Feat. Whitney Houston) — Kygo
Trumpets — Jason Derulo
Lover (Remix) — Taylor Swift, Shawn Mendes
Some Nights — Fun
Black & White — Niall Horan
Happy Now — Kygo, Sandro Cavazza
I Like Me Better — Lauv
Call My Name — Cheryl
I'll Be There — Walk Off the Earth
Africa — Tyler Ward, Lisa Cimorelli
Never Seen The Rain — Tones And I

PLAYLIST

Falling Like The Stars — James Arthur
The Cure — Little Mix
No One — Alecia Keys
Empire State of Mind (Part II) — Alicia Keys
Us — James Bay, Alicia Keys
Sexxx Dreams — Lady Gaga
London Boy — Taylor Swift
Talking Body — Tove Lo
Perfect Symphony — Ed Sheeran, Andrea Bocelli
Welcome to New York — Taylor Swift
Sexual — NEIKED, Dyo
Bon Apetit — Katy Perry, Migos
Alors On Danse — Stromae, Kanye West
Run — Leona Lewis
Time To Say Goodbye (Con Te Partito) — Lucio Quarantotto, Francesco Sartori, Sarah Brightman, Andrea Bocelli
PILLOWTALK — ZAYN

To Listen: Click Here

ACKNOWLEDGMENTS

Thank you to my husband, Stephen, for being my biggest supporter.

Roman, my little smooch. You are the absolute light of my life. I'm so blessed to be your mammy. I never thought it was possible to love somebody so much. You're the best thing I have ever done in my life. Everything is for you.

Mam and Dad, thank you for the continued support. Dad, thank you for always being a champion of my writing and helping me whenever I need you.

Samantha, Marc, Taylor, Isaac, Archie, and Elias, love you all.

Liz, thank you for being my super-agent and friend.

Neda and Ardent Prose, I am so happy that I jumped on board with you guys. You've made my life infinitely more organized.

To my TILLSTERS. Thank you for the endless love and support. You are my safe haven and I adore you all.

Thank you to all the AMAZING bloggers that have supported my career from the start, and the ones who help share my work and shout about it from the rooftops. You're appreciated more than you'll ever know.

And finally, to my readers. I adore you. You let me write whatever I want, whether that be light or dark and always support me 100%. I never underestimate how special that is to a writer. I love you all lots.

ABOUT THE AUTHOR

Tillie Cole hails from a small town in the North-East of England. She grew up on a farm with her English mother, Scottish father and older sister and a multitude of rescue animals. As soon as she could, Tillie left her rural roots for the bright lights of the big city.

After graduating from Newcastle University with a BA Hons in Religious Studies, Tillie followed her Professional Rugby player husband around the world for a decade, becoming a teacher in between and thoroughly enjoyed teaching High School students Social Studies before putting pen to paper, and finishing her first novel.

After several years living in Italy, Canada and the USA, Tillie has now settled back in her hometown in England, with her husband and son.

Tillie is both an independent and traditionally published author, and writes many genres including: Contemporary Romance, Dark Romance, Young Adult and New Adult novels.

When she is not writing, Tillie enjoys nothing more than spending time with her little family, curling up on her couch watching movies, drinking far too much coffee, and convincing herself that she really doesn't need that last square of chocolate.

FOLLOW TILLIE AT:

https://www.facebook.com/tilliecoleauthor

https://www.facebook.com/groups/tilliecolestreetteam

https://twitter.com/tillie_cole

Instagram: @authortilliecole

Or drop me an email at: authortilliecole@gmail.com
To sign up to my newsletter:
http://eepurl.com/bDFq5H

Or check out my website:
www.tilliecole.com

Printed in Dunstable, United Kingdom